MERCY RING  BOOK ONE

JACKSON

NYSSA KATHRYN

An NW Partners Book
Cover by Deranged Doctor Design
Developmentally and Copy Edited by Kelli Collins
Proofread by Marla Esposito and Jen Katemi

❀ Created with Vellum

Sometimes it's the oldest wounds that cut deepest.

River Harp fell in love with her brother's best friend, a boy who was practically part of the family...a boy who broke her heart before leaving town. Sixteen years later, he's back for her brother's funeral. And River wants nothing to do with the man. At least, that's what she keeps telling herself.

Because there are problems in her life much bigger than Jackson's return. Like the fact her brother is still alive—and she's the only one who believes it. River will do whatever it takes to uncover the truth and find Ryker. Even if it means seeking help from the man she's spent almost two decades getting over.

As a teen, Jackson Ford had one plan: get the hell out of Lindeman, Washington, away from his abusive drunk of a father, and never return. Fate had other plans, however, and now he's back to bury Ryker, his Delta Force teammate. His brother in every way but blood.

At the funeral, she's the first person he sees. The *only* person he sees. Walking away from River once was hard enough, even if it was for her own good. Walking away a second time may prove impossible...especially after he realizes she's digging into her brother's suspicious death.

When River's search for answers puts her in the sights of dangerous men, Jackson will do anything and everything to keep her safe. Even if it means losing his heart—and his life—in the process.

ACKNOWLEDGMENTS

Thank you to my team. Kelli, you're a rockstar when it comes to developmental edits. Thank you for making sure my story makes sense and my characters make intelligent decisions. Marla and Jen, thank you for finding all those mistakes that I read over a hundred times and miss. Thank you to my ARC team. You guys are amazing and push me to write the next book. Thank you to my husband for your patience and support, and my daughter Sophia, for giving me reason.

PROLOGUE

*S*ixteen Years Ago

RIVER WATCHED Jackson from across the yard. The dark night cast shadows over his face, but it didn't detract from how good-looking he was. If anything, it made him more handsome. More dangerous. More...everything.

She swallowed the lump in her throat. Tonight was her last with him. Last for a while, at least. Because tomorrow he was leaving with her brother to join the military.

A little part of her heart broke at the thought. Okay, not a little part. A big, gigantic chunk. It cracked and crumbled at the thought of never seeing him walk around the school halls again. Never waking up to see him sitting at the dining table beside her brother, Ryker.

The man was basically a staple in her house. Her parents treated him like he was their own because, well, his own father didn't.

She pulled at a loose thread in her dress, very aware that the tremble in her fingers had nothing to do with the cold and everything to do with what she planned to say to Jackson.

Michele leaned close. "When are you going to give it to him?"

River gasped, dragging her eyes away from Jackson to look at her best friend. "Chele! Someone could hear you."

The yard was packed with people. Most a year older than her, seniors from Ryker and Jackson's grade.

Michele's eyes softened. "No one's listening." Her gaze skittered across the yard, then back to River. "I think you should do it soon."

Was that her heart having a little attack at her friend's words? "Why? Because you think I'll chicken out if I wait too long?"

Michele raised a brow.

Okay. Maybe her friend had a point. She'd liked Jackson for so long. Obsessed over him basically since the first time she'd laid eyes on him freshman year. She still remembered that moment so clearly. It had been her first day at a new school, only having moved to town the week earlier. And there he'd been, across the cafeteria. She didn't know what had pulled her gaze in his direction. The romantic part of her liked to think it was fate. But that was dumb, wasn't it? Because when they were together, all they did was argue. And yet, the second he left the room, she felt his absence like the weight of a rock on her chest.

And that had been her life. For three long years.

"I'm not going to chicken out," she eventually said, not sure if she was trying to convince her friend or herself.

Hell, she hated being scared of anything. Growing up with a fearless brother like Ryker made her want to be just as brave. But, for some reason, when it came to Jackson, she felt fearful of everything.

His laugh floated across the yard, dulling the sound of music and voices. Her gaze skirted back to him, noting the crinkles beside his eyes. The way his lips tilted up and his entire face lightened.

When he stepped away from the group, she tracked his movement, watching him right up until he disappeared inside the house. *Her* house.

Michele nudged her shoulder.

She was right, this was her chance.

Nerves trickled down her spine, trying to keep her from moving forward, but she shoved them away, taking a quick, steadying breath before walking into the house.

Jackson's footsteps on the stairs peppered the air. She already knew where he'd be headed. Ryker's bedroom. The room with his stuff. The room right beside hers.

She moved up the stairs silently, forcing the air in and out of her lungs with each step. She'd just reached the top when she caught sight of him slipping into Ryker's room.

River moved into her own room, grabbing the small journal from the top drawer of her desk before slipping out into the hall and then into the room beside hers.

Immediately, her breath caught.

Jackson's back was to her, and he was shirtless. Thick cords of muscles stretched across his shoulders.

Her mouth went dry. She'd seen him without a shirt before, and each time it had little parts of her belly flopping. He'd always been more muscular than most guys his age. But over the last few months, he'd continued to get bigger and stronger.

He'd just shoved another shirt over his head and turned when he stilled. Their eyes clashed, and it almost felt like a physical blow to her abdomen. It stole her breath and rendered her silent.

"River." He frowned, scanning her face, studying her. "What are you doing in here?"

Suddenly, the courage she'd been trying to channel slipped, and every strong part of her felt weak. Every brave fissure of her soul wanted to run and hide.

She forced her spine to straighten.

Be brave, River.

She took a small, slow step forward. "I made you something. I wanted to give it to you before you go tomorrow."

Another step forward. Then she stretched out her arm and handed him the small journal. The tremble in her fingers was still there, and it had her tugging her hand away quickly, not wanting him to see.

He studied the journal as she studied *him*. His honey-brown eyes. His strong jawline. She took in every little part.

His gaze shot up. "What is it?"

"A book I made for you. It's probably silly." She shook her head, not wanting him to see exactly how much it meant to her, how much time she'd spent planning and executing it. How much his reaction meant to her. "I took photos of all your favorite things. I know you don't like this town very much, so I focused on the people. The ones who make you smile."

She knew he wanted to get out of here. Away from his drunk of a father. To not be reminded of the fact that his mother had left him when he was so young.

She nibbled her bottom lip, so damn nervous she was scared her knees would buckle.

Jackson flipped open the first page. His gaze scanned over it. She didn't need to look down to know what he saw. Pictures of him and Ryker on skateboards. They were always on those things. Skating around town. To school. Shops.

He turned the page. The next was him and Ryker in the ring at Larry's Boxing Club. He hadn't said the words out loud, but she knew it was Jackson's favorite place. It was the only place he ever looked truly happy and free.

Jackson flicked through every page, never uttering a word, his face never changing. When he reached the last page, he paused longer than the others.

The last photo was of River, Ryker, Jackson, and her parents. It had only been taken a couple of nights ago. Their final dinner together. God, the house would be quiet without them.

Jackson traced the writing below the picture. She ran her finger along a stitch on her dress, trying to stop herself from any nervous fidgeting. She'd spent hours debating what to write on that page. Eventually, she'd gone with something simple.

Stay safe. We love you.

When he looked up, he was frowning. "You made this?"

"Yes." She'd spent so long planning. So long walking around town, searching out every little thing she knew he loved. She lifted a shoulder. "I always have my camera so…it wasn't hard."

Usually, she snapped shots of the trees swaying in the wind. The sky as it shifted from blue to orange and purple. That stuff fascinated her. But for Jackson, she'd made an exception.

Sucking in a breath of courage, River stepped forward, watching the way his pupils dilated. "Before you go, I need you to know something."

She paused, her tongue suddenly heavy in her mouth. Why was this so hard? They could usually talk and banter all day, every day.

This is different, a quiet voice whispered. *This has the power to change everything.*

"I love you." The words fell from her lips in barely a whisper.

She was only seventeen, but she knew what she felt was love. The emotion was heavy and all-consuming and so utterly devastating that she could barely breathe or think around the man.

His mouth opened but quickly snapped shut.

Be brave, River, those same words whispered in her head again. She listened, taking a final step closer, slipping her fingers around his neck, and kissing him.

∼

"I LOVE YOU."

The words floated through the air, seeping into Jackson's skin, penetrating his chest.

5

No one had ever said those words to him before. Not in his entire eighteen years of life. His asshole of a father definitely hadn't. And his mother had disappeared so long ago that he couldn't even remember what she looked like.

He'd always known that River was attracted to him. How many times had he caught her gaze lingering on him from across a room? But he'd tried to ignore it. Always terrified of what might happen if he didn't.

Now, standing here, in a home that wasn't his, being thrown a party by a family who didn't belong to him, he couldn't help but want something he'd never allowed himself to want before...her.

Jackson was still in shock, still processing the way her words touched a part of his heart that had never been touched, when River stepped forward. She placed two small hands around his neck before tugging his head down and pressing her lips to his.

For a moment, Jackson was still. So damn still, he didn't so much as breathe. The small book felt heavy between his fingers. A book that had captured the only good things he'd known in this town.

Then River leaned her body into him, pressing her soft body against him. She swiped her warm lips across his. And suddenly, that thin thread of control he always held so tightly snapped.

His hands slipped around her back, tugging her closer, the book remaining firmly in his fingers.

He'd kissed girls before, but this was different. *She* was different. She was the hot sun on his frozen heart. The gentle curves to his rough edges.

His tongue slipped between her lips, and Jackson lost himself. He kissed her like he couldn't get enough. Like, if he released her, this moment would be erased, never to have existed.

How many times had he dreamed about touching her like this? Kissing her? Taking her as his own? So many that even looking at her had begun to feel too damn difficult.

And this kiss lived up to every fantasy. Every desire. She

invaded all of his senses. Almost making him forget who he was. Who *she* was.

Almost.

A quiet hum slipped from her chest. It was enough to allow small tendrils of reality to trickle back into his ravaged mind. He forced his brain to remember why he'd denied himself this girl for so long.

Because she was perfect. Strong-willed. Intelligent. She had a family who loved her. Whereas he…he lived in a trailer park. He had nothing to his name. His family consisted of one man who drank too much and had beaten the shit out of Jackson until he'd become strong enough to fight back.

Suddenly, every reason he was leaving this town, leaving her, came back to him. Every reason he'd promised himself he was never returning.

Jackson wrenched his mouth from hers, taking a large step back. The separation had his body chilling and his heart clenching.

River's lips were red, her eyes wide and glazed.

Fuck. How could he have done that? How could he have lost control and allowed himself to take something he had no right having?

"That was a mistake," he said quickly, barely able to meet her gaze.

River frowned, blinking as her eyes cleared. "A mistake?"

"We shouldn't have done that."

There was a moment of pause. In that moment, all he could feel was hate. Hate for himself. For his own lack of goddamn control.

Instead of walking away, River's spine straightened. Her lips firmed. "Yes, we should have. You feel the same way as I do. I know you do. I felt it in your kiss."

Of course, she'd felt it. The kiss had damn near shattered him.

He scrubbed a hand over his face. "I need to go."

He tried to step past her, but she shifted in front of him. "Jackson, please. I know you haven't had the best examples of love in your life, but what exists between you and me…it's real. You love me too."

Then she placed a hand over his heart. A heart that was pounding so hard he could hear it as much as he could feel it. And he swore he could feel that touch deep in his chest.

Her voice quieted. "Maybe you're not ready right now, but one day you will be. And I'll wait for you."

She'd wait for him… This perfect woman, a woman who could have the world if she chose, would put her life on hold for *him*. A man who could very easily amount to nothing, just like his father.

He couldn't let that happen. She deserved more than he could give. He didn't even know what love was.

"I'm not coming back, River."

He could see it in her eyes. She was debating what to do. How to handle this. Because River didn't give up. To her, a problem was merely a puzzle to be solved.

His heart clenched in his chest. Because he knew what he had to do. Every part of him rebelled against it, but to save her from herself—from him—he'd do whatever it took.

"I don't love you," he said firmly, making sure his words were hard and unyielding. "I never have and never will. I'm sorry if that's not what you want to hear." So damn sorry, he felt like he was drowning. "But that's life, River. It rarely turns out the way we want."

She frowned.

"I'm never returning to Lindeman," Jackson continued. "I'm never returning to *you*."

There they were. The words that would hurt her. Crush her. Because even though she acted strong, he knew it had taken something deep inside for her to come to him tonight. To open up her heart.

And he'd trampled all over it.

Her bottom lip trembled, but to her credit, she didn't break. She didn't shed a single tear. Instead, she gave a quick nod before turning and leaving the room.

Every step she took away from him felt like a dagger to the chest. He wanted to reach out. To call her back. But he clenched his jaw and forced himself to remain where he was. Because it was true that he wasn't returning. But the other part...the part about not loving her, that wasn't true at all.

CHAPTER 1

 resent Day

RYKER LOUIS HARP. Jackson's gaze skittered over his best friend's name on the tombstone. A friend he would never see again. Never speak to or fight beside. He stared at the name so long that his eyes ached with the need to look away. Blink. Anything.

Eventually, he glanced at the date of birth and date of death. Two things telling the world he was too fucking young to die.

And then that little inscription: *A loving son, brother, friend, soldier, and defender. Rest in peace.*

Jackson wished he could feel the pain of losing the man who was basically his brother. He wished he could cry. Scream. Feel the rupturing of his chest. But all he felt was numb.

The priest was talking, but Jackson barely heard a word.

For the thousandth time, he wondered about his friend's final minutes. There was supposed to be a moment right before a person died where they saw everything, right? The highs. The lows. The moments of deep regret that tore the soul to shreds and made the tiny fragments of the heart squeeze and clench.

Had Ryker experienced that? Had he felt the impossible weight of every decision he'd made press down on him seconds before he'd lost control and his car had careened off the side of that bridge?

Jackson's jaw clenched as the casket began to lower into the ground. Suddenly, the numbness started to disintegrate, and a wild anger rose in his chest. Anger that something so fucking tragic had happened to such a good man. Anger that scumbags still breathed on this Earth while Ryker would never suck in another breath again.

Ryker may not have been his brother by blood, but in every other way, he was exactly that. The guy had taken Jackson in and welcomed him into his family. There'd barely been a day since they'd met at fifteen years of age when the two of them had been apart.

Inseparable. That's what they'd been. Finishing school together. Enlisting together. Hell, they'd even become Delta Force operators together in the same damn team.

He heard Declan's sharp intake of breath beside him at the light thud of the casket hitting the bottom of the grave. Cole, on the other hand, was silent.

Those small differences described his teammates to a T. Declan was the extroverted one who wasn't afraid to show emotion. Cole was the quiet one. Ryker had been a bit of both. The glue that kept them strong. Kept them alive on their deadliest missions.

He didn't know what the hell he was. Right now, he'd describe himself as pretty damn lost.

They weren't active operators anymore. A year ago, they'd decided not to reenlist after their last mission in the Middle East. All of them had needed to get out and take some time off. The plan had been to stay close, though. Keep in contact and talk every day.

That hadn't happened—and it made him feel raw inside that he'd missed the last year of his best friend's life.

The priest continued to talk, spewing words Jackson didn't believe in.

Finally, he dragged his gaze off the tombstone to look at *her*. The woman he'd been so damn sure he'd never see again.

River. Ryker's little sister.

She stood across the large gathering, her mother on one side and her friend Michele on the other.

Even though his heart felt torn in two, and an ache had taken root inside that he was sure would never heal, he couldn't stop how his body reacted to her. The way something deep inside him flicked on, like a lightbulb. Even after sixteen long years of separation, his chest heated at the sight of her.

An old, familiar fire pulsed through his blood. A primal need that heaved through his stomach. One he hadn't felt since he was a teenager. Because no other woman had ever made him feel what *she* did.

When the wind pushed locks of soft black hair over her face, she didn't even attempt to push them away. Her entire focus remained on the grave.

He expected to see tears and heartbreak on her face. A deep, inconsolable pain.

He didn't see any of that.

All he saw was anger. It darkened her eyes to the color of the sky when there was no moon or stars. It reddened her cheeks and straightened her spine.

Jackson's brows tugged together. He'd glanced her way a few times throughout the day, and the anger was always there. And it had him wondering.

River had always been close to her brother. One year separated them in age, but growing up, a lot of people mistook them for twins. Ryker had been her brother first, friend second. Every chance the man had, he'd contacted his sister. Returned home for holidays. Checked in to see that she was okay.

Questions skittered around in his head. What else was she feeling that she wasn't showing? Why was anger the dominant emotion? Maybe anger was her way of dealing with the pain. But something in his gut told him there was more to it than that.

She hadn't looked at him once. In fact, she'd barely looked at anyone. She'd stood by her parents and friend the entire day, silent.

When her head finally rose, she scanned the crowd. That's when he saw it. The first flicker of emotion other than anger. Surprise.

Her lips slipped open, her eyes widening.

Jackson followed her gaze across the crowd of people to a young Asian man standing at the back. When his gaze met River's, his eyes rounded slightly. Not just in surprise. But like he hadn't wanted anyone to catch him there. Like he'd been trying to lurk in the shadows without being seen.

"Mr. And Mrs. Harp have organized some food and drinks at their house," the priest said. "If you can, they would love for everyone to join them."

People started moving around Jackson, but his focus remained on *her*. On the way she immediately started shuffling through the crowd, beelining for this mystery man, a desperate look in her eyes.

Jackson could already see she wasn't going to make it. The guy was walking away, and he was walking quickly. And while every step she took was fast, there were too many people she had to weave through, and every so often, someone stopped her with a light touch on her arm. A sad smile as they blocked her path.

Jackson shot his gaze back to the man who'd just reached the parking lot. He might be walking away now, but Jackson had noted the guy's face at the service and committed it to memory. It was obvious he meant something to River.

Now that Ryker was gone, the responsibility fell on his shoulders to look after her. He owed it to his best friend. And he'd sure as hell be taking that responsibility seriously.

~

RIVER TOOK A SIP OF JUICE, barely tasting it. It could have been a cup of mud for all the attention she paid. She was too busy searching the crowd for Kenny.

Where was he? Why was he at the funeral? Did he know something?

Her gut clenched at the thought.

Her brother had officially been declared dead seven days ago. It had been a long week of comforting her parents while they mourned the loss of their son. A week of trying to work out what the hell was going on.

And a week of organizing a funeral for a man she *knew* wasn't dead.

She hadn't mentioned the last part to anyone. Not just because they'd probably think she was just a grieving sister in denial over her brother's death. But because there was clearly a *reason* behind him being declared dead—probably a very dangerous one.

Even though there was no way she'd put her parents in danger by telling them, she sure as hell wasn't going to just sit on the knowledge.

"Still doing okay?"

River swung her gaze beside her to Michele. They'd been best friends since high school and usually told each other everything. This was the first secret she'd kept in…well, since they'd met.

"I'm okay."

Michele frowned, her indigo-blue eyes darkening. "River…" *Oh boy, here it comes.* "I can't begin to imagine what you're going through right now. I feel like my own heart is breaking," her voice cracked a little bit, but she recovered quickly, "and he wasn't even my brother."

Wasn't. Past tense. Everyone had been speaking about him in past tense, and it killed her.

Michele touched her arm. "But I think it's important you feel what you need to feel."

Oh, River was feeling plenty. Confusion. Frustration. An anger so powerful that sometimes she swore she'd drown in it. The anger wasn't directed at anyone else, though. It was only toward herself. All of it. Because she was pretty sure that whatever was going on, whatever the reason Ryker had faked his own death…it had something to do with River and that damn club she never should have walked into.

"We all handle grief in our own way, I know that," Michele continued. "But you're almost acting like…"

Like he's not dead?

The words were right there on the tip of River's tongue. She only just kept them to herself.

She forced a small smile to her lips. Out of the two of them, River was the risktaker. The adventurer. And Michele was the calm. The voice of reason.

"Thank you, Chele. You've been such a wonderful friend. And trust me, I'm feeling so much, I just…" She stopped when her gaze landed on a man across the room. His back was turned to her, but she was almost certain it was him. Kenny. "Sorry, Chele, I'll be right back."

The words had only just left her lips when she was zipping through the throng of people, pushing and weaving until she reached the man.

She pressed a hand to his shoulder. "Kenny—"

The man turned, and her stomach dropped. Not Kenny. Even though he looked similar from behind in height, breadth, and hair color, he was older, and not of Asian descent.

"Sorry, I, um, thought you were someone else."

Sympathy softened the guy's eyes.

Oh God. She couldn't handle another person looking at her like that. Like they were waiting for her to break before their eyes.

She needed space. Silence.

Turning away, she headed up the stairs. But instead of moving to her old room, she went to Ryker's.

The second she stepped inside, she felt like she could breathe again. Her parents had left his room untouched since he'd left for the military.

Memories flooded her. Of dropping onto his bed and talking about nothing and everything. Complaining about dumb stuff that she couldn't even remember. Bugging him until he'd physically remove her from the room.

She smiled, touching the surface of his dresser.

Over the last year, he'd mostly lived at her house, but he still stayed with their parents on the odd occasion. There were little things that sat out here and there, like his watch, a couple of shirts...and she just knew that her mother hadn't had the strength to touch anything since he'd been declared dead.

"Where are you, Ryker?" she asked quietly.

Why was he hiding? Could he see what he was doing to Mom and Dad?

She sat on the bed, smoothing the sheets beneath her fingers. Then, reaching over, she ran her hand over the light layer of dust on the side table. The drawer was slightly cracked open, something white poking out.

Frowning, she pulled it from the drawer. A napkin with a name and phone number.

She traced her finger over the name. Angel.

Then she started tracing the number, already itching to call it. It could be nothing. A random girl had probably given him her number. Ryker was tall, good-looking, and took great care of his body. He was also funny and smart. All the things women loved, so they naturally gravitated toward him.

The thing was, he wasn't the kind of guy to keep any number. Definitely not on a napkin in a drawer. He'd enter it into his phone or just toss it altogether. More the latter in the last year, since he'd returned home.

Unless the number was important. So important that he wanted to keep it, but not in his phone.

At the sound of footsteps approaching the doorway, River jumped to her feet, spinning around while hiding the napkin behind her back.

Immediately, her breath caught, her stomach doing a little flip.

Jackson.

CHAPTER 2

*R*iver pushed the napkin into the waistband of her skirt, her gaze never leaving Jackson's.

Sixteen years had passed, and somehow the man looked exactly the same, while also completely different. Was that possible? His brown eyes still had flecks of honey, his hair still the shade of pine wood. And he was still tall. So unbelievably tall.

But he was bigger. And there was something harder about him. Something more intense.

She swallowed, suddenly feeling an odd mix of desire and nervous tension bubble to the surface.

He commanded all her attention. Every little scrap of it. Which was exactly why she'd avoided eye contact with him all day. Because she'd known what would happen if she looked. She'd lose herself. Like she'd lost herself all those years ago.

"Hi, River."

His deep, silky voice slid over her skin, causing the tiny hairs on her arms to stand on end. She remembered that voice well. Too well.

"Hi, Jackson. It's nice of you to finally return to Lindeman."

There was a thread of resentment in her voice. A resentment she couldn't have hidden if she tried.

One of Jackson's brows quirked, questioning. He stepped farther into the room.

God, how was he so big? He'd always been tall. What was he? Six four? Six five? But now, he'd filled out across the shoulders and chest. And his arms...even through his white dress shirt, she could see the outline of his thick muscles. He took up all the space.

His head tilted to the side, those brown eyes watching her closely. "Should I have gotten here sooner?"

Yes. The voice was a shout in her head. A shout that would never reach the air.

How was that even a question? He damn well *should* have gotten here sooner, and he knew it. Not just to visit her or her parents. Parents who had taken him in, fed him, and given him a safe place to stay on more occasions than she could count. But because for the last year, Ryker had been here, and the man had needed his best friend.

Ryker hadn't been the same since returning to Lindeman. He'd been angry and closed-off. A shadow of the brother she used to know.

She remembered the night when she'd finally sucked up her pride and called Jackson. The man hadn't answered, and he certainly hadn't called her back. That was a month ago.

She swallowed, not able to think about that right now.

"You're an adult. It's not my place to tell you what you should be doing."

This time his eyes pinched like he was confused. He took another step forward, almost as if he was stalking her. Like he thought if he moved too quickly, he'd scare her off.

He wouldn't. She didn't scare so easily anymore.

The closer he drew, the more his musky scent permeated the space. How was it possible, after so many years, that he still smelled exactly the same? Like forest and sandalwood mixed together, creating the most intoxicating scent.

No. It was some trick of the mind. It had to be.

His voice gentled, intense eyes darting between hers. "Are you okay?"

No. She wasn't okay. She'd stopped being okay the second her father had called, telling her in that gut-wrenchingly broken voice that her brother had driven his car off a bridge and died.

"Yes." One word. One lie. That was all he was getting from her.

Jackson looked at her like he was trying to solve a puzzle. It was the same way everyone had been looking at her throughout the last week. Wondering why she wasn't crying. Why her face wasn't red and blotchy, her limbs weren't trembling.

"It's okay to *not* be okay," he said quietly.

She almost scoffed. Or maybe she actually did scoff, because his brows twitched.

"Thank you, Jackson, but I don't need you to tell me it's okay for me to be *anything*."

She was being a bitch, but she couldn't help it. Where had he been while his best friend was hurting? River may not have known why he was hurting, but she was almost certain Jackson did. And she was so damn angry at him for that.

He took another step forward. "What do you need, then?"

The question had her pausing. Whatever she'd been expecting him to say, it wasn't that. "I need..." *Answers*? "Space. From the sympathetic looks and the apologies and the tears." It was too much. All of it. Especially when they were wasted emotions.

"People just care."

Yeah, she knew that. Hell, even people who barely knew her or her brother seemed to cry like they'd lost an old friend. That probably shouldn't make her as angry as it did.

"I know." She shot a quick look to the door. "I should get back."

She tried to move around him, but before she could pass, Jackson was there, blocking her way.

This time when he spoke, there was no gentleness or softness. Anger laced his words. "What the hell is *that?*"

She looked up, almost groaning out loud when she saw what he was staring at. The black eye she'd covered with about a pound of makeup. "What?"

His jaw visibly ticked. "Did someone fucking hit you?"

Ah, there you are, Jackson. The man she remembered. The man with a temper who could spit fire with his eyes.

"It's nothing. I just got caught up in someone else's fight."

Yeah, by putting her face right next to a swinging elbow. *Smart, River, real smart.*

She attempted to step to the side, but this time his fingers curled around her upper arm. And even though his hold was firm, restraining, her chest wanted to hum at the contact. Her heart sped up and her skin tingled.

With sheer force, she shut it down. All of it. She wasn't a pathetic seventeen-year-old in love with her brother's best friend anymore. She was a thirty-three-year-old woman, and she had control of her emotions, dammit.

"Who's fight? What the hell is going on?"

"Let go of me, Jackson."

"River—"

"*No.* Don't you dare do that." She wrenched her arm free, knowing full well she only got out of his hold because he let her. "You haven't been here. You don't get to step back into this town, into my life, after sixteen years away and expect answers to your questions. I'm not your concern. For all *you* know, I've had weekly black eyes since you left."

His fists clenched at his sides, and the cords in his neck bulged. But clearly, he knew her words were true. If he wanted to know what was going on, then he should have damn well been here.

The anger narrowing his eyes deepened, but when he spoke, his voice was quieter. It reminded her of the calm before a storm. "You *are* my concern. Now tell me who the hell hit you before—"

"What? Before you go find the guy and just start swinging? Or before you up and disappear for another sixteen years, only reappearing when another member of my family is declared dead?"

It was a low blow. And by Jackson's flinch, he felt it.

She almost took her words back. She almost apologized. But then memories of their last night together came back to her. Of that kiss. Telling him she loved him. And Jackson walking away. Not returning a single call of hers over those first few years. Acting like she didn't exist for over one and a half decades when, just before that, barely a day had passed when they hadn't been in each other's lives.

Suddenly, she couldn't stand to be in this room anymore. Not with him. Because even though she told herself she was stronger, even though she'd grown so much over the years, he still owned a part of her heart that no other person had ever touched.

Gritting her teeth, she walked around him, not sure if she was relieved or disappointed when he didn't grab her again.

She'd almost reached the door when he spoke.

"This isn't over, River. Ryker isn't here to look after you, so I *will* make sure you're safe."

She turned her head. "That almost sounds like a threat."

"It's a promise."

CHAPTER 3

*J*ackson leaned back in his chair, lifting the mug of coffee to his lips. He needed coffee in an IV right now. He'd barely slept.

How could he when thoughts of River plagued him? Consumed him? Tormented his damn mind?

Not just because the woman was sporting a black eye that had nearly sent him into a rage or because she wouldn't tell him who the hell had given it to her so he could beat the shit out of him. But because he hadn't been in the same room as her in over sixteen years. He hadn't heard that voice, touched that delicate skin. Yet, yesterday, he'd done all of that.

Declan and Cole sat across from him at the circular table outside Penguin Café. They were talking about something that Jackson had long ago stopped following.

She was all he could think about. Before he'd noticed the black eye, he'd almost been in a trance. So fixated on her, everything else had faded.

She'd been pissed at him. Why? Because of what he'd said the night before he left? Or was it something more recent? She'd emphasized that he'd *finally* returned. Was she angry he hadn't been back before now?

Jackson scrubbed a hand down his face. It was probably everything. He was an asshole. He hadn't felt deserving of her then, and he still didn't today.

"Tell us the truth, J, you ruled this town with Ryker, didn't you?"

At Declan's words, Jackson turned back to them. "Nope. The only reason I didn't get my ass beat at school every day was because Ryker was there."

He'd been an angry teenager. Every damn day. Angry at his abusive, alcoholic father for laying into him all the time. For not giving a single fuck about him. And at his mother for disappearing.

Anger had been just about all he could feel...until Ryker.

Cole's brows tugged together. "Yeah, Ryker was good like that. Remember our second deployment in South America? We were drinking in that dive of a bar and I almost punched the leader of that gang?"

Declan chuckled. "Yeah, with how drunk we all were, there was no way we'd have survived that one."

"He saved our asses more times than we could probably count," Jackson said quietly.

"Hell, the man carried me on his back across the Middle East on that final mission. I owe him my life." Cole's jaw tensed. "*Owed.*"

A heavy silence fell around the table. Their final mission had been hell. They'd barely made it out alive.

Jackson blew out a long breath. "We should have kept in contact more."

They'd said they would. Hell, after their last mission went to shit and they'd made the decision to leave active duty, he'd assumed they'd be in touch every day.

But they'd each returned to different states, licking their wounds, and it hadn't happened.

"We got busy," Declan said, eyes on the street beside them. "Me with my brother at his garage in Camden." He dipped his head toward Cole. "You were with your family in Chicago, recovering from your broken back."

Cole grunted. "Yeah, it took too damn long."

Declan shot his gaze to Jackson. "And you with the security work you were doing in Boston."

Jackson's jaw ticked. What he'd really been doing was trying to find a place for himself in the world that didn't involve Lindeman or the military. Trying to figure everything out. It hadn't worked. He shook his head. "We should have tried harder."

Maybe then things would have been different.

"I know what you're thinking," Cole said, leaning forward. "But the police report says his car skidded on the wet road, probably avoiding an animal. That's a tragedy, Jackson, not something we could have saved him from."

It *was* a goddamn tragedy.

Declan frowned, eyes on something across the road. "Is that your girl, J?"

His girl?

He followed Declan's gaze to find River across the street. His gut clenched.

She had a camera bag strung across her oversized purple sweatshirt. Shorts poked out beneath, and her legs…they were long and smooth and on full display. She stepped into a little shop across from the coffee shop.

His gaze lifted, scanning the sign. "Meals Made Easy," he read under his breath.

Was it another café? He saw a big open kitchen through the windows, but there were only a couple of tables. Basically, only seats for waiting. A takeaway place?

He watched through the glass as River hugged Michele. The

two had been inseparable in high school. Obviously, nothing had changed.

"She's a food photographer, right?" Cole said, breaking into Jackson's thoughts. "Ryker said something about her taking pictures of food and drinks?"

"He used the words 'food and beverage stylist'," Declan corrected.

"Same thing. She arranges the stuff and takes pictures."

Jackson didn't cast his gaze away. He couldn't. He watched as she sat at one of the two tables. Her lips were moving quickly, while Michele just seemed to be listening.

His chest ached to hear her voice again. Almost as if, after depriving himself for so many years, he was now desperate to get as much of her as possible.

"She always loved taking pictures. I never saw her taking pictures of food. The outdoors, however...she used to chase the sunsets. Do whatever she needed to do to get the best photo."

Why hadn't she followed that passion? Her pictures had been amazing back then, and she'd only been a teenager.

When he finally dragged his gaze back to his friends, Declan had a brow raised, and Cole had a smirk on his face. Both were staring at him.

"What?"

"You guys never—"

"No." The word was out of his mouth before Cole could finish. Because he knew what was coming. "We were never anything but friends."

Hell, they'd barely been that. They'd argued—a lot. Mostly about stupid shit that meant nothing.

Despite that, by senior year, he'd barely been able to look at the woman without fighting everything inside himself not to touch her. Tug her into his arms. Press his lips to hers.

He sucked in a short, sharp breath at the memories.

"Why not?" Of course, it was Dec who asked. The man was always the one to ask the obvious questions.

Jackson ran a hand through his hair. "To understand that, you'd need to grow up in a trailer park with a drunk, abusive dad. My life was everything hers wasn't." When Declan and Cole remained silent, he lifted his shoulders. "And it was always my plan to get the hell out of this town and never come back."

Cole raised a brow. "Yet, here you are."

"Yep. Here I am."

"God, woman. Whatever you have on that stove smells a-*mazing*. I don't care what I need to do, table dance, run naked down the street…I want it in my belly."

Michele laughed, setting down a wooden spoon before placing the lid on the pot. "Well, it's your lucky day, because I've made a little extra for you to take home, no dancing or nudity needed."

River's eyes almost rolled up into her head. "You are my angel. I could literally kiss your feet. This is why we can never stop being friends. I would starve."

Either that or live a very bland life.

Michele grabbed two bowls of soup from the pot before setting them on the table and dropping down beside River. Her friend ran a meal delivery business, mostly servicing Lindeman and the neighboring town of Ellensburg. The service was getting more in demand every day.

She leaned forward. "I always thought you stayed friends with me for my witty personality?"

River lifted a shoulder. "Eh, I could take it or leave it."

Michele rolled her eyes but chuckled, knowing her well enough to know River needed Michele in her life for many reasons. The main one being, because her friend kept her sane.

She pulled the spoon from the soup, sipping a bit, and this time her eyes *did* roll up into her head. "Holy cow, woman. This is so good."

Michele gave her a knowing smile. "Salt. Lots of salt."

"I thought you tried to go easy on the salt?"

Her parents had died in short succession of each other when she was little, her father of a heart attack and her mother of cancer. Since then, Michele was a bit of a health nut. Particularly careful with things like salt and sugar. Her friend was curvy, but she wasn't overweight by any means. She had hips, a generous cleavage, and curves that most women would die for.

Michele stirred the soup in her bowl. "After everything that's happened over the last few months, I decided that life's too short."

River's heart gave a little bang against her ribs. Not only was Michele going through the grief of losing Ryker, a man she'd known for years, who was like a brother, but her uncle, the guy who'd raised her after her parents passed away, had been having heart issues.

"How's Uncle Ottie doing?"

She lifted a shoulder. "He tells me he's fine, but I know the truth. And he's like the definition of health. So if he's not safe, no one is." She sighed. "I wish he would sell the shop and relax."

She took her friend's hand. "Maybe the book shop *is* his way of relaxing."

"Yeah, you're right. I know you are."

River sipped some more of the soup. So. Damn. Good. "And you haven't heard from Tim again?" Argh, she couldn't even say his name without sneering it.

Michele had gone on just three dates with the man, and each one had left her friend feeling more uneasy. The stuff Michele had told River...the things he'd said...putting her down, becoming insanely jealous of other men, even though they'd barely begun dating.

Huge red flags.

"No."

"I'm so glad you ended things," she said, shaking her head.

"Me too." Michele nibbled on her bottom lip, fingers thrumming the side of the bowl. "River, I need to ask you something."

She only just held in a groan, knowing there was something on her friend's mind she was trying to figure out how to phrase—and almost certain she knew exactly what it was. "Okay."

Michele's fingers stilled. "I want you to tell me what's going on without brushing me off with excuses that you know I won't buy."

She'd known there was only so long before Michele pushed. "There's nothing—"

"Don't you dare." Michele held up a finger, silencing River. It reminded her of what teachers would do when she'd talked out of turn at school. "We don't do that. We don't keep secrets from each other, and we certainly don't lie."

She was right. And the truth was, she'd known there would be a timeline on how long she could keep the truth from her friend.

"Fine. But you can't freak out, and you can't tell anyone else. I mean it. Not a single soul. Swear to me."

"River—"

"Nope, I'm not telling until you swear."

Michele rolled her eyes. "Fine. I swear."

River took a deep breath before leaning across the table. "Ryker's not dead."

If she was expecting shock, she didn't get it. Michele's eyes softened into the familiar sympathy she'd been getting from everyone for the last week. River already knew what was coming.

"Oh, honey. The man drove his car off Colins Creek Bridge. The vehicle then caught on fire with him inside," she added gently. "The coroner used his dental records to identify him."

She shook her head. "No, I know what the coroner's report

says." She'd asked to see it herself. Read through every single word. "I don't believe it."

She *couldn't* believe it.

Her friend remained silent, only inhaling a long breath.

"Since coming home, he's been angry," River continued. "You saw it. We talked about it plenty of times."

Michele gave a slow nod.

"But a little over a month ago, something changed. He was still angry, but it was like…the edge had worn off. Every Friday, he'd stay out almost all night. And he had all these bruises…"

Michele was nibbling on her bottom lip again. "River, I know all this. We asked him about it, remember? And he wouldn't tell us what was going on."

"Okay, but you don't know this…" She wet her lips before continuing. "The night he died, I saw him."

Her friend frowned. "When?"

"I heard a noise in his room. It woke me up. When I went in there, I saw the back of him just as he climbed out the window." River sucked in a deep breath. "Michele, I saw him at two thirty-five in the morning. His time of death was recorded as one fifteen."

CHAPTER 4

*M*ichele's eyes widened, but then she quickly shook her head. "No. That's not possible. You were probably just tired and saw something that wasn't there. You said yourself it was dark and you only saw the back of him. I see shadows all the time when I'm tired."

"I know what I saw, Chele. It was *him*." She'd know her brother anywhere.

There was a small beat of silence. Michele lifted her spoon but didn't immediately press it to her lips. "Okay, let's be crazy for a second and work under the assumption that you're correct. That he's alive. Why would the police *and* the coroner say he's dead? And where is he? Why would he let you and your parents go through all of this?"

That's what had her stumped. "I don't know. But I'm going to find out."

Michele's spoon crashed back into her bowl. "What do you mean, you're going to find out? River, you're not going to do anything dangerous, are you?"

"I'm going to do whatever it takes to find him."

Her friend's eyes narrowed. "And what exactly do you think it will take?"

"Well, I'm almost certain his disappearance has something to do with Trinity Nightclub."

"No." The hardness in Michele's voice had River blinking. "You are *not* going anywhere near Mickey."

Only she was. Mickey was the owner of the club, so it was kind of unavoidable. "I have to. It was only after Ryker went to speak to him that it started."

Michele's voice lowered to a whisper. "He's dangerous! And not just because he has no problem hitting women. Didn't you say there were gang members hanging at his club?"

She cringed internally. "I said I *thought* there were gang members there." And she was ninety-nine percent sure she was right in her suspicions.

"River—"

The door to the shop opened, and whatever her friend was about to say died on her lips when Jackson stepped inside, closely followed by two other guys. She'd never met the other two, but she knew who they were—Declan and Cole. Ryker had talked about them enough over the years that she felt like she *had* met them.

Jackson dipped his head to Michele. "Michele. It's nice to see you again."

She gave him a small smile, her cheeks tinging red.

When he turned his attention to River, his tone deepened. "River." He turned to the first guy. He had a bit of a beard going on, but his smile was wide. "This is Dec."

Declan winked at Michele before smiling at River.

"And this is Cole."

The man's smile wasn't quite so wide. He didn't have a beard but was just as gorgeous. They all were. A little clan of gorgeous, dangerous men.

When Jackson's attention returned to her, she had to swallow to wet her suddenly dry throat.

"What are you guys doing here?" she asked.

He lifted a shoulder, his gaze trapping hers. Good God, did the man ever blink? "We were sitting across the street. Smelled something amazing in here."

Yeah, right. So it had nothing to do with the fact she was here? She remembered his threat from yesterday. And it *was* a threat. It had been clear as day.

"Michele sells ready-made meals," River said.

His gaze finally left her to land on Michele, and she suddenly felt like she could breathe again.

She. Was. Screwed.

"Is that right?"

Michele rose to her feet, smoothing her hands on her jeans. "Yes, um…would you like to take some home with you?"

Jackson shot a look to his friends.

Declan was the first to speak. "Hell yes. If it tastes half as good as it smells, I'll be one happy man."

If possible, the red in Michele's cheeks darkened. Her gaze lingered a second longer on Declan before she quickly looked away.

River rose, too. "Aren't you all staying at the lodge?"

Jackson raised his brows. "Been asking about us?"

He wished. She'd been doing as little "asking" about Jackson as possible. "No. Mrs. Albuquerque was talking about it at the grocery store." And if River had stepped closer to the group of women to overhear the conversation, well, that was involuntary.

Jackson's brows tugged together. "That old woman never liked me."

"She doesn't like anyone."

Jackson had always felt like the locals looked down on him. They didn't. When he was a kid, they'd felt sorry for him. But now? He was a hero. Not that he'd be sticking around long enough to learn that part.

She folded her arms over her chest. "When are you leaving?"

There was a ghost of a smile on his lips. "Why? Trying to get rid of me?"

"Depends if you outstay your welcome or not."

Muffled laughs from behind Jackson floated to her ears. If she expected anger from him, she didn't get it. In fact, he almost looked amused.

Michele cleared her throat. "Ah, I'm going to get those meals ready."

"I'll help you, darlin'." Declan followed her behind the counter.

Jackson stepped forward, and his voice lowered. "I see not much has changed."

That's where he was wrong. "A lot has changed, Jackson. I'm not the same girl I was. In fact—"

River stopped at the sight of a car driving past. Wait, was that Kenny behind the wheel?

Before she could stop herself, she was grabbing her stuff and running out the door. She was seconds from stepping onto the road when strong fingers wrapped around her arm, tugging her back.

The car disappeared down the street.

Dammit! She needed to talk to him and find out what he knew, but he wasn't answering her damn calls. His presence at the funeral had confirmed what River already suspected—that Ryker had started frequenting Mickey's club.

She spun around. "What the hell?"

"You're asking *me* what the hell?" Jackson looked just as frustrated as she felt, his fingers still tightly wrapped around her arm. "You were seconds from running smack bang into traffic."

River tried to control her breaths, frustration churning her gut.

Jackson stepped closer, and even though his hold on her was

firm, his touch was gentle. How was that possible? "That guy was at the funeral yesterday. Who is he?"

His quiet words had her sucking in a quick breath as she tried to ward off the sudden tugging at her heart. "He's none of your business."

Dang it, those words hadn't come out nearly as firm as she'd wanted.

Annoyance flashed over his face. "He sure as hell *is* my business. Because you keep chasing him."

"Wrong. What's happening in my life is *my* business."

His jaw ticked. He was getting angry. *Well, guess what, buddy? I'm already there.*

"You asked me how long I'll be staying in town. I'm staying as long as it takes to figure out what the hell is going on with you."

The man hadn't seen her in years, yet he knew...something.

"You'll be here for a long time then. Because I won't be telling you a damn thing."

Even though her words were firm, her insides were a jumbled mess. Because there was rarely a time when Jackson didn't get exactly what he wanted, and they both knew it.

WHEN RIVER TURNED AWAY from him and started walking down the street, the air rushed from his chest in frustration. Was the woman dismissing him? *Hell no.*

He caught up to her easily, matching her steps as they walked. "You could just be honest with me and save us both the time."

"Or—and this is a crazy idea—you could just leave me alone, Jackson. Go back to wherever you've been living for the last year and get on with your life."

"You know I can't do that."

She raised her brows. "Can't? Or won't?"

"Both."

A grumble sounded from her chest, and even though he was frustrated, it had his body heating. That little sound sucked him back sixteen years to when they'd fought about anything and everything.

"Your hair looks nice," he said softly.

She stumbled over her feet at his words, and his hand was once again on her arm, straightening her. He quirked his lips.

She shot him a quick look before tugging her arm away and continuing to walk.

"Your hair used to be long. It's a lot shorter now. I like it," he continued.

It used to be down to her butt, but now it sat just below the shoulders. He had a feeling he'd like any hairdo on her, though.

For a moment, River seemed lost for words, clearly not expecting a compliment. "Thanks."

"I like the tattoo on your wrist, too." He definitely hadn't missed that. It was a tree. And he was almost certain he knew which one.

She stopped, spinning toward him. "Are you being nice to me because being an overreaching jerk wasn't working?"

His lips twitched again. "No, but glad to know exactly what you think of me."

"Jackson—"

Suddenly, a man walked around the corner, causing both of them to look up.

Immediately, Jackson's lungs seized, tension slamming into his gut. Almost instinctively, he tugged River behind him.

He'd always hated her being around his father.

Brian Ford studied him. "Well, who do we have here? I heard you were back in town. Didn't want to give your old man a call?"

Not in a million fucking years. "No."

Brian's gaze swung to River, snaking down her body, and it took every scrap of strength Jackson had not to throw a fist in the guy's face.

"Don't fucking look at her."

"Jackson…" River's voice was quieter now.

His father's brows rose. "Back in town for two seconds and already thinking you can boss me around like you're better than me? That what the military taught you?"

No. The military taught him self-control. Otherwise, the man would be on his back with a black eye right now. "We need to go, Brian."

"Brian? I don't even get the title of 'Dad' anymore?"

"You lost that a long time ago." Right around the first hit. "Glad you don't reek of beer, at least."

He put his hand on the small of River's back. "Let's go."

He was glad when she didn't argue with him, instead taking a step forward.

When his father took a quick step of his own, blocking her way and almost causing River to collide with him, Jackson shot forward, shoving the man back—hard. "Get the fuck away from her."

He laughed. Actually *laughed*. "I see you're the same little shit you were when you were a teenager."

River's hand went to his arm. "Jackson. Let's go."

Her touch, her soft voice…they were the only things that kept him calm. "Stay out of my way. Or you'll regret it."

Something passed between them. Something dark and dangerous. At least the man had the smarts to keep his mouth shut this time.

After a beat of silence, Jackson's hand once again went to the small of River's back, and he led her away from his messed-up father.

That was his genetics. *That* was the reason he hadn't returned to this godforsaken town. And the reason River was still too damn good for him.

CHAPTER 5

"I can do that, Mom." River slid her hand beneath her mother's, taking the kettle from her fingers.

Just like every other day since her brother's alleged death, her parents' house was completely silent. Nothing like it used to be. She hoped that her presence helped at least a little bit. That they weren't completely drowning in their grief.

Her father was out with friends right now. Two days had passed since Ryker's funeral, and it was his first outing. She'd basically had to force him because, otherwise, he wouldn't leave the house. Neither of them would.

Her mother gave a small nod. "Thank you, honey."

River filled the kettle with water and set it on the stove. When she turned back around, it was to see her mother still standing by the sink, staring into the living room, seemingly looking at nothing.

Her gut clenched. She hated seeing her mom like this. A shell of the woman she usually was. Usually, her mother was the most vibrant person in the room, buzzing around, talking nonstop about her garden, the weather, the neighbors...

River took slow steps back to her mother before placing a gentle hand on her arm. Even that seemed to startle her.

"Mom, maybe you should go have a rest. I can bring you a cup of tea in bed." There had been dark circles under her mother's eyes since the news about Ryker. She'd also lost weight. Pounds off her face. Her body. And she didn't really have them to lose. "I'll bring you something to eat as well. Maybe some of that soup Michele dropped off."

A small frown marred her mother's brow. And when she glanced at River, she almost looked as if she wasn't actually seeing her. "Okay. Thank you, dear. That's probably a good idea."

Her mother walked out of the room, and every step the woman took had the fiery anger in her chest burning hotter.

It seemed anger was all she could feel anymore. Anger at Mickey for pulling Ryker into whatever shit he had going on at the club. Anger at her brother for doing this to their family. And anger at herself for getting involved with Mickey in the first place.

Stupid. So damn stupid.

All of it just fueled her determination to figure out what had happened and fix it.

Once the water had boiled, River prepared the tea and heated some soup. When she stepped into her mother's room, pain filled her chest.

Her mother was asleep, but her cheeks were shiny from the tears she'd cried.

Swallowing the lump in her throat, River moved across the room and placed the tea and soup on the bedside table. Then, walking to the closet, she grabbed another blanket to lay over her mother.

River bent down and pressed a soft kiss to her mother's head before whispering, "Don't worry, Mom. I'll work this out."

She meant that with every fiber of her being.

When she left the room, she closed the door softly. On the

way back to the kitchen, River paused at Ryker's room before stepping inside. Just like the day of the funeral, she ran her fingers over his dresser. His bed. When she reached the bedside table, thoughts of the number she'd found came to mind. She'd called it so many times over the last two days that she'd lost count. No one had answered.

She wasn't going to stop, though.

Reaching into her pocket, River pulled out her phone and called the number again. It rang so many times that River almost hung up—until she heard a voice.

"What do you want and why do you keep calling me?"

For a moment, River was silent, so shocked someone had answered that words failed her.

The woman on the phone got louder. "Seriously? You harass me for two days and when I finally answer, you don't say shit?"

River gave herself a mental shake, forcing words from her mouth. "Is this Angel?"

"Who wants to know?"

She wet her lips. "My name's River. My brother is...*was*," God, it felt wrong saying that, "Ryker."

There was a short pause. And even though she couldn't see the woman's face, she almost felt her shock through the line.

"Angel?"

"Don't ever call me again."

The line went dead—and River sat there for a full five minutes looking at her phone, wondering what the hell she was going to do next.

RIVER YAWNED. It was one of those eyes-half-shut yawns that had her wishing she could lay her head down and drift off to sleep.

God, you're a grandma, River. It was one a.m. Surely every thirty-three-year-old should be able to stay up past one in the morning without falling asleep in their seat, right?

She must be the exception. Either that, or she was just exhausted. It had been midnight when her lids had first threatened to shut.

She glanced to the back exit of the nightclub, watching as a couple stepped outside to make out. And by "make out", she meant have sex against the wall.

What was this, the eighth couple? Ninth? Who the heck knew? She'd lost count after five.

When the guy's hand crept up the woman's skirt, she dragged her gaze away. Ugh. Could the woman at least get a kiss before he started groping her?

Then she gave herself a little shake. *Stop being a jealous cow, River. It's not their fault you haven't had sex in...*

Well...a while.

Blowing out a long breath, she leaned her head back against the headrest of the driver's seat. "Where are you, Kenny?"

She had no idea which shift he was working tonight—or if he was working at all. She'd only dated Mickey for a few months, and during those months, had spent as little time in the club as possible, so she had no idea of Kenny's schedule. It seemed most bartenders finished anywhere from eleven to three thirty in the morning. Heck, he could have to work later than that, for all she knew.

She almost groaned at the thought. *Please, baby Jesus, don't let it be three thirty in the morning.* She was pretty sure she'd be passed out with dribble running down her cheek by then.

She shot a glance at the copious amounts of candy wrappers on the passenger seat. Her weak attempt to stay awake.

"You guys have been no help," she muttered. Other than giving her a bellyache, that was.

The plan was to trail Kenny back to his house and then ask— no, *demand*—he give her answers. That was a good plan, wasn't it?

It had to be. It was all she had. He knew something. She didn't need to be told that to know it.

When her phone dinged from the middle console, she lifted it. Michele. Of course, it was. The woman had been messaging all night. Heck, all day.

Michele: Are you still waiting for him?

Her friend worried too much. Maybe she shouldn't have told her about this amateur stakeout.

River: Go to sleep, Chele. You've got a lot of cooking to do tomorrow.

Michele: I can't sleep until I know you're home and safe.

She kept one eye on the back door of the club and the other on her phone. She could *not* miss him.

Michele: Also, I don't know how he got my number, but Jackson messaged me, asking if I knew where you were.

She straightened.

He *what?*

The man had already called her phone earlier this evening. That same shiver of awareness had cascaded through her limbs at the sound of his voice. Then he'd asked… No, not asked, growled at her, demanding to know where she was, like he was her keeper or something.

So, obviously, she'd done what any normal person would do and hung up on him and blocked his number. She'd probably unblock him tomorrow. Maybe. Possibly.

River: You didn't tell him, did you? Please tell me you didn't.

Even as she typed the text, her eyes began shooting around the parking lot, expecting to see him storming toward her.

Michele: Of course not. You asked me not to tell anyone, so I haven't and won't. But I was thinking…maybe you should tell him what you're doing. He could help.

She almost scoffed.

River: If he believed me—and that's a big if—he would make sure I was as far away from this as possible. I can't let that happen.

She absolutely wouldn't let that happen. Jackson hadn't been in this town for years or around Ryker for the last twelve months. She had. If anyone could solve this puzzle, it was her.

Michele: Just think about it. And text me when you get home. xox

Her friend wasn't going to sleep. Which was probably fair. She wouldn't sleep if she was in Michele's position, either.

River: I will. x

Sighing, she turned her gaze back to the door. Mr. and Mrs. Lovebird were still going at it. God, all she wanted to do was march right past them and into the club to demand answers.

Yeah, because that worked out so well for you last time, River.

She shook her head. Mickey had basically laughed in her face and told her to get lost.

She hadn't. Of course she hadn't. But then, he'd known she wouldn't because he knew all about her temper. It was a similar temper to his own.

He'd had his big goons on standby, and the second he flicked his fingers, they'd grabbed her and all but tossed her from his office.

She grit her teeth. And what had she done? She'd stormed right into the middle of a fist fight that had broken out in the club. She touched the healing bruise on her eye. At least it was fading.

Memories of how Jackson's expression had darkened in anger when he'd seen it flashed in her mind. He'd always been like that. So quick to want to fight her battles. And silly teenage River had mistaken that as a sign of his undying love.

Stupid.

She hated thinking about that last night before he'd left. Remembering how vulnerable she'd made herself. How open. It hadn't been easy. In fact, it had taken every little bit of courage she'd possessed.

And what had Jackson done? He'd stomped all over her heart and walked away. Left town. Not ever returning. Not until now, of course.

That wasn't love. It wasn't even close to it.

She was just scanning the exit again when she finally saw him. Kenny.

Her hands went to the wheel, grabbing it tightly as he walked across the lot to his car.

Yes.

Scrunching low in her seat, River watched him slide into his car. The second he started the engine, she started hers. She had no idea how to trail someone while remaining hidden, but heck, it couldn't be too hard, could it? And Kenny had once told her he didn't live far from the club, so it would be a short drive.

He pulled onto the main road. It was empty, so she slowed, keeping as much distance as she could between them. Every turn had her holding her breath, praying she didn't lose him.

Kenny had worked at Trinity Nightclub for over a year. He'd also been the only staff member who was nice to her while she dated Mickey.

She needed answers. Why was he at her brother's funeral? Why was he now avoiding her?

Kenny turned the next corner, and when River followed, she barely had time to slam her foot on the brake, missing his car by the smallest fraction.

The driver's-side door of his car opened. Kenny stepped out, and he looked…angry.

Crap.

River hurried to get her seat belt off and climbed out.

Kenny's hand went to his waist, like he'd been about to reach for something, before quickly dropping back to his side. "River? What the hell are you doing?"

She stepped closer. "Please don't be mad. I just want to talk."

"So you follow me home?"

Her gaze flicked back to his waist. "Wait, you don't have a gun, do you?"

His jaw tightened. "You need to go home. Don't follow me again."

When he turned, River ran, rushing in front of him and barricading the driver's door. Maybe it was stupid. Okay, not maybe. Definitely. The guy was clearly armed, and just because he'd been nice to her once upon a time didn't mean he wouldn't hurt her.

But desperate times called for desperate measures.

"Please, just tell me what you were doing at Ryker's funeral. Was my brother spending time at the club?"

He ran a hand through his hair, staring at the road in frustration. "River—"

"Please, I need…something! *Anything*."

His eyes shot back to her. "Yes, he spent time at the club. But that place is dangerous, and you need to stay away."

Knew it! "What was he doing there?"

"Leave it alone, River."

He reached around her for the handle but she slid to the side, blocking him. "*Please*, Kenny!"

Kenny's voice lowered, and a sliver of unease slid down her spine. "I'm not joking. You need to stay the hell away from this. I liked Ryker. That's why I went to his funeral, to pay my respects. But you can't let anything going on at that club touch you."

Before she could respond, he shoved her aside roughly, got into his car, and sped off.

For the first time since receiving that call from her father, a little trickle of doubt weaved its way into her mind. Doubt about Ryker still being alive. About what she'd seen in her house the night he'd supposedly died.

And with that doubt came something deep in her chest that started to ache.

Immediately, she pressed her hand there and her eyes shuttered. No. He was alive. Because if he was dead, she'd know. She'd *feel* it.

Swallowing the doubt and crushing the pain, River opened her eyes and marched back to her car.

The entire drive home, Kenny's words rolled over in her mind. He was wrong about Ryker being dead, but the rest...her brother *had* been going to the club. That much was confirmed.

Now she had to figure out why. It had to be something dangerous, like Kenny said, if he refused to tell her.

It was always on Friday nights when Ryker disappeared, returning with bruises. What happened at the club on Fridays?

Suddenly, something came back to her. A memory from her time with Mickey.

The basement.

On one of the rare occasions she'd gone to the club, she'd seen people going down there. *Lots* of people. And she was almost certain that night had been a Friday. When she'd asked Mickey what they were doing, he'd told her not to worry about it.

Something in her gut told her that basement was where she needed to go. That was where she'd find answers.

She couldn't just rock up to the club again, though. Mickey hadn't said the words, but she knew he wouldn't welcome her back with open arms. She'd need another way in. She never wore makeup or skimpy clothes like the women who frequented the place, but maybe if she tried to blend in, she could get past at least the door security undetected.

She needed to sleep on it. Let the idea sift through her mind.

She pulled into her driveway, stepped out of her car, and moved toward the front door. The key barely touched the lock when the large figure of a man suddenly appeared beside her.

River screamed, but the sound cut off in her throat when she saw who it was.

"Jackson! What the actual hell?"

His eyes were narrowed. "Where have you been?"

CHAPTER 6

*J*ackson's fingers drummed on the car door, his eyes never leaving the road.

Where the hell was she? It was past one in the fucking morning.

He'd swung by to check on her hours ago, but she hadn't been home. And when he'd called, not only had the woman hung up on him, but she'd also blocked his damn number!

Next, he'd texted Michele—and it was her response that had him waiting outside River's house.

Michele: I can't tell you, but she's safe right now.

It was the "right now" that really got him. Why add that onto the end unless there was the possibility she *wouldn't* be safe later? He was almost tempted to march right over to Michele's house and demand the woman come clean on River's location.

Dec and Cole had already done a drive-by of all the obvious spots in town—Michele's house, River's parents' place...hell, even the bars.

For anyone else, he wouldn't care this much. But this was River. Ryker's little sister. The woman he'd spent so many of his teenage years with. The woman who never failed to find trouble. At least that had been the case when she was younger.

Clearly, nothing had changed.

In the back of his mind, he knew there was the possibility she was dating someone, and that could be why she wasn't home. He'd assumed she wasn't because there'd been no guy with her at the funeral. But maybe there was a good reason he hadn't been there. Or maybe she was dating casually.

The thought had his insides rebelling. She deserved better than casual hookups.

He'd rarely asked Ryker about her over the years. He hadn't wanted to know if she was with anyone. He'd never felt good enough for her, but at the same time, was any guy?

The thought of someone else dating her...fuck, it was a blow to the chest.

He knew he had no business feeling that way. It was exactly why he'd stayed away from this goddamn town.

Regardless of whether she was dating, she was still up to something. And whatever that something was, it had to do with Ryker. He didn't need to be told to know.

Jackson sucked in another breath, glancing into the rearview mirror again.

Where the hell are you, River?

Suddenly, headlights from a car coming down the street had him straightening in his seat.

When her yellow Beetle pulled into the driveway and she climbed out, Jackson didn't hesitate. He was out and up the path in an instant. He wasn't trying to be quiet—hell, he was pretty sure an old man with low hearing would have heard him coming. River didn't.

The second he stopped beside her, she screeched, her hand going to her chest. "Jackson! What the actual hell?"

"Where have you been?" He probably shouldn't have growled the words at her, but fuck, he was tired and sick of worrying.

Just as he expected, her lips thinned, her shoulders pushing back. "That's none of your business."

The woman liked saying that to him. She must like being wrong.

"Are you going to open the door?"

"No. Because I know the second I do you'll just waltz inside like you own the place and then I'll spend the next twenty minutes kicking your ass out."

He almost laughed. She couldn't be more right.

"Let's just get this over with because I'm tired and ready for bed." She crossed her arms over her chest. Her ample breasts pushed up and the silky-smooth skin above the neckline of the black T-shirt tempted his gaze.

Desire slammed into his gut but he forced his body to calm. "Where have you been tonight?"

"Out."

Goddamn, this woman. He took a step forward. Her eyes widened a fraction, head tilting back to look at him.

"I'm tired and out of patience," he said quietly. "So, know that I'm not messing around when I say I'm not leaving until I get the answers I want."

A slow smile curved her lips. "How about I call the police on your overbearing ass."

One of his brows lifted. "You're going to call Fred?"

The smile fell from her lips. "Fred's on?"

"He is." Fred was good friends with her father. And Jackson knew for a fact that they told each other everything. "When he asks why I'm here—which we both know he will—I'll tell him exactly what I think is going on with you."

Her eyes narrowed. "And what do you *think* is going on with me?"

His tone gentled. "I think you're getting yourself into trouble. You already have a black eye, meaning either someone hit you, or you were in the wrong place at the wrong time, and that place was probably a dangerous one. Somewhere you probably shouldn't have been. How long until you put yourself in that situation again?"

The slight widening of her eyes told him he was right on the mark.

"We both know what will happen next, Rae."

A gasp slipped from her lips at the use of her nickname. There was once a time Rae was all he called her. It was her middle name. And for some reason, he'd preferred it. Maybe because he was the only person who used it. Maybe because her expression had always softened at his use of it.

His hand twitched to reach out and touch her. "Just tell me."

She briefly looked away, her chest rising and falling quickly. She knew he was right. That she was out of options. Still, instead of answering, she unfolded her arms and poked a finger into his chest. "You don't get to show up and boss me around."

"Incorrect. When it comes to you and your safety, I get to do whatever needs to be done."

"Why? Because you care so much about me? Because you care about Ryker?"

He frowned. "Of course. I care about both of you." Too damn much. Hadn't that always been the problem?

Her humorless laugh caught him off guard. "Then where have you been, Jackson? Where the *hell* have you been?"

"I was an active operator in—"

"No. I'm not talking about the first fifteen years, although, yeah, a visit to town to see how me and my parents were doing would have been nice. I'm talking about for the last twelve months. Ryker needed you. He needed all three of you! He was home, but he never really came back. He was angry, all the time. Where the hell were you then?"

Guilt crashed through his thin veneer of indignation. It chilled his skin and tensed his muscles. "You're right," he said quietly. "I should have been here."

Some of her anger faded, and for a moment, he almost thought her gaze softened. Then she blinked and the anger was back. As if she needed it to be there to protect herself. "Why weren't you?"

Because of you. Because of my father. Because of this town and how I feel when I'm in it.

He swallowed the words. Words that made him a selfish bastard. Words that felt too heavy to admit. "I didn't want to return."

Those pretty dark eyes darted between his. Then he saw… sympathy? "They don't see you the way you see you."

Ah, she was talking about the locals and only the locals. But yeah, that was the third reason to stay the hell away from Lindeman.

A moment of silence passed. The urge to touch her intensified. To feel her soft skin beneath his fingers. Maybe it was because he'd been feeling so weak. Ever since hearing the news about Ryker, he'd felt like a part of his chest had been torn out. Maybe that's why he reached out, curving his fingers around her neck. Because he couldn't *not*.

Mistake. Big mistake. His blood began to roar at the mere contact. Awareness pulsed down his arm.

"Please tell me what's going on, River." The words came out raspier than he'd meant. Huskier.

Maybe his touch weakened her. Because her mouth cracked open—and words he was sure she didn't mean to say slipped out. "I think there's more to what happened on the bridge than we've been told. And I'm trying to find out the whole story."

He frowned, thumb caressing her skin almost of its own volition. He should remove his hand. He knew he should. But she wasn't pulling away, so he just…couldn't.

God, he was weak. Only with her, though.

He forced himself to focus on her words, tossing them around in his head. "What else could there be?"

"I can't tell you." Her words held less conviction this time.

She wet her lips. His gaze darted down. And something clicked in his chest. Something sharp and dangerous that he had absolutely no control over.

"Jackson—"

The word had barely left her lips when his head lowered and his mouth took hers. It was like an explosion of desire and need splintered inside his body, propelling him to claim her.

Beneath his hand, he felt the pulse in her neck. It was fast, pounding against his touch. The beat of her heart matched his own.

When she tried to take a breath, he took advantage, slipping his tongue between her lips and deepening the kiss.

Maybe it was the groan that came next, or maybe it was the way she tasted—like apples and maple syrup mixed together. Whatever it was, it had him lifting her body, tucking every part of her front against his, pushing her back against the door.

Her breasts pressed to his chest, her hands slipping into his hair.

He growled deep in his throat, devouring every inch of her mouth. Nipping. Sucking. Then his lips wrenched from hers, traveling down her neck, kissing and licking. "Rae…"

The moment the word was out, he felt her stiffen. A second later, her hands went to his chest, pushing. "Jackson, we have to stop."

His lips left her skin, but he didn't immediately put her down. He studied her face. "What's wrong?"

Her eyes widened. "What's wrong? We can't…you and I shouldn't…" She shook her head. "I need you to put me down. *Now.*"

She was right. Of course she was. But the sensible part of his brain had stopped functioning the moment he touched her.

Another beat passed before he slowly slid her down to the

porch. Her softness grazed him, sending a new wave of electricity —torture—rippling through his system.

He watched as she swallowed, straightening her clothes. "You shouldn't have done that."

She was right. But the more time he spent around the woman, the harder it became to stay away.

"You need to leave," she said quietly. She turned and took a half step forward, slotting her key into the lock.

His hand closed over hers, his front pressing to her back. "Tell me where you were tonight, and I will."

There was a short exhale. "I was at Trinity Nightclub."

His brows tugged together. "What were you doing there?"

Three breaths. And then her words. "Ryker was spending time there. I think the answers to what happened that night are in that club."

His hand moved to her shoulder and he turned her to face him. "Why do you think that? And why do you think there's more to the story?"

"Because I do, okay? Because I've been here, in Lindeman, for the last year with Ryker and I just…I know. There's something going on at that club, something dangerous, and Ryker got involved."

There was more she wasn't telling him. So much more. But it was late, and he was twitching with the need to kiss her again. So he stepped back, determined that the next time he asked, he'd get more information.

"I don't want you going there again."

Her jaw tensed. "Jackson—"

He took a small step forward, returning to her again, and immediately her eyes widened. She took a quick step back, hitting the door, almost as if she was scared of him getting too close. Scared of his touch.

That was fair enough. Their connection scared him, too, and hardly anything scared Jackson. "Promise me."

Her lips pressed together. "Fine. Is there anything else you would like?"

"Unblock my number."

A ghost of a smile touched her lips. Yeah, she'd known that would piss him off. "And if I say no?"

"Then I watch you. And when I'm not watching you, one of the guys on my team will be watching."

The smile dropped. She knew he wasn't bluffing. He'd never taken her safety lightly.

He lifted a brow. "Deal?"

"Fine."

"Good." And then, because he was so damn weak, he bent down, pressing a kiss to her cheek, right beside her ear.

There was a small gasp from her before he spoke again. "Now, go inside and lock the door behind you."

CHAPTER 7

*R*iver knocked on Michele's apartment door. Her friend had already buzzed her up, so she knew she was here. The second the door tugged open, River waltzed in, dumping a bag on her friend's kitchen table before spinning around.

"What are you doing tonight?" she asked.

Michele's steps were cautious as she followed. "Well, the plan was to plonk myself on the couch, eat an entire tub of Ben and Jerry's ice cream, and read my new book. Why?"

"You know how you were worried about me the other night when I went to stalk Kenny at the club by myself? At first you insisted on joining me, but I said absolutely not, it'll be a late night and I don't want you involved in this?"

"Yes…" Michele said the word slowly.

"I'm hoping you'll forget what I said and be my wing woman. AKA, my eyes while I explore the basement at the club."

A little huff slipped from Michele's lips. "River, we've been through this. It's too dangerous—"

"It's not. I swear. I'm going to wear skimpy clothes, cake on the makeup, and keep my head down. Mickey won't even know I'm there." *Hopefully.*

Michele tapped her foot. It was a nervous habit of hers that River had grown used to. "What's in the bag?"

"Outfits and makeup."

Her friend sighed. "River—"

"I know what you're going to say. And trust me, if I had a choice, I wouldn't be going anywhere near that place. But I don't." She stepped forward, placing her hands on Michele's arms. "Saving my brother is not a choice. It's something I have to do. And it's fine if you don't want to join me. I will one hundred percent understand."

In fact, she felt guilty even asking. There was no part of her that wanted to put her friend in danger. But she also knew her chances of getting in and out of that basement unseen were a hell of a lot higher with another person watching her back.

Regardless of her friend's decision, she was going down there tonight. And she'd find out exactly what Mickey was doing. No matter what it took. No matter how many breaths of courage she needed to suck in.

Michele's head tilted to the side. "How exactly do you plan to get down to his basement? If whatever is happening down there is so top secret, won't it be locked?"

"I have the lock code."

Michele frowned. "How do you—"

"I heard Mickey tell a guy and memorized it."

She hadn't given it much thought since, but there must have been some small part of her that had known she would need it one day.

For a moment, Michele was silent. She could see her friend's mind ticking, unsure what to do.

River nodded, dropping her hands. "That's completely okay, Chele." And it was. Would it help to have someone there, someone who could give her a heads-up if anyone came her way? Yes. Would not having someone there stop her? Absolutely not.

River grabbed the bag.

"River, stop. Of course I'm coming. Who else is going to pull your ass out of the way the next time you decide to step in front of a flying fist?"

She spun around, eyes softening. "Are you sure?"

Michele rolled her eyes, and River almost laughed. She'd been getting a lot of those eye rolls from her friend lately.

Chele stepped forward, swiping the bag from River's fingers and dropping it back onto the table. She pulled out a skirt—and her eyes almost bugged out of her head. "This won't even cover my ass!"

River smiled. "That's the point, Chele. No one will look at my face if my ass and breasts are on display."

She winced. "Breasts?"

"Every woman there dresses like this. I always felt *overdressed* while I was dating Mickey." Probably why he'd wanted her. The woman who gave up nothing. Argh. "Don't worry, yours is more conservative."

She pulled out Michele's outfit, and her friend's shoulders sagged in relief. It was a pair of skintight pants with a low-cut top. "That's better."

River almost laughed. Michele grabbed the clothing and started toward the bedroom.

She frowned. "Where are you going?"

"Ah, into the bedroom to get ready."

This time River did laugh. "Chele, it's not even six o'clock. The place isn't open. We'll leave at eleven. Maybe eleven thirty."

"Oh, Lord. I'm gonna need some coffee."

"Me too, please. Make it a double shot."

∽

JACKSON WRAPPED his fingers around the hot mug of tea. He hardly felt the warmth, not while sitting in Mr. And Mrs. Harp's home, knowing Ryker would never set foot in here again.

Mrs. Harp set down a plate of cookies in the middle of the table. "How have you been, dear?"

She looked better than she had at the funeral, but she in no way looked good. The joy that usually lightened her eyes was missing. The laugh lines now just looked like exhaustion.

He swallowed the guilt that crawled up his spine. Guilt that he hadn't kept in touch with them. Guilt that he hadn't visited once over the years. They'd completely welcomed him into their home. Fed him. Given him a safe place to sleep whenever he'd needed it. Treated him like a second son.

"I'm doing as well as I can be," Jackson said, knowing his voice came out too gruff. "How are you both?"

Mrs. Harp cast a glance toward her husband. He cleared his throat. "It's been tough, son. You never think you're going to bury your own child." A sheen covered his eyes before he gave his head a shake and blinked it away. "It's been tough," he repeated.

Mrs. Harp touched his forearm, giving it a squeeze before turning back to Jackson. "We were wondering if you know why he was so angry when he got back? His entire life, he was so laid-back and calm about everything. So gentle and easygoing. Even after deployments. But the Ryker who returned home that last time…the smallest things would set him off."

Jackson sucked in a deep breath. Ryker hadn't told them. He'd suspected as much, so it wasn't a surprise. The man internalized his pain. When they said he was angry, he was sure they meant a mostly silent anger.

"Our final mission didn't go to plan." Fuck, that was an understatement.

He couldn't tell the Harps the whole story; most of it was classified.

Operation Green Thumb. Even the name tasted sour in his mouth.

"We were sent to eliminate a high-value target in the Middle East. We'd led a handful of operations there in the past, and throughout that time, Ryker had bonded with a local family to the point where they'd have him over for dinner when we were in the country."

His insides recoiled at the memory of what happened.

"We got our target but before we could leave, there was backlash from the guy's family." Specifically, from the target's brother. Jackson shook his head. "They found our location and we were attacked." It was the closest Jackson had ever come to death. The closest any of them had. Not that he'd be sharing that part with the Harps. "Dec was shot, I had to shoulder-carry him back to the US base. Cole broke his back, and Ryker carried him most of the way. It wasn't until we returned to US soil that we found out."

"Found out what?" Mrs. Harp asked tentatively. Her voice was low, like she wasn't sure she wanted to know anymore.

"The family Ryker knew...their home was blown up. The bomb took out their house, as well as a few others on the street. All families with young kids."

Mrs. Harp's lips slipped open. "And they all...*died*?"

He gave a sharp nod. It was all he could muster.

Mrs. Harp covered her mouth, and her husband wrapped an arm around her shoulders.

"I'm sorry." He wasn't sure what he was apologizing for. Maybe all of it. Any part he'd had to play in his friend's resulting anger and then his death. But the words felt inadequate. Hell, any words would be inadequate.

"What can I do?" he asked. Because there had to be something. Some small way he could help this family who had done so much for him. When he'd been a teenager, they'd even talked about adopting him. Taking action against his father. But Jackson had refused. By that stage, he'd been big and strong enough to fight back and was just biding his time before leaving town.

Mr. Harp took a deep breath. "For as long as you're in town, we'd like for you to watch over River."

Jackson frowned. It almost sounded like they knew she was involved in something she shouldn't be. Did they know she'd been investigating her brother's murder? "Of course. Do you think she needs watching over?"

The couple exchanged a look—and an uncomfortable feeling pitted his gut.

Mr. Harp sighed. "A few months ago, River dated a guy who owns a nearby club. About a month before Ryker's death, she came home with a black eye. Ryker lost it."

Jackson tensed. Was it the same asshole who'd given her the black eye she had at the funeral?

Mr. Harp cleared his throat. The anger on his face was unmistakable. "Ryker said he'd take care of it and make sure she didn't return to the guy *or* his club. With everything that's happened, we're just scared…" He paused. "Not that she'll go back to him, *per se*, but that she might do something reckless while she's grieving."

"Call it parent intuition," Mrs. Harp added.

They'd always known their kids well. Too well.

"I'll look after her."

He hadn't been able to stop thinking about the woman. And after that kiss…it had him questioning everything. Pushing her away all those years ago. Running from her. He still knew who he was, knew that she was too damn good for him. But he wasn't sure he was strong enough to be around her and not get closer. Not lose himself in her.

Jackson remained with the Harps for another hour. Talking about Ryker. Reminiscing about the good times.

When he finally said his goodbyes and stepped out, he tugged his phone from his pocket and called Declan.

"Jackson. What's going on?"

"The three of us are going out tonight."

There was a small pause. "Anywhere in particular?"

"Trinity Nightclub." He still recalled the name. Everything the woman said was burned into his memory.

"What's at this club?"

"The asshole who runs the place dated River. He hit her. Ryker got involved. And it's possible he had a hand in Ryker's death."

A short, heavy silence stretched across the line before Declan broke it. "What time?"

CHAPTER 8

*R*iver scanned the busy club. It was Saturday night, so the place was packed, which was exactly what she wanted. More people meant less chance of being seen. A perfect opportunity to sneak down to an unguarded basement.

Michele tugged at her top. Yeah, she wasn't comfortable either. Michele's skintight tank was extremely low cut, and River's top…could she even call it a top? It was basically a bra.

Then there were the heels that were tall enough to make walking an absolute nightmare. And, of course, River's blond wig and the pound of makeup.

Thankfully, the man at the door had been new, but even if he hadn't, he'd barely looked them in the eye; all his attention had been on their breasts.

"I owe you, Chele." She had to yell over the music so her friend could hear her. Sheesh, she was too old for this.

Michele shook her head. "I don't mind."

Not true. Everything about her friend contradicted her words. The way her eyes pinched in the corners. How her gaze darted around the room.

A pang of guilt hit River in the chest. Maybe she should have risked the trip on her own.

Taking her friend's hand, she pulled her a bit closer. "A quick in and out, okay?"

Michele nodded.

Yep, River owed her big time.

Tugging her forward, they squeezed through the crowd. When a man touched her ass, she itched to turn around and give him a piece of her mind. That, and a solid punch in the face. She sure as hell would have any other day. But the last thing she could risk was drawing attention to herself. Mickey's office was upstairs, and he had a huge window overlooking the club.

So instead, she gritted her teeth, kept her head down, and continued moving.

When the dark, narrow hallway that led to the basement stairs came into view, River's heart sped up a notch. That was where she needed to be.

She knew Mickey had cameras on the hall, but she also knew the monitors were rarely, if ever, looked at when the basement was locked.

Moving to the bar—the end closest to the hallway—River squeezed in so they had a spot, tugging Michele with her. Kenny was just visible down the other end of the bar, but he wasn't looking her way. Good. She was almost certain he wouldn't rat her out, but why take the chance?

A woman with brown hair and a sleeve of tattoos stepped in front of them. River almost sighed when she didn't recognize her. "What can I get you, ladies?"

River smiled. "Aperol Spritz, please."

The woman nodded before turning to Michele.

"Uh...I'll have the same."

River scanned the crowd, looking for one person. Mickey.

No sign of the man. Maybe this crazy plan just might work. So far, everything had been going well...touch wood.

Once they had their drinks, River shifted her head closer to Michele's and lowered her voice. "The hall behind us leads to the basement. Keep it in your line of sight and message if you see anyone heading down."

Obviously, she wouldn't be able to get out if someone entered the basement, but she was hoping a text would at least give her the time to hide.

Michele nibbled her bottom lip. "Are you sure about this, River? It doesn't feel very safe."

Nothing had felt safe lately.

"I'll be fine. Remember, quick in and out." She mentally crossed her fingers and toes that her words were true.

Michele nodded, still looking nervous as hell. "Okay."

River squeezed her friend's arm. Then, before leaving the bar, she took a massive sip of her spritz. Some extra liquid confidence never hurt, right?

Turning, she walked toward the bathrooms. The women's bathroom was right beside the hall. At the last second, she diverted and stepped into the dark entryway.

Her steps were quick but silent. The further she got, the darker and quieter the hall became. It actually made her feel a bit safer. Or at least gave her the illusion of safety.

At the end of the hall, she shone the light of her phone on the keypad lock and typed in the five-digit code she recalled Mickey reciting. When she heard the soft click of the lock releasing, the air whooshed from her chest.

A small part of her had been worried—okay, not worried, scared shitless—that the code had been changed. It hadn't. She was in.

Quickly, River slipped inside and pulled the door closed. For a moment, darkness blinded her. She turned on the flashlight of her phone again and used it to guide her down the stairs.

At the bottom, she shone the light around the rest of the room, and a small breath escaped her lips.

Holy shit.

A fighting ring. Surrounded by wire fencing.

She took slow steps forward. The space was massive, the ring itself large and centered in the room. There were chairs stacked taller than River along the lengthy wall beside the stairs. Dozens of them. Maybe hundreds. There was a dark hallway midway down the wall to her left and what looked like maybe an office door in the back wall.

Cage fighting. That's what Mickey was hiding down here.

Moving closer, she skimmed her fingers over the fencing. Everything made sense. Ryker's bruises. The droplets of blood staining the clothing she'd found in the wash. And the way some of his anger had dissipated over the last month. The fighting had been an outlet.

Why didn't you tell me, Ryker?

Had he thought she wouldn't understand? Of course, she would have. The man had needed something to manage the anger. And Ryker had always been into his boxing. There'd been a boxing ring in town that he and Jackson had visited when they were growing up. Both of them loved it.

But what River didn't understand was…how had illegal fighting led to Ryker being declared dead?

The question had barely entered her head when her phone vibrated in her hand. River's eyes widened when she scanned the screen.

Chele: Two men coming. HIDE NOW!

Crap crap crap!

Her gaze lifted to the hallway. She could go that way, but what if the doors were locked and the men walked down the hall? She'd be boxed in. And she didn't have enough time to cross the space to see if the other door was locked.

Half a dozen kegs sat against the wall opposite the hallway, and there were the stacked chairs near the stairs. She beelined for the chairs, knowing being closer to the exit was the safest option.

As silently as possible, she moved behind the rows of chairs and crouched, only just turning her flashlight off before footsteps sounded on the stairs.

"It's fucking wild here tonight."

River recognized the voice. Johnny. One of Mickey's right-hand men.

"No shit. Mickey fucking loves it." The lights flicked on, momentarily blinding River.

She recognized the other guy's voice, too. Brooks. He'd been the one to drag her out of Mickey's office after Ryker's death and toss her right into the middle of a damn bar fight.

"About time he was in a good mood," Johnny said.

She continued listening as they reached the bottom of the stairs.

"No shit. The guy's been more of a bastard than usual lately," Brooks said, his voice darkening.

"Yeah, well, him and Elijah are having a fucking pissing contest over turf," Johnny muttered. River made a mental note to remember the name.

Rustling noises sounded from across the room. Maybe near the kegs? Thank God she hadn't chosen to hide there.

Brooks grunted. "They've both been on edge since Ryker. Especially Elijah."

River's skin chilled at the sound of her brother's name.

"That scumbag deserved to die. I hope he fucking rots in hell," Johnny growled.

A blazing-hot fire ignited in River's belly, heating her blood. Oh, how she would love to jump out and give those assholes a piece of her mind!

"Damn straight."

A door unlocked, and she heard them step inside the small room at the back. The voices quieted, footsteps disappearing.

Rising a fraction, she shot a look around the room, then up the stairs. This was it. Possibly her only chance.

As quietly as possible, River moved out from behind the chairs and climbed the stairs. Her heart pounded the entire time, and when a wooden step squeaked, she gasped, expecting them to rush out. She quickened her pace, reaching the door and all but sagging when she made it back into the narrow hall.

Swallowing, River moved cautiously toward the bar.

Michele's eyes were wide when she reached her. "Are you okay? Oh my God, I was so worried!"

River grabbed the barely-touched spritz from her friend's hand, downing the remaining alcohol before setting the glass on the bar. "I'm okay. But we should go."

Before her friend could respond, she grabbed her hand and tugged her through the dense crowd. Christ, were there even more people here now than there had been ten minutes ago?

Shoving through the masses, she'd just made it to a small clearing near the door when she saw him. The last man she expected to see.

Jackson.

What the hell was he doing here?

Cole and Declan stepped into the club behind him, all three looking big and dangerous.

She'd barely shifted her attention back to Jackson when their gazes clashed. His eyes narrowed.

Oh shit.

Michele's mouth slid open when she spotted them. River dragged her in the opposite direction. She didn't know where she was going, just…away.

They'd only taken a few steps when a figure stepped in front of her and she collided with a big chest.

River's breath caught in her throat.

Mickey.

His eyes slitted, lips pressed together. When he grabbed her, his fingers dug into her skin, bruising her flesh.

Behind him stood two of his guys. Men she knew as more of his muscle.

For a moment, fear seized her chest. Fear that he'd caught her going down to his basement. Fear of what he'd do about it.

"What the fuck are you doing here? I thought I made it clear you aren't welcome."

The air rushed out of her lungs. He didn't know. Or at least, it didn't appear that he knew. "I—"

"Get your fucking hands off her." Heat pressed into her side. She looked up to see Jackson. A very angry Jackson, who was looking down at Mickey like he was seconds from killing the guy. The muscles in his arms were bunched and his fists clenched so tightly she knew he was preparing to swing.

Mickey studied Jackson. "Who the hell are you?"

Cole stepped to one side of Jackson, and Declan crowded beside Michele.

"I'm someone you don't want to fuck with," Jackson said quietly. So quietly, his words almost scared *her*, and the guy never scared her. "Now, let go of her before I pull your arm from its fucking socket."

Good God, did the man have a death wish? No one spoke to Mickey like that.

Not that his words surprised her. Jackson wasn't afraid of anything. And the way he and his buddies stood around her and Michele...

River held her breath as she waited for Mickey's response. A beat of silence passed. Then, finally, Mickey released her. "Get her the fuck out of my club—and make sure she never steps foot in here again."

A muscle ticked in Jackson's jaw, and she just knew he was bracing himself. Trying *not* to hit the guy. "If I ever see you touch her again, it won't be just a dislocated shoulder you have to worry about. Got it?"

She could just about feel Michele shaking beside her. Declan crept a step closer to her friend.

The veins in Mickey's neck were popping. He gave a small nod.

Jackson wrapped an arm around her waist and tugged her—no, *towed* her—toward the exit. She waited until they'd stepped outside before attempting to free herself.

His arm around her waist only tightened, not allowing an inch of space. Then his head lowered to her ear. "I'm holding on to my temper by a fucking thread, River. Don't push me."

There was something in his voice that had her obeying. Something dark.

They continued to walk, right up until she realized Michele was no longer with them. Neither were Cole or Declan.

"No, Michele and I are driving ourselves home." She stamped her feet to a stop.

The growl from Jackson was loud. Before she realized what he was doing, he swung her onto his shoulder like she was a piece of luggage and continued to march down the sidewalk.

CHAPTER 9

*W*hite-hot anger thrummed through Jackson's veins. It heated his breath and hardened his jaw. Not just because that asshole had grabbed her. Bruised her. And not just because she was almost fucking *naked*. But because she'd been there in the first place. He didn't need to know much about the place to know it was a hotspot for dangerous activity.

River's knee bashed his stomach. His hands tightened around her thighs. "Cut it out, River."

She didn't. But then, he hadn't expected her to. She fought him right up until they reached the passenger side of her car and he set her on her feet.

Her chest was heaving, the creamy exposed skin rising and falling in quick succession.

He held out his hand, and she scowled. "You're joking."

"Give me your keys." His voice was calmer but held the underlying threat of what could come.

"No." She crossed her arms over her chest, anger reddening her cheeks.

From over her head, he could see Cole heading their way.

He took a step closer, his voice low. "River, when my patience snaps, I stop asking."

Her brow lifted. "Is that supposed to scare me?"

"Depends. Are you scared?"

"No."

She'd always hated people thinking she was scared of anything. For some reason, River associated fear with weakness.

Cole stopped a few feet away. Jackson reached into his pocket, tossing his friend the keys to his rental car. Declan would be at the car with Michele right now, ready to take her home.

Cole dipped his head before walking away.

Jackson turned back to River. "The longer we stand here, the longer we have eyes on us—because I guarantee you that asshole put his guys on us the second we left."

Uncertainty snaked into her black eyes. He could tell she wanted to look but didn't. Finally, she reached into her pocket and pulled out her keys.

He used them to unlock the door and River slipped inside. The drive to her place was done in silence. He had words to speak. A lot of them. But they could wait.

He drove into River's driveway. The car had barely stopped before she jumped out.

Cursing under his breath, Jackson put the car into park and climbed out. River stopped at the door, arms remaining folded. It appeared that was her new favorite stance.

He used the keys to open the door and slipped inside first.

"By all means, come right in, Jackson."

He ignored her words, doing a quick scan of the house before moving back into the living area.

River was frowning. "What are you doing?"

"Checking your place."

"For what?"

"Remember what you told me yesterday?" He stopped in front of her. "And then tonight, you walk into Mickey's club, into his

72

space, after you promised me you wouldn't. You still wondering why I scanned your house for threats?"

At least she had the sense to look a bit guilty at that. "First of all, you said you'd have me watched and I have no doubt you would have stopped me if I hadn't agreed, so I didn't really have a choice in the matter."

"Damn straight I would have stopped you." The woman wouldn't have gotten within a ten-mile radius of that place, let alone stepped inside doing God knows what while wearing a bra for a top.

"Secondly," she continued, "I'm just a woman, and in Mickey's eyes, that makes me weak. I doubt he'll come after me."

"So what do you know?"

She sighed, shooting a glance behind him in the direction of her bedroom. "Jackson, I'm tired. Can we do this in the morning?"

Something in his chest tightened at how dismissive she was being. If the woman thought she was getting rid of him, she was wrong.

He toed off his shoes before stepping around her and dropping to the couch.

River frowned. "What are you doing?"

"I'm sleeping on your couch." He tugged his shirt over his chest.

Her sharp gasp whipped through the room. "No."

When he looked up, he saw her eyes weren't meeting his anymore, they were on his chest. And they were dark.

Warmth heated his body at having her eyes on him.

"Yes," he said quietly.

Finally, her eyes flashed back up. "Jackson—"

"I need to know what's going on. The full story." Because he sure as hell hadn't gotten it last time. "But you're right. It's late, and we both need sleep."

"And you can't just come back in the morning?" For the first time since arriving in town, River actually looked worried.

He rose to his feet, and she took a step back. Was she nervous about how she reacted to him?

Me too, honey.

"I don't like you being entangled in danger."

"I have a gun," she argued.

He only just stopped the cringe. "I've seen you shoot, Rae."

She frowned, back straightening. "I was a teenager then. I'm better now."

When she finally dropped her arms, his gaze zeroed in on the reddened bruises around her arm. The muscles tensed in his limbs. He took a step forward, gently grasping her elbow.

"What are you—" She stopped when he lifted her arm.

When he looked into her eyes, it took all his strength to control his breathing. "I don't want you anywhere near that asshole. I want you as far away from him as possible."

River swallowed. For once, she was silent, her gaze skirting between his eyes.

His thumb gently stroked over the bruise. And when her gaze dipped to his lips, memories of their last kiss skittered through his mind. It had his blood roaring between his ears.

Without thinking, his other hand cupped her cheek. Touching her took away some of the turmoil in his head. It dimmed some of the suffocating fear that had consumed him when that guy had grabbed her.

His voice lowered until it was almost a whisper. "I need you to be safe, River." And he didn't just need her to be safe because he owed it to her brother. It was so much more than that.

"Why?"

"Because the thought of losing you from this world…it's like losing a part of myself."

The good part. The part that made sense.

Her mouth slid open, a short gasp escaping her lips. For a

moment, he wasn't sure if she was going to kiss him or kick him out.

She did neither. "I'll get you a pillow and blanket."

When she moved away from him, his hands dropped. And he was left wondering if she was escaping from him before they did something stupid...like kiss again.

RIVER ROLLED ONTO HER BACK, closing her eyes.

Good God, she was tired. She'd barely slept a wink all night, way too aware of the large, sexy man in her living room.

Her cheeks heated at the memory of his thumb skirting over the skin on her arm. His hand on her cheek...

She scrunched her eyes tighter, only just holding in the groan. She'd thought he'd kiss her again. And what was worse, a part of her had *wanted* him to.

She could not let those glorious muscles and honey-brown eyes sucker her in. Not just because sixteen years ago, he'd ripped her heart from her chest and trampled on it. But because he'd been absent from her life ever since.

Nope. No way. No how.

Pushing up into a seated position, River frowned. Was that bacon she smelled? No. Jackson would be too busy beating his chest and warming up his voice for another round of arguing to cook any food.

She climbed out of bed, barely sparing her sleep shorts and tank top a glance before heading into the kitchen.

Okay, maybe she was still asleep because it looked like a bare-chested Jackson *was* cooking bacon on her stove. And Lord Almighty, did he look good. His shoulders were broad, his biceps thick, and when he reached for the tongs, the muscles in his back rippled.

Not. Good. Certainly not for her low self-control.

When he turned his head, he smiled. Not a half smile or a smirk. A full, white-teeth-on-display, hint-of-a-dimple-showing smile.

She hadn't seen that smile in...well, a long time. And it completely disarmed her.

"Morning, Rae. Hungry?"

A secret trill hummed through her veins at the way he used her middle name. It had always been his special name for her. And she loved it. A reaction she would never tell another living soul.

She walked slowly across the room, studying the set table and the already poured juice. "Okay, who are you and what have you done with the brooding bear of a man who dragged me out of the club last night?"

He turned back to the stove and his chuckle filtered through the room right into her chest. "Maybe the bear had a good sleep and calmed down."

Hm. Must have been a *really* good sleep.

He turned off the stove, lifted a plate of bacon and eggs, and set them on the table. Next, he grabbed toast from the toaster and popped them on the plates. "Take a seat, and I'll grab the coffees."

He was making coffee, too? Figured. Couldn't be the perfect dreamboat of a man without coffee.

River sat behind a plate, watching with wary eyes as he moved around the kitchen. She knew exactly what he was doing. The man was aware his tactics last night hadn't worked, so he was trying something different. Not wearing a shirt was probably another way of disarming her. And it was working. She'd always been a sucker for semi-naked Jackson.

He placed a coffee in front of her before stepping away and grabbing his shirt from the couch, tugging it over his head.

And even though she'd just been internally grumbling about his bare chest, disappointment washed over her abdomen when it was covered. She forced her attention to the food, placing some eggs on her plate.

It wasn't until Jackson was opposite her that she broke the silence in the room. "So, is this where you ask me to tell you all my secrets?"

To be honest, she was coming around to telling him anyway. After last night and the way Mickey had grabbed her arm, not to mention the guilt she'd felt about dragging Michele to the club... yeah, she probably needed Jackson in her corner. But she refused to be pushed out of everything.

"You can tell me now or later, I don't mind."

She swallowed a forkful of scrambled egg. Oh, jeez, did the man have to be a good cook, too? "Why are you being so nice to me?"

His brows rose, mouth tilting up at the edges. "Should I be less nice?"

"Yes." His anger was easier to deal with. She had no defenses against nice Jackson. He should be growling at her to spill her guts until he got each and every word he was after. He should be as stone-cold mad as he was last night when she'd returned to that club after telling him she wouldn't.

"Maybe I realized that anger wasn't the best approach."

With her. He didn't say the words out loud, but he didn't have to. And he was right. His anger had always stirred her own. Made her dig in her heels and resist whatever he wanted.

She popped a piece of bacon into her mouth. It was the perfect amount of crispy and soft.

"How's the photography going?" he asked.

Now her brows rose. He was asking about her work? "Good. With the rise of social media has come the rise in food and beverage photography."

"How'd you get into it?"

"I styled the meals for Michele's business and uploaded them to her social media accounts. People saw and started asking if I could do the same for them." She lifted her shoulder. "I wasn't earning any money from landscape photography, so food styling started paying my bills."

Photographing food wasn't her passion. Not even close. She loved nature. But she'd quickly realized that if she wanted to be semi-independent and move out of her parent's home, she had to adjust her professional expectations.

She swallowed another mouthful of bacon. "It was actually how I met Mickey."

Jackson paused, fork midway to his lips. "You took pictures for him?"

She nodded. "I styled and took photos of the drinks at the club. That was about four months ago. He flirted with me. Asked me to dinner, and we just...started dating. It was casual."

She watched as Jackson's eyes darkened before he spoke. "When did he start hitting you?"

Her mouth slid open. "How did you—"

"I visited your parents yesterday."

Of course. Ryker had been awake when she'd gotten home that night and had seen the bruises immediately. Her dad had seen them the next day. Both of them had lost their minds.

"He only hit me the one time. I broke up with him that night and told him he was never going to touch me again."

She was pretty sure Jackson's teeth actually ground against each other. "Did Ryker visit the club that same night?"

"Yes. He was so angry when he saw my face. He marched straight down there, and no amount of begging him not to go could have stopped him."

"Good," Jackson growled. The way he said it had the fine hairs on her arms standing on end.

She pushed the scrambled egg around her plate, no longer hungry. Suddenly, she straightened. "Want to go for a walk?"

She needed air and sun and nature. All the things that calmed her.

Jackson studied her for a moment. He knew. He'd always known about her need for the outdoors. He gave a short nod. "Sure."

She quickly went to her room and threw some clothes on before they stepped outside.

The calm was immediate. It washed over her limbs, warming her skin. A few minutes of silence passed before she finally looked up at him. That's when she almost tripped over her own feet. Jackson was looking back at her. In that same dark and intense way he often did.

"What were you doing at the club last night?" he asked.

"You first."

He dipped his head. "That's fair. You mentioned you thought there was more to Ryker's death than we knew and that the answer was at the club. And after your parents mentioned you'd dated that asshole owner, I wanted to check the place out myself." He nudged her shoulder, and just that small contact had awareness skirting up her arm, into her chest. "Your turn."

She swallowed. "After Kenny—one of the bartenders—confirmed that Ryker had been visiting the club, I remembered that something was going on in the basement. On Friday nights, people used to line up to go down there. Mickey wouldn't tell me what that was all about."

She paused, gaze catching on a small bird as it landed on a branch in front of her.

"It was Friday's when Ryker used to disappear all night," she continued quietly.

"Don't tell me you snuck down there, Rae."

"I had to."

His exhale was loud. "Dammit, River! What if he'd caught you?"

"He didn't."

Jackson touched her arm, pulling them both to a stop. "If he killed Ryker, what do you think is stopping him from killing you?"

"That's the thing. I don't believe Ryker's dead."

CHAPTER 10

*J*ackson remained utterly still as he studied River. The woman was serious. She really thought her brother was alive.

Suddenly, it all made sense. Why she hadn't been upset at Ryker's funeral. Why she kept returning to this club even when she knew it was dangerous and she wasn't welcome.

She was trying to find him and bring him home.

River's eyes never left his, as if she was daring him to tell her she was wrong.

"Why do you think he's alive?" he asked quietly.

She frowned. "You're not going to give me a look of pity while telling me you know this is hard but there's no way he's alive?"

"Not until I hear the entire story." He wanted every little detail she had, even though he knew it was almost impossible for the man to be alive. Not after being declared dead by a coroner.

She took a deep breath. "I saw him. At two thirty that night."

It was Jackson's turn to frown. "That's not possible. He died at—"

"One fifteen. I know." She took a small step closer. The sounds of the birds and the wind faded. Her voice was all he heard. "I was in bed, unable to sleep, when I heard a noise from his room. I wanted to talk to him, so I got up. When I opened the door, I saw him climbing out the window. It was dark, and I didn't see his face. But it was him."

Jackson's stomach clenched, dread stabbing at his chest. "Shit, River. It could have been one of *them*. One of Mickey's guys."

She was already shaking her head. "No. It was him. Pretty much all I saw was his back, but I know my brother. And I'm sure he tried to get out quickly because he heard me coming. Besides, if he was a bad guy, why would he run? And what would Mickey or his guys even want from his room?"

Was she trying to convince him or herself?

She swallowed. "It was him, Jackson."

He blew out a long breath, running his gaze along the street above her head. He'd give anything for her to be right. For the man he considered a brother to be alive.

But he knew the chances of that being the case were slim to none.

"This isn't about grief, Jackson. At the time, I didn't know he'd been declared dead, so I had no reason to doubt what I saw."

"Did you go straight back to bed after?" he asked.

She shook her head. "I tried calling him, but it went to voicemail. I eventually went to sleep, telling myself I'd ask him about it in the morning."

He gave a slow nod.

"Do you believe me?"

His muscles bunched because he knew what she wanted to hear. What she was desperate to hear. He could lie. But at the same time, he couldn't. Not to River. Not about this. "I don't know."

A partial lie. Because he was certain Ryker was dead. But now, there was a trickle of doubt surrounding the circumstances of his death. Maybe there was more to that night than had been reported.

To River's credit, she didn't look disappointed by his answer. Maybe she'd been expecting a resounding "no".

"Who else have you told?" he asked.

"Just Michele."

Not a surprise. If he'd been expecting anyone to know, it was her.

She wet her lips before she started walking again. "I think what I found in that basement is connected to all of this."

He walked beside her, only needing one step for every two of hers. "What did you find?"

A beat of silence. "A cage-fighting ring. Which makes sense. Ryker was coming home with bruises and black eyes."

Ryker was a good fighter. They both were. Even as kids, they'd spent way too much time in Larry's ring.

"That doesn't explain why his car went off a bridge."

"I know." Her features hardened. "But I plan to find out."

Hell no.

This time, he stepped in front of her, blocking her way. "You are not investigating this. You've told me. I'll tell Dec and Cole. We'll take care of it."

"This is exactly why I didn't tell you. I knew you'd say that. I can figure this out."

Goddamn, this woman. "No. If you're right, there's dangerous shit going down in that place. I want you as far away from it as possible."

Hell, if it were up to him, he'd have her shipped to another damn state.

Her arms crossed over her chest. "I'm not staying out of it, Jackson."

He took a step forward, hands gripping her hips. When he spoke, his words were low and clear. "Leave it to us, River."

When her eyes darkened, he sucked in a breath, knowing she didn't respond well to intimidation. She responded to calm rationale.

His grip on her softened, along with his voice. "Please, Rae. Trust me to get to the bottom of this."

Some of the anger faded from her features. When her hands went to his chest, desire rippled inside him. "I'll trust you. But if I can help, I will. I have to."

Her words were firm. And he knew that, for the moment at least, there was no talking her down. It would have to be enough. For now.

Her fingers grazed against his chest. And when their gazes clashed, his breath almost stalled. Because in her eyes, he saw everything. The teenage girl he'd fallen in love with but had denied himself. The strong, courageous woman who loved hard and fought for those she cared about even harder.

Before he could stop himself, he dipped his head, capturing her mouth.

River's hands immediately went to his shoulders, her fingers digging into his skin.

When her tongue slipped between his lips, he growled deep in his chest. Taking. Tasting. Giving.

For a moment, time stood still, the past and present merging. He was both the teenager who needed her but couldn't have her and the man who was just realizing he'd never stop loving her.

They kissed and touched, grazing each other's skin like they needed to feel every inch of the other person, neither of them caring that they stood by the side of a street.

When they finally came up for air, he lowered his head, touching his forehead to hers.

He couldn't lose her. He'd do whatever it took to protect her, while also finding out exactly what happened to her brother.

"She really believes he's alive?"

Jackson's fingers tightened on the wheel at Cole's question. "Yes."

But it couldn't be true. The second he'd left her place, Jackson had gone down to speak to the coroner in person. The man had reiterated what he already knew. Ryker had been identified through his dental records.

"But I'm starting to believe maybe his death wasn't an accident, and we're going to find out."

"Damn straight," Declan said from the back seat.

He pulled up out front of the club. It was only four in the afternoon, but he was counting on the owner being there. The hard part would be getting inside.

The three of them climbed out of the car, heading toward the door. He'd barely raised his hand to knock when it was pulled open. It was one of the assholes who'd stood behind Mickey last night.

"We're closed."

He went to pull the door shut, but Jackson stopped it with his foot. "We're here to see Mickey."

The guy's lips thinned. "He's not expecting any visitors, so fuck off."

He tried pushing again, but Jackson put a hand on the door, too, holding it firm and easily keeping the thing open.

The guy's chest expanded. "You fucking deaf, buddy?"

Jackson kept his features completely neutral. "We're here to speak to Mickey. And we're not leaving until we do."

The man's free hand fisted at his side. Jackson's muscles tightened, preparing for the guy to swing. He could feel his team tensing around him, ready for whatever came next.

The ringing of a phone cut through the tense silence. The guy's fingers un-fisted to answer it.

"Yeah, boss?" His jaw ticked. Then there was a quick nod. "Got it."

When he looked back to them, his jaw was still rigid. "He'll see you."

Declan smiled. "See? All's good."

Jackson almost laughed. Trust Declan to smile in a situation like this.

There was a small grunt from the guy before he led them inside. The place looked huge when it was empty. There were a couple of people milling around. Mostly security-looking guys.

The muscle who'd answered the door led them up a spiral staircase. At the top, they walked to a door and knocked.

"Come in."

Jackson was the first to step inside. A large office. There was a big desk on one side of the room, and on the other, a huge window showing the entire club downstairs.

He cast his gaze back to Mickey.

The guy smiled. "You guys were with River last night."

Jackson's muscles bunched. He didn't even like River's name falling from the guy's mouth. "We were. We were also friends with Ryker."

If he expected a reaction, he didn't get one. Mickey's features remained completely clear as he walked around his desk.

The guy who had led them to the office remained inside the room, two other guys stepping in behind him, closing the door.

Jackson only needed a glance their way to know they were armed. Guns in holsters beneath jackets.

"You must be upset about your friend," Mickey said.

Jackson's jaw clenched. He opened his mouth, but Cole spoke before he could.

"What was Ryker doing here every Friday night?"

Mickey smiled, but it came out as more of a sneer. "I would've thought you'd have that figured out by now. What with River finding the cage last night."

Jackson's eyes narrowed.

Mickey's gaze shot back to him. "What? You thought I didn't

know? The second that bitch left my club, I checked the camera feed."

Jackson shot forward a step, both his fists clenched. "You watch your fucking mouth."

The guy frowned before laughing. "Ah. I should have known by the way you jumped to her rescue last night. You two are together, no?"

"Leave her out of this. How'd you get Ryker into the cage?"

"*Get him?*" He looked at his men, all of them chuckling like Jackson had just told a joke. "The man came here in a rage. Wanted to knock my teeth out or some shit." He shook his head. "His anger…it went deeper than just River. I could see that."

Mickey walked over to his window, glancing out.

"River had told me that her brother was a soldier. I knew he could box, and I needed a fighter, so I made him an offer he couldn't refuse. Fight in my ring. Make some money. And release some of that pent-up fury."

Guilt once again stabbed at Jackson. Guilt that the only way Ryker had felt he could deal with his rage was with his fists. That Jackson hadn't been around to help exorcise all that anger.

"So he came every Friday night and got in the ring?" Declan asked.

"He did. Won me a shitload of money, too." He shook his head. "But that ended when he went and got himself killed. Stupid asshole. He was a sure bet. And now that he's dead, I'm a fighter down. That's one less fight each week."

This time it was Cole who took a threatening step forward, but Jackson held his arm out, stopping him.

"How does it work?" he asked.

Mickey studied him. "The cage fighting? The guys start at the bottom and work their way up. One fight a week. He was halfway through the other fighters. And he was annihilating every opponent." The guy shook his head. "Fucking impossible to replace."

"I'll take his place." Jackson felt the eyes of his guys on him, but they remained silent. He needed an in. A way to get into that basement and find out exactly what Ryker had gotten caught up in. Because if there was any truth to this guy or his club having a hand in Ryker's death, Jackson would be getting to the bottom of it—and murdering the fuckers.

Something flashed through Mickey's eyes. Something questioning but also…excited.

Jackson could have laughed. Mickey was a betting man. A money man. A businessman. And he liked the idea of fresh meat in his club. He liked the idea of another sure bet.

"You want to fight in the cage?" Mickey asked.

"I'm just as good a fighter as Ryker."

Mickey studied him. Weighing his options. He would know he shouldn't let Jackson or his friends anywhere near the club. Not if he'd had a hand in Ryker's death. But if he was as greedy as Jackson thought he was…

He took a small step forward, not missing the way the guys by the door reached for their guns. "I can be just as profitable as Ryker. I was a Delta. I do what I need to survive. You put me in that ring, and I'll slaughter any unlucky bastard you put in front of me."

For a moment, there was silence. He wanted to say yes; Jackson could see it on his face.

"Done. You fight from where Ryker left off, though. That means your first opponent is Thunder. He's a mean fucker. And the fight doesn't stop until someone's beaten into submission or unconscious. Still want to play?"

"Yes." Hell yes.

"Boss." Mickey didn't look at whichever guy said his name. "Elijah won't like that."

Elijah…River had mentioned him. She'd overheard one of the guys in the basement say something about a pissing contest between Elijah and Mickey.

Mickey scowled at the guy. "Fuck Elijah." He turned back to Jackson. "People are charged for admittance and that money is divvied up between the night's winners. The higher your ranking, the bigger your cut. I take a cut, too."

Jackson didn't care about money. He cared about answers. "Great. I've got some conditions of my own."

Mickey almost looked amused. "Do you? Go on then."

"My guys are allowed in the audience." He took a small step closer. "And you keep your word about leaving River the hell alone. You don't touch her. You don't talk to her. You don't so much as lay a fucking eyeball on her."

The guy threw back his head and laughed. "I don't want that bitch."

Jackson's hand itched to reach for his own gun. He only just stopped himself. "I'll see you Friday night."

CHAPTER 11

*R*iver crouched, adjusting the lens of her camera until she got the shot. Okay, not one shot, she never took just one. She took dozens. The afternoon sun was striking through the wildflowers in a way that had the outer edges of the plants turning a golden-orange shade.

Beautiful. So damn beautiful.

She'd always loved the way the setting sun could enhance a photo. Add warmth and depth and texture.

She had no paid shoots booked today, so she was doing what she always did on her days off. Getting lost in the tranquility of nature. She needed it now more than most days. She needed the grounding and the calm, and the awe.

She switched the angle of the shot, making the sun the subject, and turning the wildflowers into dark silhouettes. Beautiful. And so simple. If only everything in life was as simple as nature.

She'd spent years studying photography. The ins and outs of getting the perfect shot. The small details and the rules of editing. But even though she'd done all the classes, *excelled* in all the classes, she wouldn't say they'd been necessary for her to create the perfect shot. She'd always had a way of composing a photo in her head before snapping a picture. Adjusting until she got the perfect angle and lighting. The courses had mostly just improved her technical skills, giving her more of a framework to create within.

River moved her camera again. Then she paused, trickles of awareness sliding over her skin.

Jackson. He was walking down the trail, and his eyes were on her. She almost stood. But the light was hitting his side in a way that had him looking almost...angelic.

She snapped a photo. Then a few more.

As he drew closer, she lowered the lens, focusing on his steps. On the way his feet dug into the path. The way little specks of dust flew into the air with each one.

Magic.

"How do I look?" His deep timbre trickled through her limbs, penetrating the quiet that had been with her all afternoon.

"Like a soldier disturbing the stillness of the earth." Because the earth *had* been still before his steps. There was a little wind, a light rustling of the leaves, but that was it.

River rose to her feet slowly, looking up—way up—at Jackson's face. She often forgot how tall he was. He easily towered over her five seven.

"How'd you find me?" she asked quietly, dropping the camera to her side.

The corner of Jackson's mouth lifted, and it almost took her back in time. As a teenager, he hadn't smiled much. But when he had, she always memorized it. Stored it inside her and cherished it.

"Your text said you were in your happy place."

She'd almost forgotten about that. He'd texted her not that long ago asking where she was. She shouldn't be surprised he remembered this spot. She'd come here a lot when she was younger. Sometimes with Ryker and Jackson, sometimes with

Michele. But mostly by herself. Her favorite pine tree was here. The same one she had tattooed on her wrist when she'd been drunk and twenty-one and feeling spontaneous.

"It's crazy, isn't it? I've been walking down Umtanum Canyon since I was a teenager, and I'm still not sick of this place." She glanced over the wide expanse of land. At the calmness of the trees and flowers. Was becoming sick of a place like this even possible?

She looked back to Jackson. He was silent as he studied her.

She gave a small shake of her head. "It must seem silly to you that I love this place so much. You've traveled the world. Probably seen a million and one amazingly beautiful places. I shouldn't blame you for not coming back."

His hands were shoved into the pockets of his jeans, his large biceps bunching. "It wasn't so much about wanting what was out there, as wanting to be away from here. From my father. This town."

She swallowed, and some of the anger she'd been holding toward him wilted. "Was living in this town so terrible?" Didn't she and her family offer him some good memories? She certainly had some with him.

"It was more that I made a promise to myself when I was a kid that when I was out, I was out."

But by doing that, it wasn't just this town or his father he'd sworn off. And that was something he knew. An intentional decision he'd made.

"What are we doing, Jackson?" She hadn't meant to say those words, but now…she needed to know. They'd kissed twice. And both kisses had been addictive and heart-pounding and soul-awakening. They'd been everything she knew they could be.

His brows drew together as he took a small step forward. "I don't know. But when I touch you, it feels right."

She swallowed. It felt right to her, too. But it also felt scary. Because she could so easily drown in those kisses. And where did that leave her when he left? Because he would leave. His hatred for this town and his desire to get out had always been his greatest motivator in life.

"Have you seen your dad again?"

And just like that, the light left his eyes. But she'd known it would. Known that they'd be pulled out of their bubble and back to reality. "I haven't. And if I don't see him for the rest of the trip, it will be too soon."

Trip. The word burned her, even though she knew it shouldn't.

She gave a short nod, mostly because it was just about all she could muster.

The muscles in his arms rippled. "Have *you* seen him?"

He'd never liked her anywhere near his father. The few times she had been was when everything in him was darkest.

"No. I rarely see him around town. I don't think anyone does."

A short nod of his own.

When they'd been in school, she'd seen his bruises and black eyes. He'd never admitted anything to anyone. She was pretty sure her parents had even tried to make him talk so they could do something to help. She'd always suspected he was just biding his time to get out of town, not wanting to be thrown into the foster care system or risk anything disrupting his enlistment.

His gaze lowered to her camera. "How are the pictures looking?"

She lifted the camera, opening the display screen. Jackson moved beside her, and almost immediately, awareness shot through her limbs. His side touched hers. His heat penetrated her clothes.

Giving herself a mental shake, she slowly flicked through the photos she'd taken.

"Christ, River. They're amazing."

She wasn't one to get embarrassed, but at that moment, her cheeks heated. "Thank you." She expected him to move away after the last photo. He didn't. And when she looked up, his eyes were stormy.

"Why don't you sell your photos?"

"I tried. I wasn't making money." She'd quickly realized that maybe doing what she loved was a pipe dream.

"You should try again," he said firmly.

She almost laughed. "I spent years trying, Jackson. Failing to make it a viable career wasn't for a lack of effort."

"Still. You should try again."

Her lips tilted up. "Maybe."

He gave her a knowing smile before he started moving down the trail the way he'd come.

She frowned. Did he just expect her to follow?

She glanced up at the sun, knowing it had to be getting close to dinnertime. Fine. She'd follow, but only because she was hungry.

She jogged to catch up to him. "Are *you* living your dream? You all left the military without explaining why. What have you been doing since?"

He lifted a shoulder, eyes focused ahead of him. "I did some security work."

He said that with about all the enthusiasm of a snail. "And is that what you intend to keep doing?"

He hesitated. And the hesitation was all the answer she needed. "I have no idea what I'm going to do."

"So I'm not the only one not living my best life."

He gave a small chuckle, and it had her tummy doing somersaults. "No. You're not the only one."

"Well, maybe we'll both get there at some point." She was half joking. She'd probably be taking photos of food until the day she died. Honestly, there was so much work, she was turning jobs down most weeks.

"So," she said quietly. "You ever gonna tell me how your meeting with Mickey went? That is why you're here, isn't it?"

When he didn't say anything, she looked up. The man was frowning again. Damn, she was a sucker for a sexy brooder.

"I will. But first, I have a question."

Oh, jeez. This was going to be one of those would-rather-cut-off-my-left-hand-than-answer kind of questions, she could feel it. "Okay."

"Why did you date him?"

Yep. She was right.

"The guy's a dirty scumbag," Jackson added, sneering his words.

Oh, he definitely was. She lifted a shoulder. "Because I was lonely. And he didn't come across as a dirty scumbag at the start."

"You dated him for months, Rae."

Yeah, she'd been an idiot. "It was casual dating. I rarely went to the club, so I barely saw that side of him. When it was just him and me, we bantered. Had fun. I only noticed he had some anger issues in the last month. The second he hit me, I called it off."

The veins in Jackson's neck popped out.

"Your turn. What happened when you spoke to him today?"

Jackson took a moment to answer. Whether he was trying to control his anger or just considering his words, she wasn't sure.

"Mickey confirmed he offered Ryker a place fighting in the ring. He fought every Friday night and was slowly working his way up the ranks. People place bets on the fighter they think will win. Mickey was making a lot of money off him."

She stepped over a large rock, scoffing. "Well, I'm not going to feel sorry for him now that he's not."

"I offered to take Ryker's place in the ring."

Her foot caught on the next rock. She started falling, but Jackson grabbed her arm and tugged her back to her feet seconds before her face collided with the dirt.

She swung toward him. "You *what?*"

"I needed a way to get into that basement. This is it."

"Jackson, you're not a cage fighter! Ryker was coming home

black and blue every week. He had blood all over him!" She was yelling, but, dammit, she couldn't help it. It was too dangerous.

He almost looked like he was fighting a smile. "I've been trained by the best, River. I can take care of myself in the ring."

She was already shaking her head, fear crawling up her throat. "No."

"It's done."

An angry breath escaped her throat. He was going to do it no matter what she said. She couldn't stop him. "Fine. But if you're going to be down there, so am I."

This time, he didn't just smile, he outright laughed. "No, River, you're not. You're not going anywhere near that place."

"Yes. I am. I'm not sitting at home, twiddling my thumbs while you get your ass kicked in a cage, wondering if you've been knocked out for good! I want to be there. And you need to make that happen with Mickey."

"No."

River's jaw set. "You know what? I don't need your permission. I got into that basement once—I'll do it again."

She started to walk away, but the hand that was still around her arm tightened, holding her in place, giving her no space. "River, it's too goddamn dangerous."

"I don't care! I need to be a part of this. And if you're putting yourself in danger, then so am I. You choose, Jackson. I go with you and the guys, or I go on my own."

His lips thinned, his body almost vibrating. "Fine. But you stay with Dec and Cole the entire time. Do you understand?"

"Fine."

CHAPTER 12

The wooden steps creaked beneath Jackson's feet as he headed down into the basement. It was finally Friday night and one of Mickey's guys, Brooks, led him to where he needed to go.

He scanned the room, noticing a small crowd had already gathered, even though he was early. There were rows of chairs lining every side of the ring. The wire cage around the raised platform was high, easily seven feet tall.

Impenetrable. That was his first thought.

Dec, Cole, and River weren't due to arrive for another hour. He'd already spoken to Mickey about her attending. The guy wasn't happy, but when he realized it was both of them or neither, he'd reluctantly conceded.

Jackson had barely reached the basement floor when he felt eyes on him. Like hot beams hitting him from the side.

Immediately, he shot his gaze to the corner of the room, spotting three men. All looked to be in their early forties. All looked less than impressed by the sight of him.

Who were they? Was one of them Elijah?

He dragged his gaze away, but not before committing each man's face to memory.

"There are rooms down this hall," Brooks said, walking forward without checking that Jackson was following. It seemed a lot of people weren't impressed by his appearance. Brooks had been sneering at him since the second he stepped foot inside the club.

"How many other fighters are there?" Jackson asked.

"Nine. Five fights a night. Because of the…nature of the fights, every fighter only goes one bout, then waits until next week."

The guy seemed happy about that. Pleased about people getting their asses kicked.

Asshole.

Cage fighting was a mix of different forms of martial arts. The fighters wore shorts and hand wraps. It was dangerous. And most fighters didn't last the average three to five rounds.

Brooks shot a look over his shoulder. "Wait until you see Thunder. He's massive. And he doesn't fight fair or show mercy." He stopped outside a door, smiling.

The guy thought Jackson was going to lose. Well, Brooks was in for a little disappointment.

"Good. The dirtier the better. I got a lot of pent-up rage to get out of my system. And it's no fun taking down an asshole who's smaller, is it?"

The smile slipped from the guy's mouth.

Jackson looked away, casting a quick glance down the long, narrow hall. There were multiple doors off to one side, and right at the end were some stairs.

Where did they lead? Back into the club?

Jackson looked back to the guy in front of him. "Where do those stairs go?"

"That's none of your fucking business."

Brooks opened the door, and Jackson stepped into the room.

It was larger than he'd expected. Four guys stood around the space, some wrapping their hands, others getting changed.

"We never place you in a room with your opponent," Brooks said, stepping inside behind him. "The rest of the guys have another room down the hall. Bathroom's two doors down. We'll call you when it's your turn. You're the third fight."

"Who the fuck's this?"

Jackson turned his head to see a bald guy in shorts standing up from a bench. Tattoos covered his body from head to toe.

"This is Ryker's replacement."

The guy scowled. "He just gets to go straight into his position?"

Brooks' eyes narrowed. "Take it up with Mickey, it was his call." Then Brooks left.

The guy's gaze remained on Jackson, studying him, before his jaw hardened and he sat back down. He shook his head. "Why the fuck do I care if you wanna get fucking killed tonight?"

So Jackson getting his ass beat was the common consensus then. Turning, he lowered his bag to the nearest bench.

"Shut the fuck up, Wall."

Wall grumbled. Jackson shot a look at the man who spoke. The guy was big, probably close to six four. Tattoos covered half his chest and his right shoulder, and he had a piercing in his right eyebrow.

He looked up, catching Jackson's gaze. "Ignore him. It took him a long time to reach his rank and he's a jealous fucker."

Jackson nodded.

The guy straightened. "I'm Erik."

"Jackson. You been fighting here long?"

"Maybe a year." He lifted a shoulder. "It's good money and I'm a good fighter, so works out well."

"You had a lot of experience in a cage?"

He laughed. "I was a professional boxer for a while, so yeah, you could say I have some experience. Although this is a completely different ballgame."

Yeah, so he'd been told. He tugged his shirt over his head. "You fought Thunder before?"

The guy sneered. "Yeah, the guy's a mean son of a bitch. He likes the front kick to the face and the side kick to the knees. Protect those points. He won't hesitate to do some permanent damage."

Jackson stored those tips away. "Thanks."

The guy nodded before turning back to his own bag.

Jackson spent the next half hour wrapping his hands and warming up. He wanted to get out of the room. See what else was there. No one had told him he couldn't, so when everyone else was busy, he moved into the hall, heading away from the fighting area. The first thing he did was slip up the stairs. He tried the handle on the door at the top, not surprised to find it locked.

Next, he moved back down the hall, scanning the empty rooms. A couple held filing cabinets and beer kegs. A couple more were locked.

He did a quick scan of the desks, noticing most were empty. He was betting the important stuff was in what River had assumed was an office beyond the ring. A room he was sure would be locked.

When he reached the main room with the cage, he saw that more people had arrived. He scanned the crowd for Dec, Cole, and River but didn't spot them. What he did see was Mickey deep in conversation with some guys to the side of the room. And not just any guys. The ones who'd been watching him when he arrived in the basement.

Mickey seemed to be speaking quickly, and even though Jackson couldn't hear what he was saying, he could tell the guy was angry. They all were.

When Jackson looked past them, he saw a man leading a small

group toward the office. His entire body iced over when he realized who it was.

His father.

～

RIVER WAS SANDWICHED between Jackson's friends as they moved through the club, Cole in front of her and Declan behind. Neither of them smiled. Both scanned the place like they were waiting for a threat to jump out at any moment.

Which was fair enough. The place was packed.

When they reached the hall, there was a line to get to the basement. The men remained silent. She kind of felt like a celebrity shielded by her bodyguards. The thought almost had her laughing.

When they reached the front of the line, she recognized Johnny by the door and almost groaned. She didn't like any of Mickey's guys. In her opinion, they were all jerks with guns and too much power. But she disliked Johnny in particular. There was just something about him that made her suspect he was a slippery bastard.

When Johnny's gaze fell on her, his eyes narrowed.

Yeah, I don't like you either, buddy.

His jaw ticked, but he nodded them through. The second River stepped onto the top step, her eyes widened. From what she could see of the room, the place was packed. Like, *packed-*packed. God, there had to be a couple hundred people here, at least. Some sat, a lot stood around talking, waiting for the first fight to start.

Cole turned his head. "Stick close."

Uh, was it even possible to get away in this crush?

When they reached the bottom, the guys shifted closer as Cole led them over to some seats. Any closer, and they'd both be touching her. Full-on body against body as they walked.

When a guy rushed past, he brushed against River, shoving her straight into Declan, who caught her.

Cole grabbed the guy, getting in his face before giving him a strong shove. "Watch it."

The guy's chest puffed up, but there was a hint of fear when he saw how big both Cole and Declan were. He walked away quickly.

Yeah, she was definitely safe with these two.

When they reached the chairs, River almost breathed a sigh of relief as she sat down.

"You okay?" Declan asked.

She was quickly realizing Declan was the talker between the two. The lighthearted one. Cole, on the other hand, was a brooder.

"I'm okay." *Kind of. Not really.* Okay, she was totally crapping her pants at the idea of Jackson stepping into that cage and fighting some guy who had probably spent a large chunk of his life fighting criminals.

Why the hell had he agreed to this? Surely there were other ways to get the information they needed. Fighting in this club had ended with Ryker's funeral, for Christ's sake.

She bit the inside of her cheek, trying to calm her nerves. A second passed before Cole's hand covered hers, lifted it from her leg, and gently straightened her fingers before releasing her.

She looked down, seeing the red nail marks on her skin. She hadn't even realized she'd been digging her nails into her own thigh.

Declan nudged her shoulder. "He'll be okay."

"How do you know?"

"Because I've seen Jackson fight. He's been trained by the best and he's fought the meanest assholes in the world. He knows how to take a hit, and even more than that, he knows how to give one."

Cole crossed his arms. "This time tomorrow, he'll be bragging about his battle scars to anyone who'll listen."

River scoffed. "Well, it won't be me. After tonight, I never want to hear about this fight again."

The logical side of her brain knew they'd probably be back. That the Ryker puzzle wouldn't be solved in one night. But the part of her brain that didn't want to think about Jackson getting hurt was in denial. A solid, Jackson's-never-stepping-in-that-cage-again denial.

When the crowd started to quiet, River glanced up to see Mickey walking into the ring. Her lips thinned at the sight of him. God, she couldn't stand the guy. Not just because he'd hit her. But because if a man hit a woman once, he'd do it again, and had probably done it before. She imagined what would have happened if she was a woman of lower self-worth and had stayed with him.

Her fingers curled into fists.

"Welcome, everyone. Tonight we have five excellent matches lined up for you, including one exciting new fighter." Mickey scanned the crowd, eyes falling on River for a second before moving away. "First up, we have the Tornado and Mike. Let's get loud for them."

The crowd did exactly that. Yelling and cheering as two men stepped out from the hall and climbed onto the platform. Jesus, they were huge, both in height and breadth. And they looked... rough. As in, there was no way in hell she'd want to be caught dead in a dark alley with either.

She shifted back further into her seat, suddenly loving that she was sandwiched between two former Deltas.

Both men in the ring spent a moment glaring at each other, puffing their big chests like they were animals in the wild. It wasn't until Mickey ducked out, closing the cage door behind him, and a whistle blew, that they started inching toward each other.

River sucked in a sharp breath at the first hit. The punch was thrown by Tornado. It was hard, and it was powerful. And it took her by surprise. For some reason, she'd expected a pause before fighting. Weren't they supposed to dance around each other? Take a few moments to intimidate their opponent?

Even though Mike's head flew back, he rebounded immediately, throwing a punch of his own.

The fight continued like that, fast and violent. At one point, Tornado lifted Mike off the ground, flipping him over his shoulder. He quickly followed it up with a stomp to the ribs.

River cast her eyes away, wincing. That's when she saw him— Jackson, standing in the hall, watching the fight. Studying it.

Her next breath was more of a shudder. Because soon, that would be him in there. Fighting a man just as big. Just as dangerous.

As if he felt her eyes on him, Jackson tore his gaze from the fight and looked straight at her. For a moment, they just remained like that. The roaring crowd, the lights, the action, all of it faded around them, as if it were just the two of them. Her heart was pounding with the need to go straight over there and march him out. Put him in a little bubble of safety.

He winked at her, and a smile curved his lips as if he could see her fear and was trying to ease it. It didn't work. Not even a little bit.

When the second fight rolled around, it was much the same as the first. A flurry of fists and blood and gut-wrenching violence.

Every minute that passed had the bile in her throat rising. She pushed it down.

You asked to be here, River. Deal with it.

But she'd only asked because she'd known that sitting at home would be worse. Instead of watching Jackson get the crap beaten out of him, she'd be imagining it. And it would have been all the worst-case scenarios. The panic would have suffocated her.

When the second fight finally finished and Mickey returned to the cage, River bit her lip, tasting blood. Her fingernails bit into her thighs again, tiny gasps of air rushing in and out of her chest.

Declan leaned down and whispered into her ear, "Breathe."

She gave a quick nod, knowing full well she wouldn't be sucking in any easy breaths until Jackson was safe.

The man himself entered the cage, shirtless, cords of muscle bulging from his chest and arms.

Then his opponent stepped in.

And yep, River was pretty sure she was going to throw up right there and then. Not only because the guy was just as big as Jackson and looked like he'd just been released from prison, with scars and tattoos riddling his body, but because River was certain this guy wouldn't be fighting fair.

CHAPTER 13

The second Mickey left the cage, she expected them to go at each other like previous fighters had. They didn't. They walked around each other in a circular motion. Watching. Assessing. Waiting for the other person to make the first move.

It was Thunder who eventually did, lunging forward and swinging. Jackson stepped aside, barely missing the hit, causing Thunder to fall into the wire cage.

She swallowed at the sight of Thunder's face, suddenly understanding where the name came from. His expression was all thunder.

He ran at Jackson this time, fist cocking back, ready to hit. Again, Jackson dodged, but this time Thunder didn't fall into the cage. Jackson grabbed him from behind, tugging him back and putting him in a choke hold.

Jackson held the guy for a good ten seconds as Thunder's face reddened and he bucked and kicked. Finally, Jackson let go, kicking him forward.

When Thunder turned, he looked... River couldn't even describe it. It was worse than any anger she'd seen before.

This time when Thunder charged, he did it so quickly that Jackson couldn't dodge the man. Thunder grabbed him around the midsection, sending them both to the floor.

River's breath caught in her throat at the sight of the powerful men grappling. Any time either man got on top, hard punches were thrown. Punches that whipped the other man's head back and had River full-body flinching in her seat.

Jackson was good. And so damn dangerous-looking. Hell, he was like a stranger out there. He only ever let Thunder get in a single hit or kick before flipping their positions, going on the offensive once again. For every hit he took, he gave three back, at least. At some moments, it was as if Jackson anticipated his opponent's move before the guy even made it.

River shut her eyes for a second, needing to catch her breath. When she opened them again, both men were on their feet, and Thunder was throwing a punch. Jackson blocked it with his arm, countering it with a hard high-kick to Thunder's head.

Thunder fell back into the fencing, and Jackson charged, throwing one hard punch to the guy's face.

That was it. Thunder fell to the ground, out cold.

The air whooshed out of River's chest. Jackson won. She could finally breathe again. But the nausea was still there, swirling away in her gut, threatening to crawl up her throat and choke her.

She managed to sit through the last two fights...just. The second the final one finished, she turned to Cole. "I need to go to the bathroom."

He gave a short nod, both he and Declan rising, leading her through the rows and down the small hall. They'd almost made it when someone passing in the hall yanked her arm, pulling her to a stop.

Surprise filled her when she saw who it was. Brian Ford. Jackson's father.

Declan was immediately between them, his voice low and deadly. "Let her go before I break your fucking arm."

His fingers let go, but his gaze held hers. "What the hell are you doing here?"

She straightened her spine. "Why? You don't want me here?"

His eyes narrowed. "No one does."

She raised a brow. "And why is that?"

He took a small step forward. Declan did the same, looking moments from punching the guy. Cole remained firmly by her side like he was waiting to tug her away.

Brian sneered at her. "If you don't know, you're stupider than I thought."

Before she could respond, he turned and continued down the hall.

River frowned. What the hell? What was he doing here? Was he involved in whatever had happened to Ryker?

The idea did nothing to quell the nausea.

She pushed inside the bathroom and moved straight to a cubicle, expecting to be sick. She wasn't. Instead, she managed to just...breathe. To be still in the quiet of the empty stall. To calm her racing heart and gurgling gut.

She felt the vibration of her phone in her pocket. It had vibrated a few times, but she hadn't been able to tear her gaze away from the fights. She tugged it out and saw it was Michele. The woman had texted her three times.

Michele: Is he okay?

Michele: Oh Lord, he isn't, is he?

Michele: River, I need you to answer me right the heck now!

Taking a final calming breath, she quickly typed out a response.

River: He won. He received a few hits and kicks to the side but he's okay.

At least, as okay as one could be after fighting in that ring.

Michele: Oh, what a relief! I'm so glad. Get home safe xox

Her hand went to the lock on the door, and she was about to leave the stall when the bathroom door opened and voices sounded.

"Angel, you need to calm down," a woman said.

River's breath caught at the name. *Angel.*

"I can't!" said a different voice. A distressed voice. A voice she recognized as the woman who had answered her call. "All I could think about while that new guy was fighting was that it should have been Ryker!"

The tiny hairs on River's arms stood on end at hearing her brother's name.

"Yes, you can. You have to."

"It's my fault. It's *my* fault he's dead!" River's skin chilled. "I'm the one who told him about the kegs."

River frowned. Kegs?

"You need to get it together," the other woman said, all calm gone, her voice almost pleading. "If they find out you're the one who told him, they'll kill you too!"

A deep breath. "I know."

River opened her door. A blond woman with tears streaming down her face and a brunette with a pixie cut both looked up in surprise. The brunette frowned while the blond turned away, wiping the tears from her face.

River opened her mouth, but before she could utter a word, the door to the bathroom opened, and Cole stepped inside. "We need to go."

There was an urgency to his tone. One she hadn't heard before.

She shot a desperate look back at Angel. "But—"

He grabbed her arm, tugging her outside with an unbreakable grip.

What the heck was going on?

River was seconds from getting mad at the guy when she saw it.

Chaos. Punches being thrown in the crowd. Chairs being crashed over people's heads.

Her jaw dropped.

Suddenly, Jackson was there, throwing a protective arm around her shoulders. Then the three men shoved their way through the violent crowd, Jackson shielding her body with his own the entire time.

THEY MADE it out of the basement...barely.

Jackson's fingers were tight around the steering wheel, his gaze continually shifting between the road and the rearview mirror. Not just because someone could follow, but because he felt uneasy.

The second the fight broke out, dread had engulfed him. Suffocated him. River had been all he could think about. Was she okay? Had she gotten caught in the crowd? He trusted his guys to keep her safe, but the need to be with her had drowned him.

He shot numerous looks toward River during the drive, noticing she seemed just as unsettled as him. Neither of them spoke. Not the entire way to her place.

He continued to check the roads behind him, adding in a few extra turns as he went and making sure no one was following.

It wasn't until he stopped in her driveway that he finally spoke. "River—"

"I don't want you fighting in that cage again."

His jaw tightened as he turned off the car. A beat of silence passed before he spoke. "I need to go back next week."

She spun toward him. "Are you serious? Jackson, those guys wouldn't care if they stomped on your neck and killed you! And your next opponent will be bigger and stronger. Probably another man who looks like an ex-con."

"I can handle myself."

She scoffed, shaking her head. "You think you're made of steel. That you're invincible. You're not."

She unbuckled her seat belt quickly, but he didn't miss the way her fingers shook. His gut twisted at the sight. When he didn't immediately climb out with her, she bent down, putting her head back in the car.

"Get your ass out here, Jackson. I'm cleaning those cuts."

A bit of tension leaked from his gut, and he almost laughed. Unbuckling himself, he climbed out. River was already at the door. She'd barely unlocked it before he was stepping inside ahead of her.

Just like last time, he walked around the house, checking every room. Every space. When he got back to the living room, he was glad to find the woman still on the porch.

Finally, she listened to him.

"All clear."

With a quick nod, she stepped inside, closing and locking the door behind her before moving down the hall. Jackson sat on the couch, stretching his muscles. He was stiff. He'd taken a couple of hits in the cage, but not as many as he'd been expecting. His opponent had been strong and fearless, but he'd also been cocky.

Jackson, on the other hand, had been tactical. And once he'd learned how the guy moved, and what his preferred mode of offense was, he'd been able to anticipate what was coming.

River placed a first-aid kit on the coffee table before sitting beside him. Her jaw was still set, worry lines shadowing her eyes. There was also that same little tremble in her fingers that hadn't eased.

She grabbed an antiseptic wipe and pressed it to his cheek. He barely felt the sting as he studied her face. "When the fight broke out and you weren't in your seat, I was worried."

That was a lie. He wasn't just worried. He'd damn near lost his mind.

Her gaze remained firmly on his cut before moving to another on his chin. "I went to the bathroom. I thought I was going—" She stopped, shaking her head. "Cole and Declan were right there."

"They would protect you with their lives," he said quietly. That's why he'd had no reason to be so worried. But with River, he wasn't able to shut it off.

"I know." Leaning forward, she grabbed a new wipe. "I didn't like seeing you up there. But I also need to stay involved." She paused. "Promise me, Jackson. Promise you won't push me out. Shield me from anything."

This time when he met her gaze, he saw it. The desperation. The fear she couldn't hide.

Those eyes killed him when they were being tough, but when they were vulnerable, they tore his damn heart out. "I'll keep you as involved as I can."

She seemed to consider that for a moment before giving a quick nod. She went back to dabbing another cut.

"We'll figure this out, Rae," he said quietly.

He used her childhood nickname, and her eyes softened, meeting his once again. "I already have no idea what happened to Ryker. I can't lose you both." Her chest heaved with a hitching breath, and he was almost certain she was only just holding it together.

He took hold of the hand that had been cleaning his cut, immediately swiping the pad of his thumb across her palm. "I'll be okay."

She shook her head. "You say that, but you don't know. You can't. And it scares the crap out of me."

Unable to stop himself, Jackson lifted his other hand, grazing the side of her face. She leaned into him, and damn but it heated his chest. "I'll be careful."

For a moment, there was silence. Stillness. But a million different emotions ran between them. Each one heavy with emotion.

"Good...because as much as you need me to be okay, I need you to be okay more." Then she did something he didn't expect. She leaned in and kissed him.

CHAPTER 14

*R*iver swiped her lips across Jackson's. She needed to kiss him. Touch him. Confirm that he was really here and okay.

For a moment, Jackson was still. It wasn't until her hand grazed down his cheek that he released a growl from deep in his chest. Then he was kissing her back, his hands going to her hips, tugging her closer.

Yearning spidered up her chest, drowning out every other emotion. The fear. The panic. The gut-wrenching dread. It all disappeared, and she was left with him. Only him. She let herself get lost in the man, forgetting everything that came before.

When his tongue slipped between her lips, tangling with hers, she couldn't hold back the moan. It was low and heated and whipped through the silence.

Her hands grazed over every ridge and muscle of his chest, while his fingers dug gently into the flesh of her hips, slipping beneath the material of her shirt. They were a flurry of movement and emotion and need.

Suddenly, it wasn't enough. There was too much space between them.

She climbed onto his lap, immediately feeling his hardness press between her thighs. A dull throb began to pulse in her core.

"River." The word sounded guttural and torn from his chest. His hands slid up the bare skin of her back, burning her. "If we're going to stop, we need to stop *now*."

The only thing River wanted to stop was the night from ticking away. She wanted to hold on to this moment—to him— for as long as she could.

Her hands went to the base of his shirt, sneaking beneath the material, then slid up his heated stomach. His chest. "No stopping."

Two words. That was all she could manage.

Another deep growl from his chest, then in one fluid move, he stood, lifting her with him so her entire front pressed to his chest. She wrapped her legs around him, needing to be closer, but never feeling close enough.

She continued to kiss him as he moved, her fingers threading through his hair, the soft wisps brushing against her skin.

Then the world tilted, their lips separated, and she was on her mattress, Jackson above her. For a moment, she closed her eyes, inhaling his musky scent, a scent to which she'd become addicted.

When warm hands touched the side of her face, her eyes flickered open, and the look on his face had her pausing. He'd always been intense, but right now, he was...more. Bigger. Fiercer. Primal.

"You're sure you want to do this?" he asked, his warm breath whispering across her cheeks.

"I feel like I've waited a lifetime for you."

Half her life, she'd been waiting for this man, telling her heart to forget him but never really letting go.

The specks of honey in his eyes darkened, almost turning charcoal. His head lowered slowly, this time kissing her chin. Her neck. Each touch soft and delicate. Like he thought if he kissed her too firmly, she'd shatter.

She leaned up as he tugged the material of her shirt over her head, then his hands went to her jeans, first undoing the button and zipper, then tugging them down her legs.

She hummed as he pressed a trail of kisses down her stomach, thighs, and calves, until finally reaching her feet. Her shoes dropped to the floor with a thud.

When he lifted off the bed, she watched, unable to drag her gaze away as he stripped off his shirt, then his jeans.

The beginnings of bruises reddened and darkened his skin.

The marks of a warrior.

She swallowed as his head lowered back to her ankle, pressing a light kiss against her skin. He continued to pebble the kisses back up to her hip bone and stomach, stopping above her bra.

The air caught in her throat. One of the bra cups was tugged down. When he captured a hard nipple between his lips, her breath whooshed from her chest, her back arching.

The heat that pooled in her belly turned to lava, and she writhed and moaned as his tongue worked her.

He sucked and played. Her back arched as he reached behind her, unlatching her bra. Cool air touched her breasts, then his mouth lowered to her other nipple. The stormy need in her lower stomach grew as she grabbed on to his shoulder, digging her fingers into his flesh.

When his hand slid down her body, gliding beneath the material of her panties, she could have sworn her heart stopped in her chest. Then he swiped his finger across her slit. She jolted, a tornado of heat and desire swirling through her abdomen.

He swiped again and again, rotating between long brushes and circular swirls. He pushed her higher, demanding more while that mouth never left her nipple.

"Jackson…"

Suddenly, a thick finger pressed to her entrance. Her thighs widened, nails digging into his shoulders.

He slid into her slowly, and the throbbing inside her rippled and expanded. His lips trailed back up her neck as he began to push in and out, thumb caressing her clit. When a second finger slid inside, she almost broke as she writhed more violently beneath him. His mouth sucked at the soft skin of her neck. His fingers moved rhythmically for endless minutes.

It was torture of the best kind. The kind you pull close and hold on to for as long as possible.

Suddenly, it was too much. She pushed at his chest, but he didn't move. Instead, his brows tugged together and he paused. She gave another push, and this time he rolled onto his back.

In much the same way Jackson had, River stood, shimmying out of her panties, loving the way Jackson's eyes flared. Then she crawled over him slowly, finding his mouth with her own. Her right hand skittered down his chest, slipping into his briefs.

When her fingers wrapped around his length, his hand went to her hip, fingers digging into her flesh. He was hard and tense beneath her.

She began to explore, gliding down his length, familiarizing herself with him. She listened for every sharp intake of breath, learning what he liked. Her mouth slid down to his neck, suckling his skin in much the same way he had to her.

He was practically vibrating, his breaths deep and his length thickening in her hand with each stroke. Whenever she reached the tip, a shudder rocked his powerful frame.

Suddenly, she was flung onto her back, her hand ripped away from him, and pressed into the mattress.

"You're killing me, Rae."

He kissed her again, this time harder. When he rose from the bed, a short whimper released from her chest. His gaze didn't leave hers as he took off his briefs.

Her breath caught at his size.

He reached for his jeans, tugged a foil wrapper from his wallet, and donned the condom quickly. Then he was above her again. His length, heavy between her thighs, teasing her entrance.

She widened her legs, loving the way he nestled between them so perfectly.

His eyes were dark and intense as he watched her. "You're so goddamn beautiful, River." He pressed a final kiss to her lips, then slowly, torturously, he slid inside, stretching her.

Her eyes closed, breaths hot as they shuddered from her chest. When she was completely filled, he paused, taking her mouth once again, giving her time to adjust.

When he took a moment too long, she rocked her own hips. A deep, primal growl vibrated from his chest. Then he lifted out of her, before thrusting back in.

A long, deep whimper tried to escape her throat but it was silenced by his mouth against hers. He thrust again, and it was just as powerful. Just as earth-shattering.

His hips began to move in a rhythmic motion, every thrust claiming her. Annihilating.

She scraped her fingers down his biceps, lifting her hips to meet his. His fingers went to her nipple, grazing and plucking until it throbbed.

She tore her mouth away and tilted her head back, trying to breathe but barely able to get air. She was close. So damn close that her limbs trembled and her toes curled.

Jackson's lips found a spot behind her ear, and the second he nipped her, her world splintered into a million pieces. River cried out as the orgasm exploded through her core.

Jackson kept thrusting, his hand never leaving her nipple, mouth still latched to that spot. She was still throbbing around him when finally, his body tensed above her. The rumble that tore from his throat shuddered through his chest as he shattered.

The only man she'd ever loved. The only man she'd ever craved. Hers. For tonight at least.

Finally, there was stillness, their deep breaths the only sounds to disturb the quiet.

River remained where she was, almost scared to move. To lose him. To lose this moment.

Then he kissed her again, one final kiss that snaked into her chest, penetrating her heart. And she knew that what had just happened tonight would change everything. It had to.

JACKSON HELD RIVER CLOSE, listening as her breathing evened out.

He needed to get up, wash himself, and check that everything in the house was turned off and locked up. But that could wait. Right now, he couldn't move.

This was what he'd been afraid of. This was why he'd stayed away. Because he knew the second he allowed himself to get close to her, the second he gave himself permission to *have* her, it would be too damn hard to let go.

He wasn't the kid he used to be. That kid had felt like he had nothing to offer.

But his father was still here. Danger still surrounded them. And that scared the hell out of him.

CHAPTER 15

*R*iver rolled onto her back, groaning as small flecks of sunlight hit her eyelids. She cracked one eye open.

What time was it? Late morning?

God, she needed about a million more hours of sleep and then a good gallon of coffee.

She was just rolling back onto her belly, about to let herself get that extra sleep, when a scent permeated her nose. Jackson's scent.

Her eyes shot open as memories of the previous night assailed her. Of the fight. Of Jackson coming inside. And what happened after...

River jackhammered into a sitting position.

Holy Jesus, they'd had sex.

Her gaze skirted around the room, her heart clenching. He wasn't here. In fact, it almost looked like he'd *never* been here. There were no clothes. No phone or wallet.

She touched the mattress beside her. Cold.

Had he left? No. Maybe he was just in the kitchen or living area.

She was just climbing out of bed when she saw it. The note on the bedside table. Slowly, she reached for it, and her eyes skimmed over his masculine writing.

Good morning, Rae. Just had to pop out and do some stuff with the guys. House is alarmed. Chat later. J xox

Okay, so he hadn't skipped out on her without a word, but still, it was only…she reached over and grabbed her phone.

Holy crap, it was ten o'clock! How had she slept until ten-freaking-o'clock? She had work to do! Pictures to edit! Pictures that were due to a client by midday.

River rolled out of bed and had the speediest shower of her life before throwing clothes on and moving into the living area.

She went straight to her little work nook, which sat in the corner of the living room. It was where she kept her computer, her camera, and everything else she needed for her job. Basically, it was where her life sat.

She clicked into the folder that held the photos she needed to edit. They were for a little café in Riverbend that she'd traveled to last week. River had done some work for them before and got on really well with the young owner, Betty.

To be honest, she doubted Betty would be upset if she was a bit late getting the shots to her, but that wasn't the point. She was a professional, and if she'd promised her client she'd have images to her by a certain time, then that's when she'd get them.

She checked her phone one last time, noticing there were no messages from Jackson, before shoving it away and pushing down any and all thoughts of the man. Of last night. Of his absence this morning.

She got to work.

Over the next two hours, River kept her butt plastered to the seat, well, except for one short break to make a coffee, but only because if she hadn't, the withdrawal would have killed her.

When the final photo was edited, she shot a quick look at the time. Five minutes until they were due. Her heart gave a little kick as she attached the zipped file to an email and sent it to the client.

Done. Take that, deadline. And she had a whole—she glanced at the time again—two minutes to spare.

She was just leaning back in her seat when her phone rang.

She lifted her cell, still smiling. "Hey, Chele."

"Did you hit the deadline?"

River almost laughed. "You know my work schedule better than I do, don't you?"

"Oh, I definitely know your work schedule better than you. Remember Mrs. Tabor?"

River cringed. Michele just had to remind her of that, didn't she? "That was one time."

She'd arranged to go to the woman's restaurant, but on the day of the shoot, she'd been so worried about Ryker, she'd forgotten all about it. She'd rocked up to Michele's shop, begging for food, only to have her friend remind her about the shoot she was about to miss. Thank God she felt the need to update Michele on every little thing she did with her life, including her work commitments.

"Yeah, well, I feel responsible for you now," Michele said, the sound of what River assumed were dishes hitting countertops in the background.

She chuckled before rising to her feet and moving across to the kitchen. She dumped the half-finished, now-cold coffee in the sink before returning to her seat. "No need, my friend. I have my life well and truly under control."

If you call sleeping in until ten and only just hitting deadlines having your life under control.

"I'll pretend I believe you." More clattering of dishes. "So, are you going to tell me what happened at the club last night?"

"Oh my gosh, it was crazy, Chele. Those fights…" She shook her head. She couldn't even explain them. "They were scary. And the guys stepping inside the ring were big and strong and absolutely terrifying."

The dishes in the background quieted. "You said Jackson was okay though?"

"Yeah, he took a few hits, but not as many as his opponent." She almost shuddered, remembering the hits he *did* receive. Even one had been too many.

Michele sighed. "That's good. I was worried."

"You and me both."

"Did you find out anything about Ryker?"

She straightened, the conversation from the bathroom suddenly coming back to her. Crap. She hadn't told Jackson yet.

"Actually, I did. I went to the bathroom, and I overheard this woman, Angel, talking about him." She frowned. "She didn't say much, but she knows what's going on at the club. She told Ryker, and she blames herself for getting him killed. I really need to speak to her. Maybe she'll tell me, too." River shook her head. "I was so close to doing just that. Then a fight broke out and everyone was running."

Michele gasped. "A fight broke out?"

"Yeah, but I was okay. I had three big soldiers hovering around me. I was more protected there than at the grocery store."

"So you got home okay?"

"I did." She nibbled her lip, debating over how much to tell her best friend over the phone. "And Jackson came in."

There was a beat of silence. "Really?"

"Mm-hmm. I cleaned his cuts."

"And then he left?"

"And then we had sex."

The second the words were out of her mouth, Michele screamed. River scrunched her eyes closed, a smile a mile wide tugging at her lips.

"You're not messing with me, are you? Because if you are—"

"Nope. No messing. We kissed, then Jackson lifted me off the couch like he was Tarzan and I was Jane, took me to the bedroom, and we had the most amazing, blow-your-brains-out sex."

River chuckled at Michele's excited screams, not surprised at all that her news had sent her usually mild-mannered friend into hysterics. Michele had lived River's roller coaster of emotions all those years ago. The young love. The heartbreak. The years of trying to get over the guy.

"But it's not all good news," River interrupted.

Michele silenced. "Why? What happened?"

"Nothing. He just...he wasn't here when I woke up."

Another pause, this one heavy. She could almost picture her friend frowning. "What do you mean he wasn't there when you woke up? Where was he?"

Wasn't that the golden question? "I'm not sure. He left a note—"

"What did the note say?"

"Something about popping out—"

"No," Michele interrupted mid-sentence. "I know you memorized the thing. I want exact words."

Jeez, her friend knew her way too well. "Fine. The note said, 'Good morning, Rae. Just had to pop out and do some stuff with the guys. House is alarmed. Chat later. J xox.'"

"No mention of last night?"

Yeah, she'd noticed that too. "No." Even just a little "last night was nice" would have set her nerves at ease.

"Maybe he's just waiting to see you in person to tell you how amazing it was. Don't go trying to talk yourself into last night being a bad idea. He's changed. I can see it, and I know you can too."

She ran her finger along the keys of her computer, little flickers of uncertainty rising up in her chest. "What happens after I figure out all this Ryker stuff, though?" Because they *would* figure it out eventually. "He hates this place. Will he just leave town again?"

Michele's voice softened. "I don't know, honey. I think that's something you need to ask him."

She bit the inside of her cheek. She couldn't ask him if he was going to stay in town with her forever and always after they'd had sex one time. That was the definition of stage-five clinger, right?

"Maybe. All right, I should go, Chele. I'm gonna visit Mom and Dad. I'll talk to you later." Suddenly, there was the sound of a door opening and closing. Then the rush of wind through the line. River frowned. "Are you out?"

"Yeah, I've been baking at home all morning. Just stepping out for some fresh air and to clear my head."

A flicker of worry touched River's chest. "Is everything okay? Is your uncle okay? Wait, you haven't seen—"

"No. I haven't seen Tim. And Uncle Ottie's fine."

River frowned. It kind of sounded like Michele was leaving something out. Which was crazy. The woman never hid anything from her.

"Do you want me to come over? I can bring hot coffee and candy. Or we could just skip straight to the wine?" Was there such a thing as too early?

Michele chuckled, but there wasn't a lot of humor in it. "You're an amazing friend, River. Thank you. But no, that's okay. I'm just going to walk Pokey and chill out today."

River smiled. Pokey was her Great Dane. The dog was almost bigger than her. "You sure?" she asked.

"Yes. I'll call you later."

River sighed as she hung up.

Her friend had been through so much in her life. Losing her parents at a young age would have been heartbreaking. Then this past year, with her uncle being diagnosed as high risk for a heart attack, dating that jerk Tim, and now all this stuff with Ryker…

He wasn't her brother, but with Michele being so close to River, it was inevitable that she'd grown close to Ryker, too.

Turning in her seat, River aimed her camera at the small peace lily that sat in a pot beside the television. Her house was full of plants. She figured if she had to be inside, she might as well bring the outdoors in with her.

She took a few photos and had just zoomed in when she stilled, frowning.

Was that a light in the plant?

Slowly, she placed the camera down, moving closer. She'd barely crossed half the room when she stopped, lips slipping open, and her skin chilling.

Quickly, she moved three steps back again, hips colliding with the desk. Turning, she snapped up her phone before walking —*running*—outside to call Jackson.

CHAPTER 16

The agent held the door open for Jackson, Declan, and Cole. "This place has been empty since Larry passed away six years ago."

Jackson stepped into the large, dark space, closely followed by his friends.

His chest clenched as memories flooded him. Of Larry letting him step inside the ring when he was still just a kid. Of the old man teaching him how to punch and kick and block an attack. He'd seen the anger in Jackson. He'd taught him how to be smart with his fists. Use them as protection against his scumbag of a father.

He owed a lot to the old boxing coach. The guy had trained him without asking for a cent of payment. Let him work out his resentment in a safe space. And then later, when Ryker had moved to town, he'd stepped into the ring alongside him.

He looked up, noticing the cobwebs spidering across the ceilings. Ceilings that didn't look quite as high as they once had.

When he glanced back down, his jaw clenched at the collection of dust on the entrance desk. On the formerly well-kept boxing ring. Even the heavy bags that still surrounded the ring had dust all over them.

Larry would have hated it.

His gaze shot to the back of the room. There were closed doors that led to changing rooms on one side and a small kitchen on the other. And between them was another closed door, which led to Larry's old office.

"Jill hasn't been back since he died?" The words felt raw in Jackson's throat. Not only did he owe a lot to Larry, but he also remembered everything his wife had done for him. She'd always been around. Offering food and snacks. Always a smile on her face.

Jackson should have come back, at least once, to say thank you to them before the old man had his heart attack. Jill had moved to Colorado after the death of her husband to be near family.

The agent shook his head. "No. I sense that it's too painful for her. She's had a lot of offers to purchase the place, but no one wanted to keep it as a boxing club so she's turned them all down."

Declan crouched on his haunches, running a finger along the edge of the ring. Dust coated his skin. Cole kept his fists in his pockets as he circled the large room.

The agent cleared his throat. "The place obviously needs some tidying up, but Mrs. Mercy has agreed to rent it to you while you're in town. The rent she's requested is low, given the state of the place."

Jackson nodded, not caring about the work it would take to clean the dust and cobwebs. If he was going to enter that ring again and come up against someone bigger and stronger, he needed somewhere to train. And being inside this place right now, he felt something. It went deeper than nostalgia. Like he'd always been meant to return.

Cole bent under the rope and stepped inside the ring. "And we can rent it for as long as we need?"

"Yes." The agent chuckled. "Mrs. Mercy sure doesn't seem willing to rent it to anyone else, so having you guys use it beats the place sitting empty." He fiddled with a folder in his hands. "I'll step out for a bit and give you guys a chance to look around and chat."

He handed Jackson the keys before leaving. Jackson moved across the room, unlocked the office, and stepped inside the small room.

Memories blasted him. The room looked untouched. Papers were scattered across the desk. There was even the old land-line phone. He'd always given Larry shit about how damn messy he kept the space. The old guy hadn't cared one bit.

The guys stepped inside the room behind him.

Declan chuckled. "Not much of a bookkeeper, huh?"

"He used to say that any minute spent in here, was a minute lost out there in the ring."

The ring was his life. People would travel from all over Washington State to be trained by the former boxing specialist. And before boxing, he'd gone straight from school to the military. It had been Larry's constant talk about his time in the military that had put the idea into Jackson's head. The man had changed everything for him.

He lifted a piece of paper, tracing Larry's handwriting with his gaze. "I keep thinking he's gonna walk right on back in here."

"If the guy loved this place so much, he would have hated to see it empty like this," Cole said quietly.

"I see why she hasn't sold, though. He also would have hated this place being turned into anything other than what it was." Jill was holding out hope that someone would come and recreate what Larry had built from the ground up.

They went back into the main room, and this time it was Jackson who stepped into the ring. For a moment, he felt like that twelve-year-old kid again. Angry at the world for the hand he'd been dealt in life.

"I still remember that first day," he said quietly. "My dad had just beaten the shit out of me again, and I walked in here and demanded Larry train me."

"What did he say?" Declan asked.

"He stood there for what felt like endless minutes. It was the only time I ever sweated under someone's stare." The guy might have been older, but he'd been big and could lay a guy out without blinking. "Then he told me to get in the ring."

Cole's brows rose. "He fought a kid who had no idea what he was doing?"

Jackson chuckled as he wrapped his fingers around the rope. "I swung a dozen times without landing a single hit. That was my first lesson. You fight with your head and take the emotion out of it."

He'd been hurting. But then, he'd spent a lot of his childhood hurting. Until he'd found Larry. Then a few years later, Ryker and his family.

"You said there was a guy you could call who might come down here and help you train?" Cole asked.

Not just train. That was mostly a pretense, and Cole and Dec knew it. His team could easily help with training. "Yeah, Erik gave me his number. Said if I needed any help before the next fight to hit him up."

For some reason, he trusted the guy. Call it gut instinct.

"Good way to get more information," Declan said, crossing his arms. "We need to get to the bottom of whatever the fuck happened to Ryker, and we need to do it soon." There was an undercurrent of impatience to his voice. An impatience they all felt.

Jackson's fists clenched. "And I need to find out what the hell my father was doing there."

He was just climbing out of the ring when his phone rang. He almost smiled when he saw it was River. He hadn't told the guys about last night. And he didn't intend to. Not yet, anyway. "Morning, Rae."

Wind rustled through the line before she spoke. "There's a camera in my house."

The smile slipped from his lips and every muscle in his body tensed. "Don't go back inside. I'll be there in less than five minutes."

JACKSON WATCHED as River downed half her beer in one go. Had they been at Lenny's Bar and Grill for any other reason, he probably would have laughed. As it was, he'd taken her here while Dec and Cole searched her house for more cameras. If there was one, he was sure there'd be more.

"How long do you think someone's been watching me?" she asked, the glass of beer hitting the table. "Since Ryker disappeared? Longer? Do you think they were for watching *him?*"

"We won't know any of those things until we find the assholes who put the camera there," Jackson said quietly. His own beer sat untouched. He needed a clear head to deal with this. Hell, even with a clear head, he was trying like hell to control his rage.

Someone had gone into River's house. Installed cameras. Watched her. It made him want to go out and hunt down the bastard.

Her head suddenly shot up. "Oh my God, do you think there are cameras at Mom and Dad's house? He spent a lot of time there—"

"The guys are checking there too. Your parents are out for the day, so neither of them will ever know."

A long breath whooshed from her chest. She shook her head, and even though she cast her gaze around the room, he could tell she wasn't really looking at anything. "Do you think it was Mickey?"

When he was silent for a beat, she cast her gaze back to him.

"I'm not sure." Not after seeing those three men at the club and hearing about this Elijah guy. He didn't need to know who they were to know they were bad news. "But I promise you, I'm going to find out."

She swallowed, giving a small nod. "Distract me. Tell me what was so important you had to sneak out this morning."

Ah, he'd been waiting for that to come up. "Is it still sneaking out if I left a note?"

"Yes." Her response was immediate and had a smile tugging at his lips.

"I went down to my father's trailer. I wanted to ask him why he was there last night."

Stepping up to the door of that trailer, though…it had been like stepping into the past. Stepping into the personal hell he'd lived through as a kid.

River frowned. "What happened?"

"He wasn't there." A part of him had been disappointed because he needed answers. But another part had almost been relieved. Because even looking at his father, let alone talking to him, felt like having his insides shredded.

"Then I met the guys, and we went to look at the old boxing studio."

River tilted her head to the side with a smile. "Larry's place?"

He nodded. River knew what Larry and the ring had meant to him. Hell, she'd gone there and watched him and Ryker train a hundred times.

"Why?"

"We're using the place to train while we're in town."

Almost immediately, his stomach cramped. Because he knew she heard what he hadn't explicitly said. That his time in this town was temporary. He couldn't stay.

Why did the idea of leaving suddenly make his gut feel like someone had punched a hole in it?

He knew why, of course. Because last night had felt right. *She* felt right.

Unable to stop himself, he reached across the table, placing a hand over hers. "I'm sorry I didn't wake you. You looked too peaceful."

She smiled, but it seemed forced. "It was probably a good decision on your part. I can be a grump in the morning."

He almost chuckled. He knew that. He remembered what she was like in the morning, thanks to all those nights he'd stayed over at her family's place.

He leaned forward. "Last night was amazing."

Something flashed across her face. Something that came and went so quickly, he couldn't quite catch what it was. "Really?"

"Yes."

He could have said more. Hell, he wanted to say a lot more. But a second later, Dec and Cole were there, sitting at the table with them.

River tried to tug her hand away, but his fingers tightened. He wanted to touch her. Hold her. Screw the future. While he was here, he wanted all of her, all the time.

"What did you find?" he asked.

"Two cameras," Declan said quietly. "The one River spotted, and one in a kitchen light."

River frowned. "So, none in the bedrooms?"

"No."

River's breath eased from her chest, and the muscles in Jackson's body, the ones he hadn't even realized he'd been tensing, relaxed. Maybe whoever set the cameras thought they'd be too obvious in a dark bedroom.

Cole grabbed Jackson's untouched beer, taking a sip before speaking. "We found a similar setup at your parents' house."

Her gasp was quiet. "How the heck did they even get in and out of both houses without being noticed?"

"When you don't have great locks or alarms, it's easier than you might think," Jackson said. For certain people, it was child's play. The question was, who were those people?

"We ordered the security system," Declan said, addressing Jackson. "It's being installed tomorrow. New locks will also be put on all doors and windows."

Jackson nodded. "Good. I'll stay over tonight."

She remained silent at that comment. He rubbed the pad of his thumb over the back of her hand.

"I don't think it was Mickey," Cole said, frowning. "Call it a hunch, whatever, but after meeting the guy, I don't think this is his work."

"Me either," River said, everyone's eyes going to her. "He's more upfront about what an asshole he is. Hidden cameras don't scream Mickey."

Declan looked across to Jackson. "What about those guys you saw in the club who were talking to Mickey?"

His gut clenched. "Brian sat with those guys once the fights started." He hated the idea of his father being involved in Ryker's death. He knew the guy was an asshole, but Brian had known Ryker since they were teenagers. "They sat in the back row, near the hall. But it almost felt like they weren't there for the fights."

He'd been standing so damn close, he'd almost expected them to get up and talk to him.

"I heard a conversation in the bathroom," River said, eyes on her beer.

Jackson frowned. "You did?"

"Yeah. A woman named Angel was crying. Saying it was her fault Ryker died. Because she told him about the kegs."

Cole leaned forward. "Kegs?"

She lifted a shoulder. "I was going to ask her about it but then we had to leave." She wet her lips. "There's something else. This woman Angel...her number was in Ryker's room at my parents' house. I found it the day of the funeral."

Jackson shared a look with Cole and Dec. "Two more leads.

We need to find out what's in those kegs, and what this woman Angel knows."

River straightened. "I want to talk to her."

Jackson shook his head. "No."

She turned a steely gaze his way. "Why not?"

"Because it's too dangerous."

River frowned. "She spoke about Ryker like she knew him. Like she *cared* about him."

"I don't care."

Her frown deepened, and she tried to tug her hand from his. His grip firmed again, the slow grazing of his thumb continuing.

Her back straightened as if she was readying herself for a fight. "I'm going to get her address, and I'm going to pay her a visit."

Like hell she was. "And how exactly would you get her address?"

Her brows lifted.

"You're not going to tell me?"

River still said nothing.

Didn't matter. He wasn't going to let that happen. All she'd done was confirm that what he'd already planned was the right decision—he needed to stick to the woman like glue. Because there was no way she was conducting any kind of investigation into this shit on her own.

CHAPTER 17

*R*iver's eyes shot open. Something had woken her. What? Was it Ryker?

She shot a quick look to her bedside clock. Three a.m. So, yes. Probably Ryker. After all, it was Friday night—or Saturday morning, depending on which way you looked at it—and this had been his normal return time for the last few weeks.

Worry tingled her spine as she pushed the sheets off. Worry about the bruises he'd have on his body. The blood staining his clothes. Blood that was his? Or someone else's?

Swallowing her trepidation, she crept out of her bedroom. She'd barely stepped into the hall when she saw him. The second he turned toward her, the air caught in her throat, and tiny pricks of ice skittered over her skin.

"Ryker..."

His eye was black, almost sealed shut. Specks of blood dotted his neck and cheeks. There were stains all over his shirt, like he'd thrown it over the top of his bleeding chest.

When she met his gaze, it was to see his one good eye slitted. "What are you doing up, River?"

"Where have you been?" She let icy tentacles of anger replace the worry. The anger felt good. Safe. "And don't give me some bullshit answer about it not being my business, because it is. You're my brother, therefore my business."

She wanted answers, and she wanted them now. Whatever decisions he was making, whatever he was choosing to participate in to make himself feel better, it clearly wasn't safe.

"As much as I'd love to debrief you on my entire fucking life right now, I'm tired and going to bed."

She tried not to flinch at the way he cursed at her. The brother she knew and loved would never do that.

What the hell had happened to him?

When he scrubbed a hand over his face, her gaze zeroed in on his knuckles. Red and raw. Like he'd been hitting something...or someone.

He tried to walk past her to his bedroom, but she stepped into his path, blocking his way. "Ryker—"

"I'm not in the mood, River."

He wasn't quite yelling, but his voice was definitely raised. And that, in combination with his size, would have scared most people. Not her. She would step in front of a speeding car to save this man. No hesitation. No questions.

"You're never in the mood. Since returning to Lindeman, all you've been is angry." He tried to step around her, but she mirrored his movement, blocking him again. "It's Mickey, isn't it? You've been visiting his club. Why? Are you working for him?"

That was the only thing she could think of. That he'd decided to work as one of his bouncers or something. What else could it be?

His jaw clenched, the muscles in his arms bunching. "I'm going to say this as clearly as I can, River. Stay...the hell...out of this."

"Tell me what this is and maybe I will."

His head lowered, face so close to hers, she just about smelled the flecks of blood on his skin. "My life."

His words were like a physical blow. For a moment, she just stood there, searching for something, anything familiar. For some little part of the brother she remembered.

There was nothing.

"What happened to you?" The words were barely a whisper torn from her soul.

Something flashed through his eyes. The first emotion in months other than anger...sorrow, maybe? "I learned the hard way that life isn't all sunshine and rainbows."

When he stepped to the side this time, she didn't stop him, knowing she didn't have words to save him. Not right now.

But before he disappeared inside his room, she splintered the silence. "I'm not going to stop, Ryker. I'm going to keep digging, keep pushing, until I know you're safe." Because, right now, she knew he wasn't. And it wasn't just because he'd been returning home covered in bruises and blood. It was something else. Something deeper.

For a moment, he paused, knuckles almost white as they wrapped around the wooden doorframe.

His head turned, eyes so dark and angry he could almost be a stranger. "You stay away from Mickey and that club." Then he slammed the door shut, the loud bang exploding through the house.

For a few long minutes, her gaze stayed on his door. Something akin to desperation seeped into her bones. Desperation to figure out what was going on. Desperation to save him from whatever demons were torturing him, both inside and out. Desperation to get the brother she knew and loved back.

RIVER'S EYES SHOT OPEN. The remnants of the dream, the memory of her brother's tortured eyes sinking into her soul, haunted her.

She sucked in a deep breath as she took in the room around her. Still dark, but not completely. Maybe early morning?

She glanced beside her at Jackson's still body. He lay on his side, his heavy arm wrapped around her waist, breath brushing against her neck.

They hadn't even spoken about where he would sleep tonight.

When night came, she'd pulled down the sheets, and he'd just slipped in with her.

For a moment, she watched him, letting the sight of him calm some of the turmoil in her chest. He'd always been the most beautiful man she'd ever laid eyes on. Even when she was a kid, a part of her had known that she'd never meet another person who made her feel quite what he did.

Blowing out a small breath, River tried to crawl out from under him, but the second she moved, his arm tightened like a band of steel, keeping her rooted to the spot.

"Are you okay?"

Holy Christmas, the man didn't sound tired at all. Had he even been asleep? Or was he just able to open his eyes at the drop of a hat and be wide awake?

She glanced beside her. Even in the darkness, she saw the beautiful specks of honey in his brown eyes. "I'm just getting a drink."

She tried to tug away again, but his arm remained, gaze still on her, searching. "I can get it for you."

She almost chuckled. "Thank you, but I can manage."

And then, because she couldn't stop herself, she leaned into him and pressed a kiss to his lips. It was meant to be a peck. But immediately, he rose, leaning into her, chest pressing her down to the mattress.

The kiss was hot and intense, his tongue sliding between her lips, dancing with hers. For a moment, she lost herself.

He raised his head, and when he whispered against her lips, his breath was warm on her mouth. "Don't take long."

A shudder coursed down her spine as she pushed up from the bed. She grabbed her phone for light and slipped from the room. Good God, but the man was going to be the end of her. She touched her mouth, swearing she could still feel his lips there.

On the way to the kitchen, her gaze paused on the front door, and suddenly her dream came back to her. The memory of Ryker stepping through the door that night was so clear, she almost expected him to come in right now.

Giving herself a little shake, she went to the fridge, tugging it open and grabbing the bottle of apple juice.

That night had been a week before she'd received the call from her dad, telling her Ryker was dead. Her brother hadn't returned to her place after their confrontation, instead choosing to stay with their parents. She'd almost wished she *hadn't* confronted him because at least when he was close, she had eyes on him. Knew he was returning home safe each night. That he was somewhat okay.

Sighing, she poured some juice into a glass before leaning her hip against the counter. "Where are you, Ryker?"

Every so often, a voice whispered in her head that maybe they were all right. Maybe he *was* gone. But she always shut it down because the pain was too crippling.

Taking a sip, she watched the moon cast a glow over the grass through the window. Was Ryker looking at that moon right now?

Lifting her phone, she called Angel, not caring about the time because the woman never answered anyway, so what did it matter?

"I told you to stop calling me."

River froze, shocked that Angel had actually answered on the first ring. Loud music boomed in the background. Was she still at the club? Was it even open at this time? "Please, one conversation, that's all I ask."

"How many times do I have to say no?"

"As many times as you need to before you say yes, because I'm not going to stop. I can't. He's my brother, Angel, and I need answers. *Please*."

There was a beat of silence. Was the woman considering it?

"Fine. Come tomorrow. I'll text you my address and a time."

River's mouth slid open in shock.

"After tomorrow, you need to leave me alone. Got it?"

She nodded even though the woman couldn't see her. "I will. I promise."

When she hung up, the text came through with the address almost immediately. River's eyes shuttered. This could be it. The moment she got her answers.

She was just setting the glass in the sink when something caused her to pause. A noise. Like the unlatching of a lock, coming from...Ryker's room?

Frowning, she took a step toward the living room when a hand suddenly clamped over her mouth, another around her waist, and she was tugged into the walk-in pantry.

River's heart catapulted into her throat. She threw an elbow into the guy's stomach, but he didn't react at all. It was like elbowing a brick wall.

Then there was a voice in her ear. "It's me."

Every muscle in her body relaxed, and she sank into Jackson, the moment of panic morphing into a form of light-headed relief.

"Someone's in your house," he said quietly. The fine hairs on her arms stood on end. His lip brushed against her ear as he continued, "I need you to stay here while I check it out."

She wriggled from his grasp, glad when he let go. Then she turned. "No. It's too dangerous. Call the police. Or your team."

Anything that meant he wouldn't be stepping out there on his own.

"There's not enough time. Don't leave the pantry."

Her heart rate tripled as he slipped out.

Air barely made its way in and out of her chest as seconds ticked by, dread knotting her stomach.

What if there was more than one person? What if they were too much for Jackson alone?

At the sound of a crash and a loud thud, River jolted. Her hand flew to the pantry door but she quickly tugged it away. Jackson had told her to stay.

But could she do that, knowing full well he could be in trouble?

Suddenly, she remembered the gun Ryker had strapped to the top shelf of the pantry. God, how had she forgotten? She could have given it to Jackson!

Stretching up, her fingers only just reached the weapon. She tugged it down and took a deep breath before cautiously moving out of the pantry.

Grunts sounded from the hallway.

She raised the gun and moved slowly toward the hall. Her breath caught in her throat when she saw the two big men fighting on the floor. Jackson threw a punch, whipping the guy's head back.

She wasn't sure if she made a noise or if he saw her from his peripheral vision, but suddenly Jackson's head flew around to stare at her. That was all it took—the guy shoved him on his ass and ran toward Ryker's room.

Jackson flew after him, and River after Jackson, but the guy was already out the open window.

For a moment, Jackson stood there, looking out the window like he wanted to give chase but didn't want to leave her unprotected. His shoulders were moving up and down with his heavy breaths.

When he turned, she almost stepped back at the sparks of fire flying from his eyes. "I told you to stay in the goddamn pantry, River."

"I thought you could be outnumbered. And I didn't know whether you had a gun and remembered that Ryker had hidden one in the pantry."

Jackson moved across the room. "What if there had been more than one guy here? Hell, there could have been an army of men in your house!"

Her jaw clicked. "Even more reason for me to come out here and help you."

Jackson's hands went to her cheeks. For a moment, his eyes shuttered, and he was silent. Like he was trying to calm himself. When his eyes opened, they were tortured. "This isn't a game, Rae. When I ask you to do something, you need to listen."

She sucked in a shuddering breath. He was right. She knew he was. "I'm sorry. I just can't handle the idea of you getting hurt."

He blew out a long breath, lowering his head and pressing his temple to hers. "Don't ever do that again."

CHAPTER 18

*J*ackson remained light on his toes, dancing around Erik, watching him closely. He'd already taken a few hard hits, but he'd given them back, too.

He was on edge. Someone had infiltrated River's home last night. And he hadn't stopped the asshole. The guy hadn't had a gun, but he'd had a knife.

What had he planned to do with it? Threaten her? Hurt her? Worse? He'd caught a glimpse of the guy's face but didn't recognize him as anyone he'd seen at the club.

Erik swung at Jackson's head. He ducked before throwing a body shot Erik's way, landing it on his ribs. The man barely reacted, dancing back a step.

Jackson swung the next two punches, letting the frustration fuel him. Drive him to hit harder. Fiercer.

It was just training, but it also wasn't. It was a way for him to release the anger. What if he hadn't been there last night? What if River had been alone?

Nothing had been disturbed in Ryker's room. It could mean that he'd been there for River. Or he'd planned to hurt her before going through Ryker's things. Either way, Jackson and his guys had gone through Ryker's room that morning and found nothing that stuck out to them.

Jackson dove forward, driving the next hit at Erik's head, then his body. The first was blocked. The second wasn't.

Erik grunted a second before Declan's voice stopped them both in their tracks.

"Time."

Jackson stepped back, deep breaths rushing in and out of his chest.

Erik frowned, panting. "You sure you need my help? You fight like a demon."

He moved to the rope, grabbed his towel, and wiped the sweat from his face. "I'll take all the help I can get before my next fight."

They'd been at it for most of the afternoon. And before Erik arrived, Declan had been inside the ring with him, drawing on the extensive combat training he'd received from the military.

Cole was shadowing River right now, otherwise, he no doubt would have stepped into the ring, too. No way was Jackson leaving her unprotected. Not after last night.

Erik nodded. "Fine with me. I'm always up for a round."

Declan pushed off the rope, crossing his arms as he looked at Erik. "How did you get involved in that place?"

He lifted a shoulder. "I heard whispers. People in the boxing community talk. I live in the area, and even though I stopped boxing professionally, I still like to get in a ring or a cage whenever I can."

Jackson hunched under the rope, stepped out, and grabbed two bottles of water from the cooler. He tossed one Erik's way.

They'd cleaned the place up but hadn't bought a fridge. They probably wouldn't, not when they weren't sure how long they'd be using the space. "Do you know much about Mickey?"

Erik scoffed. "Other than the fact the guy's a jerk? No. I go in there, keep my head down, win my fight, and leave. I'm not interested in anything else that might be going on."

Jackson paused, bottle midway to his mouth. "Anything else that might be going on?"

Erik unscrewed the cap of his bottle. "There's always other shit going on in places like that. I stay out of it."

"Do you know where the stairs at the end of the hall lead to?"

"The parking lot. Mickey only uses it for deliveries. It's usually locked."

Declan nodded. "What kind of deliveries?"

"Alcohol, I think."

Jackson and Declan shared a look. Alcohol. That meant kegs, didn't it?

Before either of them could ask, Erik was walking toward his bag. "So why did you take Ryker's spot? I'm guessing you knew the guy?"

Jackson only just stopped the flinch. *Knew.* Damn, that sounded wrong.

"We were in the military together." Jackson didn't add that they'd also grown up together. That they were in the same team. That they were as close to brothers as you could get without actually being related.

He didn't know Erik enough to trust him that much, so sticking to the truth while also being brief was smart.

Erik nodded. "Figured. You all fight like soldiers."

Declan laughed. "How does a soldier fight?"

"Tactically. And you're good at keeping the dominant position." One side of his mouth lifted. "I'd know. I was a Marine."

Jackson nodded, not surprised. You could generally tell when someone had been in the military by the way they held themselves. The way they watched their back, always aware of their surroundings.

"All right, I'm gonna head out." Erik lifted his bag from the floor. "Call me the next time you want to train."

The second the door closed, Jackson headed toward the

changing room for a shower. He stopped at the sound of the door opening again.

When he turned back, his fists clenched, fury heating his breath.

His father studied the place before turning his gaze to Jackson. "Word around town said that you'd come back here."

Jackson didn't move a muscle. "You here to tell me what the fuck you were doing at Mickey's club Friday night?"

Declan remained where he was, but Jackson could see his friend's muscles bunching.

Brian's eyes narrowed. "I'm here to tell you that if you're smart, you'll stay the hell away from that basement."

Jackson could have laughed. "Since when do you care about whether I'm smart or not?"

His father's jaw visibly clenched, but he remained silent.

Jackson took a slow step forward, his muscles vibrating. "What were you doing there?"

"The same thing as everyone else. Placing bets." His father shoved his hands into his pockets. "And now I'm doing my fatherly duty. I've told you to stay away. Any trouble you get yourself into is now on you."

Jackson was across the room before his father could turn, grabbing him by the shirt and shoving him against the wall. "Why were you taking a group of people into that office?"

"I told you," he said quietly. "We were placing bets."

"Bullshit."

Brian tried to shove Jackson off, but he didn't let the guy move an inch. "Who were those men talking to Mickey?"

Brian scowled. "They were men you want nothing to do with."

"Do *you*?"

The smile that stretched Brian's mouth had Jackson's stomach turning. "You know I like a bit of danger in my life."

Jackson's fingers tightened, and he pulled his father away

from the wall before shoving him against it again, harder. "What the hell happened to Ryker?"

His father's eyes steeled. "He got too close to something he had no business getting close to. And if you wanna stay out of the ground, you'll do as I said and stay the fuck out of this."

RIVER WASN'T HAPPY. Jackson had planted Cole on her without telling her. She knew why. Someone had broken into her house last night. Someone with a goddamn knife. But Jackson could have told her what he'd done. Even a text would have been nice. Because the sudden appearance of Cole at her side had put a serious dent in her plan to talk to Angel.

She stepped into the boxing gym, searching the large space. Seconds later, the door to the locker room opened, and Jackson stepped out. He was fully clothed, but his hair was wet and feet bare.

His gaze went straight to her, his eyes darkening as they ran over her body.

No. She would not let the man distract her. She pushed down the rising desire. "Why didn't you tell me Cole was watching me today?"

His gaze skirted behind her to Cole before skittering back. "It slipped my mind."

She almost rolled her eyes. "Nothing ever slips your mind."

He frowned. "How did you see him?"

Cole cleared his throat behind her. "I'll leave you guys to it."

There was the sound of the door closing behind her, then…silence.

Jackson took measured steps forward. "Cole's good at trailing people. You would've only seen him if he wanted you to. So…*why* did he want you to see him?"

She crossed her arms. "Don't you try to change the subject. Why didn't you tell me you were having me watched?"

His features remained completely clear. "I see it more as *protected* than watched."

"Yeah, well, it felt a bit more like six and a half feet of surprise surveillance. You should have told me. Not only is that the normal thing to do, but you and I are dating, or bed buddies, or something in that vicinity, so telling me you've got me 'protected' is the minimum I expect."

His brows lifted. "Bed buddies?"

"Jackson—"

When he reached her, his hands went to her waist, his face pushing into her hair. Her belly quivered. "Mm, you smell good."

When his lips touched her neck, she wrenched free, stepping back. "Don't try and distract me."

One side of his mouth lifted. That look was dangerous. It could easily have her dropping all her defenses, and he knew it.

He took a step toward her, but then his phone beeped from his pocket. He lifted it, frowning when he read the screen.

Oh, crap. If that was Cole ratting her out…

When his eyes turned back to her, they weren't angry, but they were definitely suspicious. "How exactly did you work out Cole was trailing you again?"

So Cole hadn't told him what happened…but he'd hinted at something. "What exactly did he just text?"

"He asked me to let him know if I need any more details."

Snitch.

Jackson's hand returned to her waist, and this time she was almost certain he was holding her in place in case she ran. "River—"

"I went to speak to Angel."

All hints of playfulness left his features. "You *what?*"

She'd expected him to yell. For some reason, his quiet words were worse. "I didn't even get inside the building. The second I

149

got out of my car, Cole was in front of me, asking what I was doing, then he said I had to check with you first." As if Jackson was her keeper or something. Cole had been one big annoying wall, blocking her way and refusing to let her pass.

"So if he hadn't been there, you'd have just waltzed on in by yourself and asked if she knew who killed your brother?"

She crossed her arms. "No. I would have asked what was in the kegs."

Finally, he reacted the way she'd expected him to. "Are you *crazy*? The woman could be involved in whatever's going on at that club! Hell, she could have had Mickey or one of his guys in there with her."

He was right. Hell, the whole thing could be a setup, for all she knew. But her brother was worth the risk. If the situations were reversed, Ryker wouldn't be leaving a single stone unturned to find her.

Her jaw set. "I need to talk to her."

Not the right answer. Not if the tensing of Jackson's muscles and the way he towered over her was anything to go by.

She hadn't asked him to go with her because, one, it would have taken a hundred and one years for her to convince the man to say yes. And two, he would have wanted to go himself. Alone. And that wasn't the deal she'd made with Angel. It needed to be her. Preferably by herself.

"How did you even get the woman's address?" he asked through gritted teeth.

"She texted it to me." She tried to turn, but this time he grabbed her with both hands, pulling her back.

"River—"

"This is why I didn't tell you, Jackson. Because I knew you wouldn't like it."

"Damn straight!"

Again, she attempted to pull away, but his hold was like steel. "I'm going, Jackson."

Was it possible the man just got even bigger in his fury? "No, you're not."

"Yes, I am!"

"You aren't, River. It's not safe, and I won't allow it."

Oh, she was getting pretty sick of this guy telling her no. Especially when Angel could be the breakthrough she needed to find her brother.

For a moment, her eyes shuttered. She took a moment to calm her frazzled mind, allowing the frustration to bleed away and the rational side of her brain to take over. Jackson cared. That's why he was stopping her. She had to appeal to that part of him.

Her eyes opened, and she touched his chest, her voice softening. "Please, Jackson. I begged Angel to talk to me, and she finally agreed. To talk to *me*. One time." The next part was hard to say, but she forced the words out. "Come with me. Bring a gun, be my bodyguard, have your guys on standby. Whatever you need. But I need to be there." She leaned forward. "This could be it. This could be where we find the answers we need to help Ryker."

This time, it was his eyes that shuttered.

Her voice lowered. "*Please*, Jackson."

There was a deep intake of breath, and then he was looking at her again. "Fine."

The air rushed out of her chest.

"But you follow my lead the entire time, and if I say we're leaving, we leave."

It wasn't ideal. But right now, her options seemed to be that or nothing. "Thank you."

CHAPTER 19

*R*iver shot a quick glance across to Jackson. Yep. Still stony as hell. In fact, it was entirely possible that throughout the twenty-minute drive to Angel's apartment, everything about him had become...harder.

"You realize Angel might just know what happened to Ryker, and this all ends today." She didn't want to get her hopes up, because if she thought she was going to find her brother, but then she didn't...well, that would be like wrenching her heart from her chest and tearing it in two.

"It's also entirely possible that she's in on everything and this little visit leads us to more danger."

"True. But to me, it's worth the risk."

His knuckles whitened around the wheel. "Ryker wouldn't agree."

"Of course not. He thinks I'm made of glass and need around-the-clock protection so I don't shatter."

Jackson scoffed, eyes remaining on the road. When the man remained silent, she lifted a brow. "Anything you'd like to say?"

"Ryker never thought you were made of glass. He knew exactly how tough you were. Me too." Her heart gave one big jolt against her ribs. "But I also know that you can make poor decisions that land you into precarious situations."

"When have I ever—"

"Tenth grade. You went to that douchebag senior's party, Greg Halper. And even though you knew exactly what he wanted, you *still* went into his pool house with him. Alone."

She cringed. Yeah, that hadn't been her brightest idea, but she'd been upset. Only a couple hours earlier, she'd walked into Ryker's room to find Jackson making out with some blond bimbo on the bed.

She'd felt heartbroken. Reckless. Emotional. And the sixteen-year-old River had needed validation that *someone* was interested in her.

Jackson's biceps rippled. "You're damn lucky I saw you go in there."

He was right. Greg had all but thrown himself on top of her, and Jackson had torn the guy off before beating the crap out of him. "Okay, that was bad decision-making, but I was a teenager. I'm not anymore."

Jackson raised a brow. "Yet you're still making dangerous, emotionally driven decisions."

"Shouldn't all decisions be emotionally driven?"

"No. Most should be made with your head."

"*Pfft.* Is that some military spiel?"

"No, it's a 'this is how you stay alive' spiel."

"Same thing. By the way, how would *you* know whether or not the decision I made with Greg was driven by emotion?"

He shot a look her way, and her stomach clenched. "I saw your face when you walked into Ryker's room that night, when you saw me with that girl. But even if I hadn't, I knew how you felt about me."

She frowned, a mixture of embarrassment and confusion swelling in her stomach. "Even before I—"

"Yes. Even before you told me."

He pulled the car to a stop in the parking lot of a large, old apartment building. For a moment, neither of them moved or spoke.

There were so many things she wanted to say. So many questions she had for him. How long had he known? *How* had he known? Had he seen some lovesick look on her face? Had Ryker realized and told him?

Now wasn't the time for that.

Pushing it all to the back of her mind, she undid her seat belt and was about to climb out but paused when Jackson reached beneath the driver's seat and tugged out a gun. His eyes never met hers as he climbed out of the car and holstered the weapon. When his door closed, she climbed out of her own side. She'd barely closed the door when Jackson was beside her, hand on the small of her back.

"Remember, if I say go, we—"

"Go. I know." How could she forget? He'd reminded her a gazillion times.

His hand remained on her back as they headed inside, his heat penetrating through the thin material of her shirt. Jackson's eyes never stopped flicking around.

River took in the interior of the building. It was rundown, and that was putting it mildly. The lights in the foyer were flickering, and the place smelled musty and moldy.

Jackson led her into the elevator, pressing a button. His hand never left her, not the entire way up to the sixth floor. She shot a couple peeks in his direction, and each time his expression looked just as stony as it had in the car.

When they reached Angel's floor, Jackson stepped out first, shooting a quick glance down the hallway before that hand returned, and he led her out. They stopped outside her apartment.

Jackson was still looking down the hall, his hand now pressed against her in a way that said he was moments from tossing her over his shoulder and running, as she raised her hand to knock.

When nothing sounded from the other side of the door, River knocked again. "Angel, are you there? It's River."

On her third knock, she hit the wood a little harder—and suddenly, the door creaked as it pushed in.

Immediately, she tugged her hand back. What the—

"I don't like this," Jackson said softly. "We need to leave."

Anxiety bubbled in her chest. "No, Jackson. Maybe she's—"

The sound of footsteps on the stairs cut her off. But not just footsteps. Voices. Men's voices.

Before she could move, Jackson pulled her inside the apartment, closing the door silently behind them. They'd barely stepped into the living room when they saw her.

Angel. Tied to a chair, bruised and battered, with crimson blood dripping from the knife wound across her neck.

River's stomach dropped and a loud buzzing rang in her ears. Her lips separated, and she wasn't sure if she was going to scream or be sick.

Before she could do either, Jackson's hand clamped over her mouth and he tugged her backward.

A door opened—a closet, maybe?—then there was darkness.

River's heart pounded against her ribs, nausea she could barely suppress crawled up her throat.

Jackson's lips went to her ear. "I need you to not make a sound, Rae."

His other hand was around her waist and arms. He held her tightly, and she was almost certain that if he wasn't, she'd have fallen to the floor. Something he probably knew.

Her heart catapulted into her throat at the sound of the apartment door opening. Then heavy footsteps hit the wooden floorboards.

"Christ, this bitch was so stupid. Who the hell goes crying

about illegal shit in a club? It's like she wanted to die." The man's voice wasn't familiar.

Rustling noises sounded. Oh God, were they moving Angel's body? She pressed her eyes closed, begging the bile to stay put in her stomach.

Jackson's thumb began to move in small, soothing circles on her arm. She breathed slowly through her nose, focusing on his touch. On his warmth against her back. And not on whatever those men were doing with the woman's body.

"How do you think she found out?" a second guy asked.

"Probably slept with Mickey or one of his guys. She was a dumb whore."

A zipper sounded.

"You think she slept with Ryker?"

River flinched at her brother's name on the lips of those murderers.

"Probably. She fucked her way through half the club. What *I* wanna know is what Elijah plans to do about Ryker's sister."

This time, it was Jackson who tensed.

"Maybe nothing. We just heard the bitch say she thought Angel knew something. There was no mention of what she knew. Now that Angel's dead, problem solved. He knows we can't go around murdering everyone at the club. It will draw too much attention he doesn't need."

"Elijah doesn't fear shit. He gets what he wants."

More movement.

"Oh, yeah? Like he got what he wanted with that fucker Josef?"

The other guy cursed. "I can't believe that asshole skipped town and now we can't fucking find him."

"I can. He was a small-time crook who only killed Ryker because he was in Elijah's debt. He knew once the job was done, he was a loose end. I would have fucked off, too."

River's insides iced over as she felt every part of Jackson behind her harden.

"Yeah, yeah." A few more rustling sounds. "Hey, why do I have to carry her?"

"Because I have a sore fucking back. And one of us needs to clean the chair and floor."

The guy grunted. "Fine."

"What about that guy, Jackson...the one taking Ryker's place? You think he's gonna figure out the same stuff Ryker did?"

"Mickey never should've let the asshole in. He's being reckless. His need to prove he's got bigger balls than Elijah is gonna get him killed."

Another grunt. "He sees the club as his turf."

"But it's not," the other man said firmly. "It's *ours* now. Something that asshole needs to learn."

Someone sprayed something, then there was the scraping of a chair.

"You done?"

"Yeah, let's go."

The second River heard the door closing in the other room, she tried to move, but the arms around her tightened, holding her in place.

Jackson's mouth went to her ear again. "Just wait a sec, honey."

They remained like that for a full five minutes, Jackson stroking her arm, his breath brushing against her cheek. When he finally released her, she opened the door slowly, and her gaze went to the spot where Angel's body had been.

Gone. And any trace that it had been there was also gone. The smell of antiseptic was strong, souring her stomach.

River sucked in deep breaths, pressing a hand to her belly. "I'm going to be sick."

His fingers twined with hers and tugged her toward the door. "Hold on for me, okay, honey?"

She continued to suck in deep breaths as Jackson tugged her out the door and down the stairs. They'd barely stepped outside when she threw up everything she'd eaten earlier that morning.

Jackson's hand was on her back, rubbing more slow circles. Calming her.

When they got back to the car, Jackson opened her door before sliding behind the wheel. They were silent the entire way back to her house. Jackson's jaw was tense and his muscles bunched.

It wasn't until he pulled into her driveway that he spoke, breaking the quiet. "Are you okay?"

Her eyes remained on the passenger window. "It's my fault."

"What is?"

"That she was killed. They were talking about my phone call with Michele. We talked just before I saw the camera. I told Michele that Angel knew something about Ryker and the club, and I needed to find out what it was."

Guilt rippled through her chest, crippling her. If she'd only kept her mouth shut, maybe the woman would have kept her life.

And right there, alongside the guilt, was shame. For feeling relieved that Cole had stopped her from meeting Angel today. Because if he hadn't, she'd probably be dead as well, right? How sick was that? To feel relieved at a moment like this.

Jackson's hand went to her chin, gently tugging her head his way. "None of this is your fault."

She watched his eyes, not able to nod because she didn't believe that for a second.

His jaw visibly ticked. "We have no idea how long the cameras were there, or what else they heard."

"I don't think I said much else in the house." She couldn't be sure though. Her brain felt foggy as hell right now.

"We learned a couple of things today. That the cameras belonged to Elijah. That he's willing to kill to protect whatever his secret is. And that he's responsible for Ryker." He dipped his head, moving closer. "I promise you, with everything I am, that I will get to the bottom of what happened to your brother—and Elijah and his men will pay."

She swallowed, giving a small nod. If there was anyone in the world she trusted to solve this, it was Jackson.

CHAPTER 20

*J*ackson cracked an egg into the frying pan. The sausage was cooked and the bread was ready to go in the toaster. With any luck, he'd have breakfast ready by the time River woke up.

He'd barely slept last night. Not after how close River had come to danger. And not after everything he'd learned. Particularly about Ryker's death not being an accident.

He scrubbed a hand over his face. River had barely talked last night, then skipped dinner and went straight to bed.

He needed to find out what the hell Ryker had become involved in, and then he needed to murder every asshole responsible, Elijah being the first.

He moved to the fridge, grabbed out the OJ, and set it on the table. If there was anything he remembered about River, it was that she loved her breakfast. And he was counting on that still being the case after last night.

He was just starting on the coffee when his cell vibrated from the island. "Declan," he said, answering the call.

"Cole took first shift, and I took second. No sign of anyone else in Angel's apartment, police included."

Not surprising. It would probably take a few days for friends or family to report her missing. "Thanks. I'm guessing it will be a while before the police discover she's dead."

"Yeah, well, her workplace isn't going to report anything. How's River doing?"

"Still asleep. I'm hoping she's doing a bit better this morning." He leaned against the counter. "I need to look inside those kegs this Friday night."

"I've got a feeling they'll be watching you. Hell, I'm waiting for you to receive the call from Mickey to say he doesn't want you back."

"It sounds like letting me in was his way of sticking it to this Elijah guy." Jackson just about sneered the guy's name. "I'd like one of you guys to stay home with River Friday night. I don't want her returning to the club."

In fact, he wanted her as far from the place as possible.

"Was planning on it."

If he'd told River that decision yesterday, he knew she would have fought him tooth and nail to remain involved. After last night, though, he had no idea how she'd react.

"Thanks, Dec."

Jackson hung up and got to work putting breakfast on the table. Then he shot a look at the clock. It was almost nine a.m. That was late, wasn't it? He hadn't heard a sound from the bedroom or bathroom.

Slowly, he moved down the hall, pausing at the bedroom door to find River still in bed but not asleep. She lay on her side, phone in hand.

For a moment, he was silent as he watched her, just taking her in. So many emotions flickered over her expressive face. Love. Hope. Fear.

And worry, so much worry that it had his heart tugging and shredding.

RIVER SMILED as she flicked through the photos of her and Ryker. She had a separate folder on her phone of just the two of them. Even before he'd been declared dead, it was her most-viewed folder. Anytime she needed to smile, this is what she did.

I miss you, Ryker, she whispered in her head, wishing there was a way she could get them to him.

Every day, something tried to knock her faith in her brother being alive. Last night was the worst it had ever been. Last night, seeing the lengths Elijah's guys would go just to protect whatever was going on at that club, hearing them admit they'd hired a man to kill her brother...she almost caved.

Her breath shuddered from her chest at the memory of everything that had happened. Angel was dead. A woman who meant nothing to her but possibly something to her brother. A woman who had only lost her life because River had said the wrong thing at the wrong time.

But the one thing that still gave her hope? The man they'd hired to kill Ryker had disappeared. That meant they couldn't receive confirmation from the source that he was dead, right?

When she flicked to the next photo, the watery smile returned to her lips. It was her and Ryker at the Grand Canyon. They'd made the trip two years ago. It held so many of her favorite memories. Memories were made in the small moments as much as they were the big. The moments of pause. The ones you think are forgettable but are often the ones held the longest.

Would they have those moments again? Even if he was alive, where was he? Why wasn't he here? Why hadn't he reassured her or her parents or Jackson that he was okay?

"We'll get the assholes who did this."

Jackson's hard words had her head shooting up. He stood in the doorway, taking up all the space. And his face, it almost looked soft in the morning light. But even a soft Jackson looked like he could tear down anyone who stood in the way of him getting what he wanted.

"How long have you been standing there?" she asked quietly.

"Not long." He walked into the room slowly, his familiar scent permeating her air, hitting her full force. He lowered to the bed beside her, hand going around her shoulder.

Immediately, she leaned into him. "I miss him."

His thumb stroked across her bare skin, leaving a trail of goose bumps. "I know. I'm sorry, Rae."

She stared into her brother's eyes through the phone. "This was our last trip before your final mission as Deltas."

"I know that too. Ryker told us all about it. It was a damn effort to get him to shut up, actually."

She chuckled. "I did the same. It was amazing." Even if she hadn't been a lover of nature, it would have been impossible not to be awestruck by the sheer magnificence of the canyon. And getting to share that with Ryker... "I remember standing at the edge and feeling so small and insignificant."

What she wouldn't give to be standing there with him again.

Jackson gave her shoulder a small squeeze. "You'll have to take me sometime."

"Oh, I would go back in a heartbeat." In fact, she'd build a little tent and spend the rest of her days there if she could. She shot a quick glance up at Jackson. "Will you tell me about that final mission you went on? The one that caused you all to leave the military?"

There was a beat of silence. "Ryker didn't tell you anything?"

She shook her head. "I asked but..."

She'd been met with that familiar stony silence. The one that almost always had Ryker walking out of the room, muttering something about needing to be somewhere.

Jackson sighed, his thumb starting to rub her shoulder again. "The mission wasn't the only reason we left. Our contracts were coming to an end, and we'd all talked about the possibility of leaving."

"But nothing had been decided."

"No." Another pause. "The mission was in the Middle East. We'd done a couple in that particular area before. During our very first trip, Ryker befriended a family. They helped hide him in their home one night when he needed to disappear quickly. Every trip after that, he made an effort to visit them. Bring them gifts from the US. Have a meal with them. Two parents and two young kids."

A sinking feeling started to grow in her gut because she already knew this story wouldn't have a happy ending.

"There was also an American aid worker who was friends with the family. The guys and I always thought she was the biggest reason he kept returning. He used to come back and talk about her all the time."

River straightened, sitting up and looking at Jackson. "Really?" Ryker had never mentioned a woman.

"Her name was Blakely," Jackson continued.

When he paused, River frowned. "Tell me, Jackson."

"That last mission, our directive was to kill a high-value target. It was pretty textbook. We took out the target, but before we made it out of the country our location was compromised, and we were attacked by our target's family. It was a long night. Dec was shot and Cole broke his back."

River gasped.

"We barely made it to the military base alive."

River covered her mouth. "Oh my God."

"When we reached US soil, Ryker made contact with Blakely." There was a flash of pain on Jackson's face, and the sinking feeling of dread started to coil in her stomach. "She was really distraught. The guy's brother bombed not only the home of the family Ryker had befriended, but all the houses around it. The entire family was killed, as well as many others that night."

River gasped. For a second, she didn't have words.

The guilt and devastation Ryker must have felt. It would have been gut-wrenching. She knew exactly how big Ryker's heart was, and she also knew just how much that would have destroyed him.

"Ryker demanded to be sent back to find the brother and kill him, but they wouldn't give him clearance."

"It makes sense now," River said quietly. "His anger. He felt responsible but was also powerless to do anything about it."

Jackson nodded before running a hand through his hair. "I should have come here to support him. I just..."

River frowned. "What?"

"I knew that my father was here, and I can't look at the man without wanting to hit him. More than that, though...I knew the second I saw you, I wouldn't be able to walk away again."

She frowned. "That can't be true. That night before you left—"

"I lied."

River's heart stilled in her chest.

"I lied because I didn't want someone like you, someone so beautiful and smart...a woman with so much potential...to be tied to someone like me, who came from nothing and could very easily have ended up as nothing. I didn't want the ugly of my life to touch you, River."

She shook her head, the ache in her chest choking her. She shuffled closer, placing her hand over his heart. "You are a good man, Jackson. And your parents..." She shook her head again, not able to comprehend their actions, let alone put them into words. "They lost everything by not treating you the way they should have. That's on them. Not you."

He gave a small nod, but it was almost like he didn't believe her.

"But regardless...you don't have to say you felt something for me before you left when you didn't." Even saying the words hurt. Not nearly as much as they once had, coming from Jackson. But at least now, the pain of unrequited love had dulled. "I heard what you said. I felt every one of your words. And…it's okay."

When he stood, her hands fell away, a flash of confusion skittering through her. Was he leaving? Because she didn't believe him?

Instead of walking out of the room, he moved to his duffel bag, riffled around, and tugged something out. When he sat on the bed, he handed it to her.

A shocked gasp slipped from her lips.

It was the journal. The one she'd made him when she was seventeen years old and in love with a man who was about to leave her.

"You kept it," she whispered.

She looked back up at him, and he gave a small nod. "I took it out every single day. It got me through some of my toughest moments."

With trembling fingers, she opened the book. The pages were worn, the photos curling at the corners. She flicked through every page, right up until the last one of her, Ryker, Jackson, and her parents. She traced the photo. The words she'd written at the bottom.

"I can't believe you kept it." She spoke the words more to herself than to him.

She'd been so nervous, holding it out to him that night, hoping and praying that he'd like it.

"I'm sorry I lied to you about how I felt. I'm sorry I hurt you. I did it to push you away. Because I didn't want you to wait for me."

She looked up, struggling to push down the emotion that clogged her throat. "Are you done pushing me away now?"

A slow smile curved his lips. The book was slipped from her fingers, and then he was leaning forward, pushing her back until she lay on the bed, Jackson hovering over her. "Depends. Do you still want me? I still come from nothing. I anger easily. And I can be a bully to get what I want."

His breath against her lips had her stomach quivering.

"I do. I want all of that." She couldn't even smile while she said it. She had a feeling the day would never come when she wouldn't want him.

"Then I'm yours."

His head dipped, and he kissed her, erasing the last sixteen years of longing.

CHAPTER 21

"*I*s Jackson ready for his next fight?" Michele asked quietly.

River sighed as she thumbed through a tub of books in Uncle Ottie's bookstore. "I hope so. He's been training every damn day. And the bruises he comes home with…" She shook her head. "I'm going to meet him down there after my shoot today."

"Great." Michele said the word almost absently as she lifted another book to add to the gigantic pile already in her arms.

River wasn't a big reader. Actually, that would be an under-statement. She'd barely finished a book in her life. Michele, on the other hand, read every single day. Mostly romance but she'd seen the odd thriller sneak in.

River glanced around the store. The place hadn't changed one bit since they were teenagers. The big wooden bookshelves still covered every wall and created several aisles. There were still the old wooden ladders leaning against walls and the same musty, old book smell.

Finally, Michele looked up, nibbling her bottom lip. "Are you worried about him?"

"So worried that I don't know what I'm going to do with

myself tomorrow night." Probably curl into a ball on the couch and drown her worries in a bottle of wine.

"Want me to come over?" The second Michele said it, her gaze slid sideways to Declan, who was standing with Uncle Ottie.

River grinned. He'd been following them around all morning, and she'd caught her friend looking at him on more than one occasion. Right now, he was talking to Michele's uncle. The older man had his head thrown back in laughter at whatever Declan had said.

"Sure. I don't know who will be with me, though. Dec or Cole."

Michele's eyes flew back to her, fingers visibly tightening on the books. "Why would that matter?"

River bit the inside of her mouth to stop from smiling. "It doesn't. I just wanted to remind you that *one* of them would be there."

Michele's smile returned. "Oh. Okay. I don't mind."

River nodded toward the books in Michele's hands. "Found anything good?" The woman was carrying so many she needed a cart or something.

Michele's eyes lit up. "*So* many good ones. I'm really loving my historical romance at the moment, and Uncle Ottie ordered all my favorite authors."

Of course he did. The guy was besotted with his niece, a woman who was basically his daughter.

Michele lifted a book. The cover featured a shirtless man with long hair blowing in the wind. He looked a bit like what Tarzan might look like if he was born in Regency England, with the English manor in the background. "I mean, really, could my night get any better?"

River chuckled. It always astounded her how the two of them could be so different yet remain best friends for so long. "Do you even have room for more books in your house?"

Michele's mouth slid open. "River, there is always room for

more books. And if the day ever comes when there isn't, well then, it's the house that goes, not the books."

River threw her head back and laughed. The woman wasn't even kidding.

The smile suddenly slipped from River's lips when a man stopped on the other side of the front window, his gaze catching hers. Her stomach dipped.

"What's wrong?" Michele asked, head spinning around.

"It's—"

Before she could finish that thought, Brian stepped into the store. A small gasp slipped from Michele's lips.

He moved toward River, but he'd barely made it halfway across the room when Declan was in front of him, blocking his way. Jackson's father was tall, but he'd lost both weight and muscle over the years, so Declan all but dwarfed the man.

"What are you doing here?" Declan asked, his voice the hardest River had ever heard it.

Brian held River's gaze for another beat before turning to Declan. "Just walking past. Thought I'd drop in and say hi." He frowned up at Declan. "You're still in town?"

"Why? Want me out?"

Brian smiled but the expression made River's skin crawl. "Do whatever the fuck you want. I said my piece. If you boys are stupid enough to stay, that's on you."

Declan inched forward but Uncle Ottie grabbed his arm.

"I think you should go," River said.

Brian lifted a brow, then his gaze trailed down her body, and it took everything in her not to squirm. "Really? Is that what you think, girl?"

Declan shoved his shoulder hard, causing Brian to fall back a step. "Don't fucking look at her. Get out."

Angry energy bounced off Brian. He didn't like being told what to do. Never had. Because he was a bully. And bullies liked to be in charge, didn't they?

"Watch yourself, boy. You're closer and closer to getting your-self a nice cozy grave, just like your friend Ryker."

Suddenly, Declan grabbed Brian by the shirt, shoving him against the door.

Michele visibly jolted, books dropping from her hands. River moved forward, not sure if she was hoping to stop Declan or not, but this time Uncle Ottie was grabbing *her* arm.

Declan lowered his head until his face was close to Brian's. "Did you have something to do with his death?"

Again, Brian smiled. Like this was all a joke. "No. He did that all on his own."

The muscles bunched in Declan's arms.

"Y'all better watch your backs." Brian's gaze flicked to her again. "Especially you."

River's heart thumped against her ribs.

"Is that a threat?" Declan asked.

Brian just grinned wider.

Declan shoved him away. "Get the hell out before I kill you."

Brian shook his head, that damn smile never leaving his face. Then he turned and left the store.

A beat of silence passed. A moment of stillness before Uncle Ottie cleared his throat. "Well, he won't be stepping into a store with *you* again, son."

River almost smiled. Trust him to break the awkward quiet.

When she turned to look at Michele, she saw the woman was holding a book so firmly, her knuckles were white.

"You okay?" River asked quietly.

Michele dragged her gaze back to River, nodding. "I should be getting back to the shop."

"Sure."

Michele paid for her purchases, and they said a quick goodbye to Uncle Ottie before stepping out. Once they were walking down the street, Michele shook her head. "That was a bit scary."

River nudged her shoulder. "We're safe with Declan."

Michele cast a quick glance over her shoulder. "Why isn't he walking with us?"

"I don't know. He muttered something about watching our backs." He was only a few feet behind, but it was enough to make her feel like they had some kind of security detail. Which she supposed they did. "Have you got much cooking to do today?"

Michele sighed. "Yes. So much that I've been thinking about hiring someone to help in the store. The orders are becoming unmanageable for just me."

River squeezed her friend's arm. "That's amazing. I remember when Meals Made Easy was just an idea in your head and you had no clue if it would pan out."

The business had started in her uncle's kitchen, for Christ's sake. And now look at it, so big her friend had to expand.

"Yeah, you're right, I'm super grateful. I just really like working by myself, you know?" She lifted a shoulder. "Classic introvert problems."

River laughed. Her friend needed her time to recharge. Something River had known for as long as she'd known Michele.

They'd almost reached her shop when Michele stumbled. River grabbed for her arm, frowning when she saw her friend's face had paled. "Hey, are you okay?"

"That's Tim's car."

River's head shot up. "Tim? As in—"

"Went on a few dates and was an asshole, Tim? Yes."

She followed her friend's gaze to a beat-up Corolla parked on the street.

Michele quickly turned to face River. "I didn't tell you this but…he came to my place the other night."

River's mouth fell open. "What? Why the heck didn't you tell me?"

"Because I knew you'd be mad."

Damn straight, she would. Was the man stalking Michele now? "What did he do?"

"Someone buzzed him up and he banged on the door, begging for me to open it for about twenty minutes. I ignored him, and he finally left."

Okay, now River was livid. That probably scared the heck out of her friend.

Suddenly, the door to the Corolla opened and there he was. What was this, a morning for assholes?

The man was a bit over six feet tall, with dirty-blond hair. He was wearing a collared shirt and neat slacks. It wasn't what he was wearing that caught River's attention, though. It was the sneer on his face. River took a half step in front of her friend, and, if possible, the sneer darkened.

He'd almost reached them when suddenly, Declan was there, standing in front of them and blocking Tim exactly the same way he had Brian.

Tim stopped. "Who the fuck are you?"

"I'm none of your damn business. Who are you?"

"Michele's my girlfriend."

River scoffed. "You're a lying sack of shit!"

His face reddened, and he started to step forward, but Declan pushed him back with two hands to his chest. The guy stumbled and fell to the ground. He was on his feet again in seconds, glaring at Declan. Even though Declan towered over him and beat him in muscle, the idiot didn't look scared. "You shouldn't have done that. Now get out of my way, man."

"No."

For a moment, Tim stood there, his fists bunched and his chest puffing up and down, looking like he might hit Declan.

His gaze shot back to Michele, his eyes softening. "Michele, come on. Give me another shot."

River could see the muscles in Declan's back tense through the shirt.

"Just go, Tim," Michele said quietly. "And don't come back."

Her friend's voice may have been quiet, but the words were

clear and firm.

When the man didn't immediately move, Declan stepped closer. "You heard her. Or do you have a problem understanding English?"

Tim stood there for another few seconds before glaring at Declan and walking backward. When his eyes met Michele's again, something dark flicked across them before he spun around and walked away.

What a psychopath.

They all waited until Tim got in the car and drove away, then Declan turned toward them. "You women magnets for assholes or something?"

River rolled her eyes, but really, he wasn't wrong. "Just this morning."

When Declan's eyes landed on Michele, he frowned. "Hey... you okay?"

Michele's gaze dragged off the road and she nodded her head vigorously. Too vigorously. "Yeah, I just...didn't expect him to show up again. Or at least, I was hoping he wouldn't."

Declan threw a quick look over his shoulder toward the man's taillights. "Who is he?"

"Just someone I dated. It was very brief."

Declan's jaw ticked. River didn't need to know him well to understand he didn't like that Michele had dated the guy. "Give me your phone."

Michele's brows rose. "My phone?"

"Yeah, honey. I want to give you my number."

"Oh." Michele stood there looking unsure for a moment before reaching into her pocket and handing her cell to Declan.

When he handed it back, his gaze was heavy as he watched her. "If he bothers you again, or shows up unannounced, you call me."

River tried to hide her smile at Michele's reddened cheeks.

Her friend gave a quick nod. "Okay."

CHAPTER 22

*J*ackson stood outside the ring, watching as Erik threw a punch at Cole. He blocked it easily, retaliating with a hit of his own. Even though Erik was more experienced in the ring, Cole held his own well.

Jackson crossed his arms over his sweaty chest. This was his only break. It was also the only break he wanted. With his second match at Trinity Nightclub coming up tomorrow evening, he needed all the practice he could get.

His gaze shot to his phone again, which it had been doing ever since he'd received that message from Declan about his father going into the bookstore.

Brian clearly didn't understand the lengths he would go to in order to keep River safe. Otherwise, he never would have dared to threaten her. And it *was* a threat.

It made him want to never leave River's side and solidified an idea that had been skittering through Jackson's head since Monday and his confession to her. An idea about staying. About creating a home in the place where he'd always sworn he'd never return.

When Cole and Erik finally stepped away from each other,

they were both breathing heavily. Cole ducked below the rope and grabbed a towel. "God, being in the ring feels good."

Erik nodded, also stepping out before disappearing into the kitchen. He came back a few seconds later with three bottles of cold water.

Yeah, Jackson had invested in a fridge.

Erik threw one to Cole and one to Jackson. "I know. Sometimes it's the only place I find peace."

Jackson frowned. "Peace?" He knew the guy was former military, but he hadn't spoken much about his time serving or why he'd left.

"Don't worry about it." He took a drink of his water before setting it on the ground. He fiddled with the wrapping on his hand. "You feeling ready to fight Benny?"

Jackson lifted a shoulder. "Do you ever feel ready?"

Erik shook his head, smiling. "Never. Make sure you rest tomorrow."

"Was planning on it. What can you tell me about Benny?"

"He's a defensive fighter, so he'll wait for you to hit first. He's good at blocking, and he has one of the best counterpunches out there so he uses it often."

Jackson nodded. He'd watched a little of the guy's fight last week and had seen bits of that.

"You have a powerful hit, though," Erik continued. "He would have seen that when you were in the cage with Thunder. It might make him question whether he can block those hits and force him to change tactics."

In other words, be prepared for anything.

Jackson shot a quick look to Cole before turning back to Erik. "You heard of a guy named Elijah?"

Erik paused, the wrapping half undone. When he looked up, his eyes were harder. "Where'd you hear that name?"

Jackson unscrewed the cap of his own bottle, not wanting the guy to think he was too invested in the topic. "Overheard one of the guys using it the other night. He sounded important."

Erik seemed to consider his words carefully. "He's there every Friday night. I've heard rumors he's into some pretty heavy shit, and anyone who crosses him dies. What exactly he does there, I don't know. Like I told you at the start, I keep myself out of those things. If you go looking for trouble, you generally find it."

Jackson nodded. Trouble was exactly what he was looking for. Because it would lead him to the guy who'd put a hit on Ryker—and why. "One more question, and I swear that's it. Those deliveries they receive. You ever seen them bring the stuff down?"

His eyes narrowed. "No. As far as I've heard, the deliveries come on Friday nights, but always before the fight."

Jackson gave a short nod. He would bet everything those "deliveries" were the kegs. What was in them, though, he had no idea.

When his phone beeped with a message, he grabbed it, his chest suddenly feeling a bit lighter.

River: Food has been styled and pictures taken. I am now thoroughly starving. Dec and I are coming by, and I'll most definitely be demanding you feed me.

He chuckled.

Jackson: I'm going to do one more round in the ring then I'll feed you the best food Lindeman has to offer.

River: Will this feeding occur before or after you have a shower? Because I'm hungry, but I also like a nice-smelling man by my side.

Jackson: We could always shower together.

When River responded with emojis, Jackson chuckled to himself again. He looked up to see Cole shaking his head. The man knew he was completely besotted with the woman.

Erik was frowning. "Your girl going to be there again tomorrow night?"

Jackson hadn't mentioned River to him, but he wasn't surprised the guy knew they were together, not with the way he'd hustled her out of there after the fight last week. "Nah, she can't make it."

He nodded. "Good. I'd keep her away, too. That place is always one step away from another brawl."

"You think it will be as busy this week as it was the last?" Jackson asked.

"Yeah, the place is always packed."

"Considering the amount of people and the five-hundred-dollar entrance fee, I was expecting my prize money to be bigger," Jackson said, again aiming for casual. He didn't care about the prize money. What he did care about was learning the ins and out of the club. If he didn't receive his share of the entrance fee, where did it go?

Erik nodded. "Mickey takes a large chunk." He straightened. "Look, I don't know what you guys are up to, but I don't want any part of it. I'm here to be in the ring."

Jackson gave a small nod. "Let's get in the ring then."

RIVER STEPPED into Larry's old boxing gym and her gaze immediately found Jackson, all six and a half feet of him. His chest was bare and it glistened with sweat. He blocked a punch before quickly following it up with his own, which was blocked in return. Every muscle in his body shook and rippled.

Her mouth dried, and the little hairs on her arms stood on end.

Holy heck, the man was a damn gladiator. She hadn't been able to properly appreciate what he looked like when he was in the ring in the club because, well, she'd been too damn worried about him dying. Now though, he looked big and sexy and powerful. He looked like a force.

When her gaze swung to the other man, she realized she'd seen him before. He was one of the fighters last week.

Jackson's gaze met hers. Only for a second, but it was enough to give his opponent an opening. The punch caught Jackson in the chin and his head flew sideways.

River gasped and started to move forward, but Declan grabbed her arm.

The guy opposite Jackson paused. "You okay?"

He nodded, not looking fazed by the hit at all. "Yeah, let's finish up though."

The guy gave a short nod before turning. When his gaze met River's, he gave her a chin lift. "Hey."

She smiled. "Hi. You're one of the fighters from the club."

"Yep. And you're Ryker's sister."

Her back straightened. "How did you—"

"You look just like him. And you're with Jackson, who took Ryker's place in the ring. I put two and two together."

Made sense. "Did you know him very well?"

"Nah, but we had a couple of conversations. Unlike most of the people there, he was one of the good guys. He mostly kept to himself."

She nodded again, not sure how to respond.

Jackson climbed out of the ring, stepping up beside her. Immediately, her attention went to the red bump on his left brow. She lifted her hand to touch the skin around it. The guy didn't even flinch.

"Are you okay?" she asked quietly.

"Yeah, it's just a bruise."

Just a bruise, my ass. "Have you got an ice pack here?"

"Yeah, in the freezer in the kitchen, but I don't need—"

"Save it, Mr. G.I. Joe. I'm getting you an ice pack."

She moved across the room and into the kitchen. It sat in the back corner of the building. There was a door inside that led to the parking area behind the gym. It was also where Larry used to take out the trash. She was pretty sure this small space had once been a mudroom or something before Larry had converted it into a poky little kitchen.

She opened the freezer door, secretly glad the guys had invested in the fridge. Because that meant they were considering staying. Or at least prolonging their stay in Lindeman. You didn't buy an expensive appliance unless you planned to use it for a while, right?

The last few days had been amazing. But there had also been the whispered reminder in her head that eventually they'd figure this Ryker stuff out...and what then? Jackson had made it clear this town wasn't his favorite place to be. He didn't want to be around his father, but the guy didn't seem to be in a hurry to go anywhere.

Would he stay for her? Or would he ask her to go with him?

Blowing out a long breath, she reached for an ice pack.

One thing at a time, River. Right now, if she wanted to find her brother, her focus needed to be on that and only that.

She was just closing the freezer door when she was hit by a small breeze. Looking at the back door, she watched as a stiff wind blew it open. Only a tiny fraction, but still...had someone forgotten to close it? And why wasn't it locked?

She took a single step forward and was about to close it when suddenly a body pressed against her back and a hand came over her mouth.

Before she had a chance to react, she was pulled outside, and her front was shoved against the back of the building. For a moment, fear clouded her mind and froze her limbs—and that small hesitation killed any hope she had of escaping. By the time she struggled against her attacker, it was too late. He'd effectively rendered her immobile. His entire front pressed against her back, forcing her so tightly against the wall there was no space to even move her head. The hand over her mouth barely allowed her to breathe.

She tried to buck her hips. To bite or scratch the man. Nothing worked. He didn't move, and she couldn't reach him.

When the sharp edge of a knife touched her throat, her body stilled, ice cascading through her limbs.

A mouth pressed beside her ear, hot breath making her stomach coil. "I have a message for you." The voice was unfamiliar, but it had a shudder racing up her spine. "Leave your brother's death alone. Stop looking into it. Don't even fucking *think* about it."

She tried to nod, but the guy's hand on her mouth, in combination with the knife against her neck, made it impossible.

The guy pushed his face into her hair. Her skin crawled. Was he smelling her?

"Just so you understand we mean business, I'm gonna need to do something. You won't like this very much, sweetheart."

His fingers latched into her hair, tugging her head off the wall before slamming her head against the bricks—hard.

Pain crashed through her skull and her vision darkened. Her body hit the ground the second he released her. She tried to scream but all she could muster was a groan.

He lifted her hand—and she felt the edge of the knife press against the knuckle of her finger.

Oh God, was he planning to—

The sharp blade sliced into her skin.

She'd barely opened her mouth to force a scream when the knife disappeared, along with the weight on her back.

Then there was the sound of scuffling.

River rolled onto her back, grabbing at her hand, feeling the blood drip from where he'd cut her finger. Her vision was blurry, fading in and out, and the side of her face throbbed with pain from where it had collided with the wall.

She scrunched her eyes, trying to make out the people fighting nearby. They were so fuzzy, moving too quickly.

She blinked. Wait. Was that…?

Her breath caught. Ryker! Or at least, she thought it might be him.

She tried blinking again, but rather than become clearer, the men blurred more. Her lids grew heavy. She tried to keep them open but it was impossible.

The sounds started to fade, and for a moment, she thought it was because she was passing out—but then she heard something else.

"River?" Footsteps drew closer. "Fuck, Rae! Baby, are you okay?"

She hadn't passed out. Ryker and the man had disappeared.

Warm hands touched her cheeks. She already knew there was blood on her head, the warm stickiness heated her temple.

More footsteps, then more cursing.

"We need to get her to a fucking hospital!" Jackson shouted. His voice was desperate. His hand went around her wrist, and he cursed again. "It'll be okay, baby. I promise."

CHAPTER 23

*J*ackson stood beside the bed as the doctor shone a light into River's eyes. She'd barely been conscious on the way to the hospital but seemed a bit better now, thank God.

The doctor nodded. "You have a mild concussion, and the wounds on your head and finger will need stitches."

Jackson tensed at the mention of her finger. The cut across the top knuckle was deep. He'd wrapped some material around it on the way here to stem the bleeding, but the cloth had already been soaked through when they arrived.

The doctor lifted her hand, removing the bandage and studying her finger for a second time, his white brows tugging together. "How did this happen, Miss Harp?"

Her gaze skittered to Jackson almost nervously before looking back at the doctor. Dread pooled in his gut. He wasn't going to like this.

"The attacker put a knife against my knuckle. He started cutting me but was stopped."

The doctor's gaze shot up to hers. Jackson's entire body

turned to stone. His muscles vibrated with the need to get up, go, find the asshole who did this, and murder him.

The doctor cleared his throat. "Well, you're very lucky to have gotten away. I'm going to send a nurse in to do the stitches. After that, the police will be here to talk to you."

She swallowed, giving a small nod.

The second the door closed, he stepped in front of her, taking both sides of her face in his hands. "How are you doing?"

Fear flashed across her eyes before she quickly hid it. And God, but that tore him apart. She was his to protect. Had been since the second he stepped into town. And he'd let her down. Fuck, the brazen asshole had attacked her while he'd been inside the goddamn building.

"I'm okay. It's just a couple of cuts. It could have been a lot worse." She paused, eyes shuffling between his. "And this isn't your fault, so don't you dare get that idea stuck in your head."

Not true. "I should have heard something. Why didn't I hear anything?"

"Because he put a hand over my mouth and dragged me outside. He was quiet. He knew what he was doing."

The muscles in Jackson's limbs tensed at the visual. He'd been picturing it since they'd found her, but hearing the words from her mouth…it was worse.

"Did you open the door?" It was a question that had been rolling around in his head. How had the attacker reached her? The door should have been locked.

"No, it was open when I got there. I noticed it a second before he attacked me because a breeze blew the door in slightly." She frowned, massaging her temple. "It's all a bit of a blur. I think he was hiding behind the door leading to the gym."

That couldn't be right. There was no way he or his team would have unlocked that door. Unless…

His limbs iced, a new fury rising in his chest.

When he felt the small shudder race up her body, he pushed it all down. *Focus on her, Jackson. She needs you.*

He shifted his hands to her shoulders and touched his forehead to hers. "We'll figure this out. No one will touch you again." When he straightened, he swiped some hair from her cheek. "How did you scare him off?"

There was a heavy pause.

He tilted his head to the side. "What is it?"

"I'm going to tell you something…and I need you to believe me."

"Why wouldn't I believe you?"

She wet her lips. "The guy was cutting my finger. I could feel the pain of the knife as it sliced into me. He wasn't going to stop, Jackson."

It took everything in him to remain as he was. To not turn and plunge his fist through the wall. She didn't need that right now.

"I could barely think or move after he threw my head into the side of the building," River continued. "I couldn't do *anything*. But…Ryker saved me."

Jackson sucked in a sharp breath. "Ryker?"

"Yes." Her gaze never wavered from his, and in those black eyes, he saw that same desperation again. Desperation for him to believe her. For *someone* to believe her.

"You actually saw him?"

She hesitated. "Kind of. My vision was blurry. But I saw his outline. I know it was him."

So no. She hadn't seen him. Not really. He opened his mouth, not exactly sure what words were about to come out, but at that moment, the nurse stepped into the room, saving him.

"Hi, guys, my name is Nurse Petra, and I'm here to do the stitches."

River's gaze was still on him. "Jackson…"

He kept his voice low. "We'll talk about it tonight, honey."

Disappointment washed out the hope.

God, he felt like an asshole. But he couldn't lie, either.

Even though he couldn't believe it had been Ryker, the question still remained—who had saved her? And why had they left? Where was the attacker?

When the nurse started working on the stitches, a text came through on Jackson's phone. He typed back a quick response, and a second later, Declan stepped inside the room.

Jackson turned to River. "I'm just popping into the hall for a second. Declan's going to wait in here."

She frowned but gave a quick nod.

The second Jackson stepped out, he saw him.

Jackson was in front of Erik in under a second, grabbing him by the shirt and shoving him against the wall. "Are you working with them?"

"Working with who?" His question was quiet.

Cole touched his arm. "Jackson—"

"*Them.* Are you working with Elijah and his guys? The men who put a hit on Ryker."

Erik's features remained neutral, but his eyes were stormy. Like he was right on the verge of fighting back. "Why the hell would you ask me that?"

"Because you were the last person in the damn kitchen," Jackson yelled. "Did you leave the fucking door open for them? Did you text to let them know she was coming? To let them know she was heading back there so they could grab her and cut her fucking finger off?"

This time, Erik's features darkened. "No. I'm not working with them. I didn't open the door. And I didn't text anyone. Check my fucking phone if you want. Or better yet, check the lock on the kitchen door. Someone broke it."

Jackson didn't release the guy. "Bullshit."

"While you and Declan came here, Cole and I have been at the gym. We checked the lock. It was tampered with from the outside."

"He's telling the truth," Cole said quietly.

For a second, Jackson didn't move. Cole wouldn't lie. He trusted the man with his life. Which meant it was true. Someone had broken in and hurt River, but it wasn't Erik's doing.

Jackson let go of the guy's shirt and stepped back.

Erik pulled a small bag out of his pocket, shoving it at Jackson's chest. "We also found these. You're welcome."

Then he turned and stormed down the hall.

Jackson lifted the bag, cursing under his breath when he saw the small cameras inside. Cameras which were almost identical to the ones they'd found in River's and her parents' houses.

RIVER LAY ON THE COUCH. The news was on in front of her but she barely paid attention. The events of the day played over in her mind. Had been playing in her mind all freaking evening.

She scrunched her eyes, trying to recapture that image of Ryker fighting the man who had attacked her. God, she wished he'd been clearer. But it had been him. She knew it. She didn't need her brother's image to be crystal clear to recognize him.

At the feel of hands on her shoulders, her eyes flew open. Jackson lifted her upper body, sitting on the couch and gently lowering her head down onto his lap.

They hadn't said much to each other since getting back from the hospital. What could they say? He was pissed he'd been in the other room while she'd been attacked, and she was disappointed that, yet again, no one believed her.

"How's your head?" he asked quietly.

"It's fine."

Even though her eyes were on the TV, she could feel Jackson's gaze on her. It had been on her all day, like he was scared she'd disappear if he looked away.

When he started to stroke her hair, her eyes shuttered again. The feel of his hands on her always had that effect. It was like the man could calm every little part of her soul with a single touch.

"Are you upset with me because I don't believe it was Ryker today?"

She tried not to flinch at his words, but it was impossible. She'd known he didn't believe her, but he hadn't confirmed it until now. Hearing him say it out loud hurt worse. "I'm not upset." Okay, maybe she was a little bit upset. "It would just be nice if *someone* believed me."

Maybe then she wouldn't feel like she was in the middle of a river, paddling a boat upstream, all on her own, seconds from running out of steam.

On his next stroke, his thumb grazed against the side of her face. It was right beside the cut, and it soothed some of the ache in her head.

"I'm sorry," he whispered.

"You don't need to be sorry for what you believe."

She just had to pray that sooner rather than later, they found Ryker. That everyone would see she was right...before she lost faith herself.

They remained like that for a while, Jackson stroking her hair, his thumb grazing the side of her face, while the TV changed to some movie she'd never heard of.

Jackson cleared his throat. "So, the guys and I were talking about what happens after all of this..."

River's breath halted in her throat, almost scared of the next words to come out of his mouth. Scared that he'd confirm her worst fear. That he'd be leaving town. Leaving *her*. It took her a few goes to force her voice to work. "Really?"

"Yeah. I told them I want to stay."

She shot up into a seated position—and immediately regretted it when pain bolted through her skull.

Jackson cursed under his breath, touching the side of her face again in that soothing way. "Careful, Rae."

She took a quick breath. "Are you serious? You want to stay? Here in Lindeman? But your father's here, and even if he wasn't, you hate this town."

"Maybe I've come to realize that staying away is just me letting him control my life. I'm not willing to do that anymore." He lifted her hand, threading his fingers through hers. "And I don't hate this town. How could I? You're here."

She felt the wetness of tears in her eyes. "What will you do here?"

"I have an idea. But mostly, I just want to be with you." His gaze skirted between hers. "I love you, Rae. You're the first person I ever loved, and I want you to be the last."

Her eyes closed, and a tear trickled down her cheek. At the feel of Jackson's finger swiping it away, she looked at him again. "I love you too. I've loved you for so long, the feeling has just become a part of me."

Fire ignited in his eyes. Then he was kissing her like she was everything he'd ever wanted and needed.

CHAPTER 24

*J*ackson's fingers strummed against the passenger door. Declan was behind the wheel but they weren't driving. They were waiting. Watching the little screen on Declan's phone. They'd used one of their connections from the military to acquire a high-tech wireless camera which Declan had planted just above the exit of the basement stairs in the Trinity parking lot. There was sound and a crystal-clear image. That was all they needed.

They'd already been waiting for a good hour, but so far, they'd seen nothing. They'd wait another hour and, if nothing happened, go to the fight.

"What I wouldn't give to be able to step into that club tonight and murder every asshole involved in Ryker's death," Declan said quietly, leaning his head back.

"You and me both, brother. But first we need to work out exactly who Elijah is and what he's up to."

If Ryker had become involved, it had to be important.

Declan nodded.

"We've got to be careful," Jackson continued. "Even though the club is Mickey's turf, and he's okay with us being here, I wouldn't put it past this Elijah guy to try something."

"That's why we're armed and we watch our backs." He turned to look at Jackson. "How was River this morning?"

His fingers paused mid-strum. "I think she's more frustrated than anything that no one believes it was Ryker."

"I mean, the question's there. Who the hell saved her?"

Jackson blew out a long breath. "I don't know. She's adamant she saw two men fighting so it had to be someone."

Declan nodded again.

"I wish she was right," he said quietly. "I would give my right fucking arm to have our brother back with us."

"You and me both," Declan echoed.

He opened his mouth to say something but quickly snapped it shut. Because really, what could he say? Ryker was dead.

"You talk to Erik today?"

Jackson scrubbed a hand over his face. "No. I'm hoping to catch him tonight." And hoping the guy didn't throw a fist in his face. But if he did, Jackson deserved it. Everything Erik had said yesterday was true. The guy had just been trying to help. Hell, he'd been helping him since Jackson walked into that club.

"Your girl had just been slammed against a wall and almost had her finger sliced off," Declan said, watching the screen on their phone. "Your anger was understandable."

True. But that didn't make it any fairer for Erik.

Jackson's eyes were also on the empty parking lot through the screen. He was starting to think nothing was going to happen when the basement door opened and three men stepped out.

Jackson straightened. Declan leaned closer to the screen. The three men were the same ones Jackson recognized from the last fight. And he was almost certain one of them was Elijah.

Before the door could close behind them, a fourth man stepped out. Jackson's fist clenched so hard, his knuckles cracked.

Brian.

He'd been sure his father was involved, both from the way he'd led those people into the office at the club and after the warning he'd served to Jackson to stay away. This just confirmed it. And it had his blood chilling in his veins.

The four of them stood around for about ten minutes, two of them pulling out cigarettes, his father and the other guy just waiting. All of them silent.

Jackson heard it before he saw it. A large truck pulling up outside the door.

When the truck stopped, two guys got out of the cab and moved around to the back. The way the truck parked, with its rear facing the club door, Jackson and Declan had a perfect view of the back.

One of the guys from the front opened the cargo door, and four more guys stepped out. Behind them were metal kegs. The truck was full of them. Some large, some small. They didn't quite fill the space, but they came close.

The driver stopped in front of one of the guys. "It's all here, Elijah."

Ah, there you are, Elijah.

Elijah nodded to one of his men, who moved forward, climbed into the truck, and unscrewed the top of one of the kegs. He stuck his hand inside, and when he pulled it out, Jackson cursed under his breath.

Money. A handful of it. The man lifted the cash closer to his face, studying it, before shoving it back inside. He did the same thing to each keg.

When he was done, he turned to Elijah and nodded.

Over the next twenty minutes, Jackson and Declan watched as the guys moved the kegs down the stairs. When the truck was empty, the six men got back in and drove away, while the others went back into the club, his father being the one to pull the door closed behind him.

For a moment, both Jackson and Dec were silent.

"So they're selling something out of the club and whoever's buying it is hiding the payment in kegs?" Declan said quietly, even though there was no one else around to hear.

"The question is, what are they selling?"

What were Elijah and his father putting back into those kegs in exchange for that kind of money?

Jackson and Declan remained in the car for another hour, watching the camera, waiting to see if the truck returned. Or if anything else went down.

It didn't.

Declan finally drove the short distance around the corner to the club. When they stepped into the basement, the place was already packed. Jackson had just reached the bottom step when he saw them—Elijah and Mickey talking. And just like last week, neither man looked happy.

He looked away before either could see him watching and moved down the hall and into the changing room. Four other fighters were already inside, Erik included. His gaze clashed with Erik's for a second before the other guy quickly looked away. He didn't look angry. But he didn't look happy, either.

Jackson dropped his bag and spent the next ten minutes getting changed. Then he slipped out of the room, beelining down the hall.

The first door he checked led to an empty room, just like last week. He quickly moved to the next—and the second he opened it, he froze.

Five people he'd never seen before looked back at him from where they stood around the empty desk he'd searched last week. And then the man behind the desk glanced up.

Brian.

His father's eyes narrowed to slits.

Before anyone could say anything, Jackson tugged the door shut. But in those few seconds, he'd already seen what he needed to see.

Guns. Bags of them on the desk. And a few open kegs. He'd also seen money being exchanged, Brian handing a wad of bills to one of the men standing across the desk.

Firearms. Elijah's men were buying firearms, then selling them elsewhere. That had to be it.

But where the hell did Ryker fit into it all?

He was just stepping away from the door, half expecting it to open behind him, when fingers grabbed his arm, spinning him around.

It was one of Mickey's guys.

"What the fuck are you doing?"

Jackson narrowed his eyes. "Unless you want that hand broken, get it the hell off me."

Instead of letting go, the guy tightened his fingers. Jackson was a second away from snatching his arm and breaking the guy's bones when Erik appeared beside him.

"He's new. I gave him the wrong directions to the bathroom."

The guy's fingers remained for a moment before dropping. He took a step back. "Don't let it happen again."

Erik shoved Jackson in front of him as they headed back to the changing room. Jackson felt Mickey's guys eyes on him the entire way.

The second they stepped into the room, he met Erik's gaze. "Thanks."

"Don't do that again. They'll murder your ass."

He was about to walk away when Jackson stopped him. "I'm sorry about yesterday. I was an asshole."

There was a short beat of silence before Erik nodded. "Don't worry about it. It was a shit day for you."

∾

RIVER DUNKED the measuring cup into the sugar canister. When she pulled it out, she was seconds away from pouring it into the bowl when Michele's sharp voice stopped her.

"What the heck are you doing?"

River frowned. "Ah...you asked me to pour a cup of sugar into the mixture, so I'm pouring a cup of sugar into the mixture."

Was she the one who'd hit her head yesterday or had Chele?

Michele took the cup from her fingers and lifted it to eye level like she was a scientist inspecting a specimen under a microscope. "This isn't a cup, River. It's not even close to full."

Well, sure, the sugar wasn't level with the top, but—

"It's needs to be exact." Michele dunked the cup back into the sugar. When she pulled it out, it was overflowing. She grabbed a knife, tapping the side of the cup a couple times before using the flat edge of the knife to smooth the top.

Okay, maybe River hadn't been that precise, but was it really necessary?

"Perfect," Michele said, more to herself than to River, before pouring it into the bowl.

"Okay, now I remember why I don't bake with you." The woman was a little dictator in the kitchen.

Michele sighed, setting the measuring cup back on the table. "Sorry, I know I'm a lot. I just...when it comes to making food, it's the one thing I'm confident in and good at, so I don't like to mess it up."

River frowned. "The one thing you're good at? Michele Joy King, I know you're not insinuating you aren't good at much."

Michele rolled her eyes. "What else am I good at, River?"

"Uh, a million things. You're good at being a dog mama to Pokey. You make those homemade cards at Christmas that make everyone in town smile. You're an awesome businesswoman. And the best damn friend I've ever had."

One side of Michele's mouth lifted. "Okay, I agree with you on the dog mama part."

"And everything else, I hope." River shot a look across to Cole on the couch. "Would you tell the woman she's amazing?"

Cole rose from the couch, moving into the kitchen. "If those cookies taste anything like the banana cake you brought over tonight, I wouldn't stop at amazing."

River gave her friend a pointed look. "See?" She reached over, grabbing the bag of chocolate chips before popping one in her mouth.

Michele shook her head this time, but the smile remained. She pushed the bowl in front of River. "The mixture needs some chocolate chips, too."

River frowned. "Okay, this time you haven't even told me a quantity. You setting me up to fail, woman?"

"You can add as many or as few as you want."

River met Cole's gaze. "So, a lot?"

"And then a few more," he confirmed.

The man knew how to bake. She poured almost the entire bag into the bowl. Michele shook her head again, taking the bowl back.

River leaned over the island. "So, Cole, give us the goss on Declan."

Beside her, Michele paused for a moment before going back to her mixing.

Cole frowned. "Goss?"

"Yeah, is he a good guy? Is he dating anyone? A playboy? Does he have anger management issues that only come out on the third date?"

Cole scoffed. "The man is calmer than a saint. Definitely calmer than me or J. And I haven't seen him date a woman since I met the guy over ten years ago."

Okay, not really the answer she was looking for, but hey, he was calm and single. "So, playboy?"

"I wouldn't go that far." Cole shot a quick look Michele's way. The woman wasn't looking at him. In fact, she was mixing the cookie batter, looking at it like it was the most interesting thing she'd ever seen. He looked back at River. "What I *would* say is, no woman has made him pause. Not to say it won't happen in the future."

Interesting. If there was anyone River thought could make a man pause, as Cole put it, it was definitely her beautiful, softly-spoken best friend.

She grabbed another few chocolate chips from the bag. "What about you? Any woman in your life?"

He shook his head. "Nope."

That was all she got? Nope? "I might know—"

"Nope." Again with that word. "Not going on any blind dates."

She pouted. "Why? Because God forbid you might meet the perfect woman and live happily ever after?"

He leaned forward. "Because I don't believe in happily ever after."

Then he grabbed the remaining chocolate chips and headed back to the couch.

CHAPTER 25

*J*ackson pulled the car to a stop outside his father's trailer.

He barely felt the bruises and cuts from the night before. The fight had been a tough one, but he hadn't come close to losing.

Even though it had been a difficult win, he'd swap being back in that cage in a heartbeat if it meant not being here.

Fuck, he hated this trailer park. There were too many shitty memories from his childhood. The constant smell of alcohol. The empty bottles. The fucking loneliness.

Being alone beat the hell out of when he *wasn't*, though. Being alone had meant he was safe from the fists that always ended with more bruises scattered across his body.

"You sure you want to do this?" Declan asked.

It was close to six in the morning. He'd stayed at the inn with Dec last night instead of returning to River, trusting Cole to protect her. Needing some space to think.

He also hadn't been sure if his father was going to rat him out for stepping into that room last night. He'd almost expected Elijah's guys to storm into the inn.

"He has the answers," Jackson said quietly. "He knows exactly what happened to Ryker, and why."

His own father. Involved in his best friend's murder. It should surprise him. It didn't. And wasn't that the most messed-up part of all this?

Jackson shook his head, anger racing through his veins. "He saw what Ryker and his family did for me. It wasn't enough that he had to be a shit father, he also had to have a hand in the death of my best friend."

And over what? Money?

Declan looked like he wanted to say something, but then the door to his father's trailer opened, and Brian stepped out, looking right at them. Like he was challenging Jackson to get out. Confront him.

Jackson swung his door open. He vaguely heard the loud exhale from Declan. His focus remained on his father. The man who'd made sure his childhood was a living hell.

Grabbing Brian by the shirt, Jackson shoved him against the metal trailer. "What the fuck is going on at that club?"

There was no expression on his father's face at all. "Don't tell me you haven't figured it out already, son?"

That three-letter word at the end...it almost broke the thin grasp he had on his self-restraint. "Don't fucking call me that. You've never been a father to me."

For a moment, Jackson almost thought he saw a flash of remorse on the guy's face. But it couldn't be. The man didn't have a scrap of humanity in him. "Because I'm not fucking father material. Your whore of a mother knew that and she still left me with your dumb ass."

Jackson didn't think. He just swung. Crashing his fist into the side of his father's face.

The older man almost crumpled, but Jackson grabbed him, shoving him against the trailer again.

"I'm not here to talk about why my mother left me with a sad excuse for a father, or why you couldn't clean your ass up and be a better goddamn person. I already know the answer. Some people are incapable of making decisions that benefit others. Some people are incapable of love." He'd let the pain of that truth go a long time ago. "Tell me about Ryker's involvement at the club."

His father spat a mouthful of blood onto the ground. "You should have listened to me when I told you to leave."

"Why? Because they're going to kill me like they killed Ryker?"

"Yes. What he's got going is too fucking lucrative to let anyone get in the way. I didn't tell him about you walking into that room last night because I didn't have to. You're digging your own grave. If you care about that little girlfriend of yours at all, you'll stop."

Jackson pulled the guy forward before slamming him into the trailer again. "Tell me what's going on right the hell now or I'll break every fucking bone in your body one by one."

The guy remained silent. Fine. Jackson lifted his leg and brought his boot down hard on Brian's foot, knowing he snapped at least one bone.

His father cried out and tried to pull away, but Jackson held him firm.

"I'll start with the smallest bones and work my way up," he said quietly. "Now, tell me what I want to hear before I break your hand."

His father remained silent, his breaths heavy. When Jackson reached for his wrist, he finally spoke.

"Firearms trafficking," Brian growled. "Elijah's the leader. He traffics a high volume of guns in and out of the country."

Declan stepped forward. "Where do they go?"

Brian tried to pull out of his hold again but got nowhere. "Canada."

"And Ryker found out."

It was a question. But it wasn't.

"Yeah. And things don't end well for people who find out when they're not supposed to." There was a sneer on his face. "So what do you think's going to happen to *you*?"

A slow smile replaced the sneer. "Go on. Hit me again for not protecting Ryker. You know you want to. *I* know you want to. I can see it in your eyes. It's the same look I see in the goddamn mirror."

The muscles in Jackson's body tensed. "I'm *nothing* like you."

"No? So you don't feel the sweet release every time you throw a punch? You don't step into that ring to appease your demons?"

Jackson lowered his head, quietening his voice. "Maybe I do. The difference is, I know when and where to throw the punch. And I know how to stop. It's called being a fucking adult."

His father actually laughed. "It's called violence, kid. It runs in your blood as freely as it runs in mine."

River crept out of her bedroom. It was midmorning. She'd only just woken up, and she could hear the hum of voices from the other room.

The birds were chirping and the sun was up. She should be in a good mood. She wasn't.

"Cole, I know you're trying to help, but it's really not necessary."

River stepped into the kitchen and stopped at the sight of Michele trying to wrestle a pan from Cole's hand.

Cole lifted a brow. "You know, when people offer to help, the polite thing to do is just say thank you."

Michele huffed, her fingers looking like steel wrapped around that pan. "Guess I'm not too polite then, am I?"

"Where is he?" River asked.

Both sets of eyes swung her way.

Michele's brows rose. "You're up."

"I am." River shot her gaze to Cole. "Where's Jackson?"

Because he certainly hadn't been in bed with her when she'd woken. In fact, his side of the bed had been cold and still made, meaning he hadn't returned last night at all. And there had been no text. No call. Nothing.

Cole let go of the pan and moved toward her. "Jackson finished late at the club, so he decided not to come back in case he woke you."

And he hadn't thought to let her know he was okay? "So where is he?"

"He stayed with Dec at the inn."

She moved further into the room. "But he won his fight?"

For a split second, Cole paused. Then he gave a quick nod. "Yes."

"Why'd you hesitate?"

Michele ducked her head and turned toward the stove.

"I didn't hesitate."

"You kinda did," Michele said quietly.

"You definitely did." Another step. "Is he okay?"

"He just sent me a text to say he's at the gym with Dec, so he must be."

River's mouth slipped open. "He sent *you* a text to say he's at the gym?"

The man said he loved her the other night but couldn't update her on his well-being after going to a dangerous club and fighting a man who could have killed him?

Cole's mouth opened, as if he'd said the wrong thing but wasn't sure what the right thing was.

"And he's fine enough to go to the gym this morning," she said, more to herself than anyone else, "but he can't send me a text to say that he's, I don't know...*alive*?"

Now she was just hurt.

When Cole remained silent, River turned on the balls of her feet and marched toward the bedroom.

"Where are you going?" Michele called.

"I'm getting changed to go see Jackson."

River took the quickest shower of her life before throwing on some jeans and a T-shirt. Then she grabbed her keys, not surprised to see Cole and Michele already by the door.

Michele gave her a quick hug. "Let me know how it goes."

"I will."

Michele walked to her car as River and Cole went to hers. They both remained silent until River was just pulling onto the street.

"Are you angry at him?" he asked.

"A little. Also frustrated. Confused. I don't think a quick text or phone call to let me know he's okay is too much to ask, considering what's been going on."

Cole gave a short nod. "Fair enough."

"I mean, it wasn't just the fight that I was scared about. The man's going to a club that led to my brother's supposed death. He could have easily never walked out again."

"True."

"And the only reason I didn't text *him* last night was because I didn't want to distract him. I didn't want to be the reason he couldn't concentrate around Mickey or Elijah or that guy he fought in the ring." She shook her head. "Even a simple 'Hey Rae, just letting you know I wasn't killed in the ring last night' text would have been nice."

"I agree."

River parked the car on the street outside the gym. "I texted him before I jumped into the shower. And you know what I received back?"

"I could venture a guess."

"Nothing. Radio silence. Diddly squat."

She climbed out of the car, moving toward the door. Cole

trailed inside behind her, and the first thing she saw was Declan lifting a bag over his shoulders.

He frowned. "What are you guys doing here? Jackson's in the locker room, and then we were leaving."

Her gaze shot to the empty containers of food from the Penguin Café. The rational side of her brain knew Jackson needed to eat. It was late morning, so of course, he'd gotten food. But for some reason, the sight of the containers had another part of her feeling even more annoyed. Maybe because he'd prioritized takeaway over her.

"We're here to yell at Jackson," Cole said calmly, folding his arms over his chest.

River flashed a look at Cole. "I never said yell."

Declan didn't even look surprised. He tilted his head toward the locker room. "He's showering."

She gave a quick nod and moved forward. "Thanks."

"We'll leave you to it then," Cole called.

River waved her hand distractedly before stepping into the bathroom.

Steam fogged the space. There were four shower cubicles. Jackson was in the third. He was turned to the side so she could only see part of him, and his eyes were closed, chin on his chest as water pummeled his back.

For a moment, she was pulled out of her frustration and confusion to just…look at the man. At his powerful, thick arms and legs. At the tightly packed muscles on his chest and stomach.

Her mouth went dry. He was, and always had been, the most beautiful man she'd ever seen. And now he was just more…everything.

She moved toward the shower. "Are you okay?"

Jackson's eyes opened and his head turned. She almost gasped at the bruise on his left cheekbone. And not just his cheekbone. Now that he was straight and facing her, she saw the dark bruises on his side, like someone had repeatedly kicked him. Also, one on his shoulder.

"What are you doing here, River?" he asked quietly.

She swallowed. "You didn't come home last night." Yes, she was referring to her house as his home, and she didn't even care. "Why haven't you texted? And where have you been all morning?"

For a moment, he was silent, a frown marring his brows. And then she saw something else.

Pain. It seemed to be tearing at his soul, torturing him.

"Jackson—"

"Come here."

She stepped forward without hesitation. The second she was within reaching distance, his arm snaked around her waist, tugging her against his body and under the spray. A gasp had barely left her lips when his mouth crashed onto hers. Like he couldn't go another second without kissing her.

For a moment, she was still, so surprised, that every muscle in her body froze. Then his tongue slipped between her lips, and his hands roamed along her body, firm and unyielding, yet oddly gentle. He tugged her hips against his, making her ridiculously aware of the hardness that pressed against her belly.

She leaned into him, groaning deep in her throat as she held his face, surrendering herself to the man she loved.

CHAPTER 26

A low sexy hum vibrated from River's chest, and it had every part of Jackson's body hardening. In one swift move, he lifted her into his arms and pressed her against the shower cubicle wall.

He needed to touch her, kiss her. He needed the reminder that there was still good in the world. Good in *him*.

Everything, from the fight last night—where every hit had felt like a knockout, where he'd felt eyes on him the entire evening—to this morning, hearing his dad confirm he'd never wanted him and his claim that they were the same…it had every part of him revolting. Souring. Churning.

He hadn't contacted River because he couldn't. Because his insides felt raw and he'd needed to breathe.

But now, seeing this woman, he realized she was his air. His goodness. She was every part of him that remained pure.

His hand lowered to her breast, cupping her, grazing her peak with the pad of his thumb.

Her cry was like gas on flames.

He tore his mouth from her lips, trailing kisses down her

cheek, her neck. There wasn't an inch of her that he didn't want to graze. Taste. Consume.

With desperate hands, he wrenched off her top, then her bra. There were too many barriers, and he wanted none. He wanted her against him, skin to skin.

When her breasts bounced free, blood roared between his ears, deafening him. He didn't know if the guys were still in the studio, and he didn't care. All he cared about was her and this moment and the impossible weight that she lifted off his chest.

Lowering his head, he took one light pink bud into his mouth and sucked.

River's cry pierced through the room, washing out the sound of water hitting tiles. Her back arched off the wall, pressing her breast farther into his mouth. She tasted like every sweet fucking treat he'd ever consumed. His body throbbed and burned for her. Craved her like he'd been having withdrawals.

He switched to her other breast, and there it was again. The hypnotic moan pulled from her throat. The dancing of her fingers along his shoulders and his back, warmed the chill that had taken root under his skin.

He kept her pinned against the wall with his hips as his hands went to her jeans, undoing the button and pushing down the zipper.

"Tell me you want this," he growled, unable to smooth his voice.

"I want—" Her voice cut off when he dipped his hand into her panties and swiped against her clit. This time her cry was louder, and he watched the flurry of emotions wash over her face.

"You," she finished with a gasp. "I want you!"

He swiped again, rubbing his thumb against her nub. Her breathing labored. Her body began to writhe in his arms. A finger went to her entrance, and slowly, he pushed inside.

Another cry. Another bit of ice thawing in his chest.

"Jackson."

He began to move his finger in and out of her, his thumb continuing to torture her clit. When he pushed a second finger inside, he paired it with the latching of his mouth on her neck. He nibbled and sucked.

There was a flurry of whimpers. Of frantic moans. Her limbs were almost shaking, and all he wanted was more. More of everything she was and had.

When he drew his head back to look at her, his heart clenched. Everything inside that had been eating away at him, haunting him…she soothed it. Calmed it. Made him feel human again.

"Now, Jackson!"

He lowered her to her feet for a second. She quickly toed off her shoes while he tugged down her jeans and panties. Then he was lifting her again. Positioning himself at her entrance.

"I don't fucking deserve you, Rae. But I'm taking you anyway."

"You do. I love you."

He sank inside, his temple touching hers when he was all the way in.

He paused, trying to calm the wild need that threatened to consume him. Her soft hand touched his cheek, and a gentle kiss pressed to the other. And there it was. The last remnants of his anger, his frustration at the world, it all faded.

He rocked out before pushing back in. Their temples remained together, the fingers of her uninjured hand shifting to the back of his head, clutching his hair. He rocked back and forth again, watching the scrunching of her eyes. The feverish need rippled over her face.

He held her tightly as he continued to thrust.

How the hell had he had the strength to stay away from her for so long? To keep that distance.

Never again.

When her head fell to the side, he buried his face in her neck, tasting her once again. His hand rose to her breast, holding her, massaging the light weight.

The soft moans and cries releasing from her throat urged him to move faster. To thrust harder.

"Jackson..."

Fuck, he loved hearing his name on her lips.

She was tugging his hair now. Nails of her other hand stinging his shoulder. Her feet dug into his back, pulling him closer on each thrust.

He pinched her nipple with his thumb and forefinger. She arched once more. He thrummed her tight peak again and again, continuing to thrust.

Suddenly, she screamed, her body shattering in his arms and around his length. He continued to rock into her as she convulsed, wanting to stretch out the moment. Make it last every second he could.

Lifting his head, he took her lips once more. The second he tasted her, he broke, his body tensing and seizing.

This woman...she both saved and destroyed him.

RIVER LEANED her head back against the car seat, loving the heat of Jackson's hand on her leg as he drove. The rest of today had been pretty smack bang-on perfect.

After the amazing shower sex, they'd dropped by her house to grab some dry clothes and her camera, and then they'd spent the afternoon together. First grabbing food, then taking it to her favorite nature spot. And the best part, they hadn't spoken a word about the club or the fights. They'd given themselves permission to have a day off.

God, she could spend every day for the rest of her life like she had today. And she loved that the anger and anxiety and frustration that had been on Jackson's face was all but wiped clean now. She smiled at the sight.

But the second the smile appeared, it faltered.

Guilt swamped her. Guilt that she was happy and smiling while Ryker was missing. Guilt that he hadn't been on her mind every waking second of the day.

Was it fair for her to find happiness while he was gone?

No. No, it wasn't.

Jackson's fingers squeezed her thigh. "What are you thinking about?"

Had the man seen something on her face? "That life isn't fair."

He frowned, taking his gaze off the road to look at her for a second. "You're right, it's not. But what made you think about that?"

"You're just…amazing. I love where we are and everything our relationship has become. But I hate that we've only found each other because something terrible happened to Ryker."

She didn't miss the slight tightening of his hand on her leg. "Ryker would be happy for us."

"How do you know?"

A ghost of a smile tugged at his lips. "Every so often, during a drunken night or when we were delirious with exhaustion on a mission, your name would come up. I'd say something about you being beautiful or frustrating or too damn perfect."

Her cheeks heated at his words, the smile threatening to return to her lips. "Really?"

"Yep. Ryker saw right through my shit. He'd mutter under his breath about us both being too stubborn for our own goods, and I'd pretend I didn't hear him."

River threw her head back and laughed. That sounded like Ryker.

"There was one night in particular when we were both dead tired, grumpy as all hell after a twenty-four-hour stakeout. He turned to me and said, 'You'd better work your shit out before it's too late.'"

River frowned.

"He didn't say your name, but we both knew what he was talking about." Jackson turned to look at her. "He'd be happy for us, River."

For a moment, tears pressed at her eyes. It had been so long since she'd spoken to her brother. So much longer than any other point in her life, even during his missions. But when Jackson talked about him, she could almost trick herself into thinking he was here. That he was waiting for them at home. Within reaching distance.

"How's your finger?" he asked quietly.

"It's fine. I don't even feel the stitches."

By his expression, she could tell he didn't believe her. She turned her hand over, carefully lacing her fingers through his. They drove in silence for a few minutes. When she eventually opened her mouth to say something, she stopped at the frown on Jackson's face. His gaze was alternating between the road and the rearview mirror.

River started to look behind them but stopped at the gentle tightening of Jackson's fingers. "Don't turn around," he said quietly. "I think we have a tail."

"What?" The fine hairs on her arms stood on end. "Can you see them?"

"Yes."

He took his hand from hers to grab the wheel and sped up the car.

She bit her bottom lip. It was taking everything in her not to look behind them. "What are you going to do?"

"Lose them and call the guys." He grabbed his phone, then Declan was on loudspeaker.

"Jackson, everything okay?"

"I have a tail."

There was a short pause. "Where are you?"

"Berkley Street, near River's house. I'm going to lose him. I want you and Cole to meet me at her place, just in case."

River sucked in a sharp breath. Just in case what? The tail beat them there? Had friends waiting for them?

"Done."

"Thanks." Jackson hung up the phone.

"Do you think you'll be able to lose him?" she asked quietly.

The next corner was sharp. He grabbed her arm moments before she slammed into the door.

"I know these streets like the back of my hand, so chances are good." His gaze shot to the rearview mirror once again.

She gave a small nod.

It didn't take him long. A few minutes of sharp turns and driving above the speed limit and Jackson slowed, glancing behind them once again.

"Is he gone?" she asked.

He gave a sharp nod.

"Do you think he was with Mickey or Elijah?"

"I don't know." A thick tension tangled in his words.

Okay, her perfect bubble of a day was over. "Did you learn something about Ryker or the club last night?"

She hadn't wanted to ask earlier, but she may as well now.

"Let's talk about it inside."

That was all Jackson said before he pulled up outside her house. He parked on the street, and a second later, Declan and Cole pulled up behind them.

Jackson grabbed a gun from beneath his seat before climbing out. Declan and Cole were already on the sidewalk.

River swallowed. All three men were glancing around the street, the house, like they were waiting for someone to jump out with guns of their own.

The house was dark when Declan opened it, he and Cole

stepping inside first. She remained on the porch, Jackson's hand holding hers.

Declan flicked a light on—and River's heart jumped into her throat. Because even from outside, she could see them.

It was Jackson who spoke first. "What the fuck are you doing here, Kenny...and who's your friend?"

CHAPTER 27

*J*ackson was seconds from pulling River back to the car when another vehicle parked on the road. *Fuck.* It was the same one that had been tailing them.

Two men stepped out.

Jackson aimed his gun at the men on the street while Cole and Declan aimed at Kenny and the other man in River's house.

"Put the guns down and come inside," Kenny said from his position behind her couch. When Jackson briefly met his gaze, he added, "We're the good guys, Jackson."

The men from the street stopped several feet away. None of them pulled a weapon, and none of them seemed particularly concerned about the guns aimed at them.

"Please," an unfamiliar voice said.

Jackson swung his attention to the man sitting on the couch. A man he'd never seen before. He didn't recognize the guys on the street, either. Certainly not from the club. In fact, they looked too clean-cut for that place. The guy on the couch wore a suit and glasses, and the two guys in the front yard were also wearing suits. If anything, they looked more like law officials. Not quite cops, but something else.

Jackson exchanged a look with Dec and Cole. Both were waiting for his decision.

He took River's hand, tugging her inside, but keeping his gun drawn. He positioned River behind his team as the two new men stepped inside the house, closing the door behind them.

"If you're such good guys, why the hell did you break into River's house? Why were you sitting here in the dark, waiting for us?"

"Because there are people who can't see me here," Kenny said, his arms crossed. "It's for my safety as much as yours."

That had Jackson pausing. "What are you talking about?"

His gaze flicked to the guns, then back to him. "Drop the guns and we can talk."

"Like hell we will. How about you tell us who the fuck you are and we'll *consider* dropping the guns."

Kenny sighed. "Jackson—"

"We work for Homeland Security Investigations," the man on the couch said, interrupting Kenny. "I'm a case agent, Agent Dwight Widow. Kenny's real name is Todd Pierce. He's an undercover operative. The guys by the door are Alan and Kevin."

"Case?" Declan asked.

"Everything we say tonight is confidential. It doesn't leave this room. Do you all understand?"

Again, Jackson and his team shared glances before nodding.

Widow leaned forward. "We're the primary law enforcement agency responsible for international smuggling operations. We work to disrupt and dismantle illegal export of weapons, so they're not used to commit acts of violence here or abroad."

River took a step closer to Jackson's side. Immediately, his fingers tightened around her arm, on the verge of pulling her straight back behind him.

"Export of weapons?" River asked.

"We've known for a while that a large-scale gun trafficking

organization is being run out of Trinity Nightclub, and that the guns are being trafficked into high-crime areas in Canada."

Exactly what his father had told him that morning.

"You may have heard of Elijah," the guy continued. "He's the brains of the operation. His men have been recruiting spectators from the cage fights to buy the guns through straw purchases. A straw purchase is when someone purchases a firearm for someone else who can't legally buy one of their own or doesn't want the paper trail attached to the sale."

The agent's eyes flicked between Jackson and his team. "The firearms are driven over the border and the money comes back in the kegs. Unfortunately, Canada is one of the biggest recipients of US firearms, and those guns are used in some of the worst crimes in the country."

"I've been undercover for about a year," Todd, the man they'd known as Kenny, added. "When we discovered the operation was being run from the basement during the cage fights, I wasn't able to get close enough. Mickey keeps me in the bar. After Ryker started in the ring, we did a background check and learned that he was former special forces."

River jolted beside him. "Was he working with you?"

Todd met her gaze. "Yes. He was happy to help. And he was able to get what we couldn't by asking a lot of questions. He even got close to a woman who knew a lot of the ins and outs of the operation."

"Angel..." River whispered.

Todd dipped his head. "Yes."

Agent Widow shifted in his seat. "It's a violation of federal law for an individual to provide a gun to someone while having reasonable cause to believe they're prohibited from possession. Fortunately, Ryker was able to identify the leader and all men involved. He was also able to identify many of those responsible for the straw purchases, who've broken the law by making false statements in connection with their gun sales."

He paused. "In other words, we needed to know all the players, and obtain as much evidence as possible for prosecution and asset seizure. Ryker made that happen."

"So why are you here telling us this?" Cole asked. "Why aren't you out there arresting them?"

The agent cleared his throat. "They move the trucks every week to throw anyone off, while the firearms are only transported once a month. We never know when. But we've finally learned a shipment of guns are scheduled to leave the club next Friday night. That's when we'll enact the sting." He stood. "And we're telling you this because you all need to stop. Stop engaging with the club. Stop questioning Brian. And stop digging. Leave it to us to bring these people down. We can't afford for this to go wrong. Not after a year of planning."

Todd nodded. "There's already a lot of tension between Mickey and Elijah over you being allowed in the ring, Jackson. Elijah's been growing more brazen, threatening the whole operation. Mickey doesn't like it. He knew letting you in, someone close to Ryker, would be a statement of sorts. We can't afford for Elijah to do something reckless."

River inched closer to Jackson. "Would us getting out of town be safer?"

Todd and Agent Widow shared a look. Widow was the first to speak. "It would. But it would also make them suspicious. Possibly make them deviate from their plan. We don't think they knew that Ryker was working with law enforcement, just that he knew too much and was former military. We don't want them finding out about us."

"So where is he?"

The agent glanced at River. "Who?"

"Ryker. He was working with you, then he was compromised, so you needed everyone to believe he was dead for his own safety. That's how it went, right?"

Todd swallowed, and the agent frowned, both appearing uncomfortable.

Jackson's stomach dipped, knowing what was coming but unable to protect River from it.

Todd moved to the front of the couch. "River...Ryker's dead."

She shook her head. "No. I've seen him. *Twice*. This is the point where you confirm he's alive."

Todd's voice lowered as he shook his head. "I'm sorry. Your brother is gone."

CHAPTER 28

*J*ackson's gaze flicked to River as she rinsed the dishes. She'd barely said a word since everyone had left. Not while they'd gotten dinner ready. Not while they'd eaten.

The woman remained silent, in her head, and he had no idea how to reach her.

Setting the tea towel on the island, he moved behind her and wrapped his arms around her waist. Her entire body tensed, her hands stilling.

He lowered his head to her ear and spoke softly. "I'm sorry."

There was a beat of silence. It was heavy and painful and strained. "You don't need to say sorry. You didn't do anything."

He pressed a soft kiss just below her ear. "I know you were hoping—"

She pulled herself out of his arms, looking everywhere but at him. "I'm going to bed."

When she took a step away, he grabbed her arm, not wanting her to leave. Not like this. "River—"

The ringing of his phone cut off his next words. An exasperated breath rushed from his chest. He wanted to let it go to voicemail, but he was certain it was his team.

Slowly, he untangled his fingers, and River left the kitchen, her back rigid. There was the light thud of the bedroom door closing, then silence, bar the ringing phone.

Tugging the phone from his pocket, he wasn't surprised to see it was Declan. "Hey."

"Hey, brother. Just wanted to check on how you're both doing?"

"Been better. A round in the ring wouldn't be terrible right about now." He had enough pent-up energy that he could probably go ten rounds.

"Meet there tomorrow morning?"

"Depends how River's doing. I'll let you know."

"You got it, brother." There was a small pause. "Is she okay?"

Jackson's gaze flicked to her bedroom door again. "The second she saw them, she thought that was it. The moment everyone revealed Ryker was still alive."

She hadn't said the words out loud, but he knew.

Declan cursed softly down the line. "I wish she was right, that Todd had confirmed it was all a cover."

"Me too. I'm going to check on her. Talk tomorrow."

"Night."

He'd barely hung up when the bedroom door opened again, and River walked out. She wore a jacket over the T-shirt she'd had on all day, as if she was going out.

He was across the room in seconds, stepping between her and the door. "What are you doing?"

For the first time since Todd had left, she looked up and met his gaze. Her jaw was set, eyes steely. She was determined. But she was also desperate. The two emotions battled on her face.

"Ryker's alive—and I'm sick and tired of people telling me he isn't. I'm going to find him."

She tried to move around him, but he stepped to the side, blocking her way. "Where?"

"I don't know. I just need to go somewhere. Do something. I can't sit here another night not knowing where he is."

The woman clearly wasn't thinking straight. Emotions were clouding her judgment. She was a step away from teetering off the edge of devastation, and she was trying to save herself by hanging onto this belief of Ryker being alive.

"You're not going anywhere, River."

"Get out of my way."

She stepped the other way, but he mimicked the movement again. He reached out and took her shoulders in his grasp. "River, Ryker is *gone*. It's gut-wrenching and soul-destroying, but it's true. And it's something you need to accept."

She took a step back, wrenching herself from his grasp. There was a wild look in her eyes now. "People need to *stop* saying that! I would feel it if my brother was dead, and he's not!"

She reached beside him for her car keys, but he snapped them up before she could touch them.

Her eyes narrowed and she held out her hand. "Give them to me."

"I can't do that, Rae."

For a moment, she stood there panting, anger reddening her cheeks. "Fine, I'll walk."

She tried to step around him yet again, but this time he swung her over his shoulder and walked back to the bedroom.

River kicked and writhed, pounding on his back. "Let me go! I need to find him!"

Jackson dropped her onto the mattress as gently as he could. She was on her feet in seconds.

"River, you can fight me all night, but I'll just keep bringing you back here. There's not a chance in hell I'm letting you leave this house. Not tonight. And not on your own until the arrests have been made."

Her chest heaved up and down. This was it. All the emotion she hadn't displayed at the funeral was about to unleash. She was going to shatter. And he couldn't save her.

He took a small step closer, his hands going to her arms and his voice softening. "You're not thinking clearly right now. And I'm sorry. So damn sorry that I can't take away your pain and grief. But I also can't let you put yourself in danger."

She shoved at his chest, but he didn't move.

"River—"

"Get out! Get the hell out of my bedroom! *Now.*"

He shot a quick look to the windows, knowing they were sealed and alarmed. If she tried to open them, he'd be notified.

Christ, he hated this. All he wanted to do was pull her close and let her lean on him. Find some sort of comfort in him.

Instead, he took a slow step back, hands dropping. Then he turned and left the room, each step feeling heavier than the last.

THE SECOND THE door closed behind Jackson, the pain in her chest rippled and expanded. A part of her wanted to call him back, but another part didn't. Couldn't. It was this strange in-between of needing to be alone but also wanting Jackson's comfort and strength and warmth.

Turning, she walked into the bathroom, closing the door behind her.

Her skin was like ice, her hands trembling as they grabbed the edge of the counter. She couldn't breathe. It was like someone had a hand around her throat, squeezing and suffocating her.

Dead. Ryker was *dead*.

That's what Jackson had been telling her all along. What her parents had been telling her. And now, damn Homeland Security was telling her.

The second they'd revealed who they were today, hope had

erupted in her chest. A hope that she'd so desperately needed. Hope that this was it. The moment her brother was proven to be alive. She'd almost expected him to walk into the room and reveal himself.

She looked up at her reflection, but the shape blurred from her tears.

Had he *really* just been in her head? The outline of him in his bedroom? The shadowy shape of him saving her outside the boxing gym? Had she wanted to see him so badly that she'd made it all up?

Her breath cut off in her throat and nausea rose in her stomach.

Dead. The word was on repeat in her head, cutting into her chest, her heart, like a dagger. She pressed a hand there, not entirely sure whether she was trying to dull the ache or hold herself together.

He didn't feel gone. He felt seconds from walking back into this house. Talking to her. Arguing about something petty and stupid that they'd both laugh about later.

Her feet itched to leave. To get out. Every part of her vibrated with the need to be out there looking for him.

But she couldn't get out. Jackson was both her protector and her captor.

Tugging her phone from her pocket, she lowered to the edge of the bathtub and, with shaking fingers, typed a text to Michele.

River: I can't stand the thought of him being gone, Chele. It hurts too bad.

The second she hit send, her eyes shuttered. Waiting. Needing Michele to tell her she believed he was alive.

The phone vibrated in her hands.

Michele: Oh, honey, I'm sorry. I know it hurts today, but I swear to you, every day it will hurt a little less, until the ache in your chest just becomes something you learn to live with.

Tears flooded River's eyes. It wasn't the message she'd been hoping for, but then, she knew it wouldn't be. Knew that no one on this earth believed he was alive except her.

Because he was gone, wasn't he?

Really gone.

Slowly, she slid down the side of the tub to the cold tiled floor. Tears flooded her eyes and her chest cracked wide open as she slowly let the ugly reality that everyone had been pushing on her sink in.

She was never going to see, speak to, or touch Ryker again.

The phone slipped from her fingers, and she tucked her head into her knees. Then she let the tears wash down her cheeks without hesitation. She let the pain in her chest flutter and swell and cripple her.

River cried for the brother she thought she'd never lose in her lifetime. The brother she'd never had a chance to say goodbye. The brother she loved like a best friend.

The tears didn't stop. They soaked her cheeks, trickling down her arms.

"Rae, honey…can I come in?"

She barely heard Jackson's words. Maybe it was because her pain was so loud. Or maybe it was because her body, her chest, her heart…it was all being torn in two. Shredded. And that was all she could focus on. All she could hear and see.

She was vaguely aware of the jiggling of the doorknob. A minute passed. Then another. Each one had the tears falling faster. She didn't remember locking the door, but maybe she had.

A second later, it opened, and Jackson was in front of her, hand going to the back of her head. "Baby…"

"I don't know how to live without him in this world." The words squeezed from her chest.

They'd been separated a lot, but she'd always known he was alive. That he existed in the world and the time would come when she'd see him again.

Jackson shifted beside her, immediately sliding an arm behind her back and another under her knees before lifting her onto his lap.

This time, she didn't push the man away. She couldn't. She leaned into his warmth and ducked her head into his neck. He felt like a lifeline. The only thing keeping her from breaking apart completely.

With trembling fingers, she grabbed onto his shirt, wanting him to be closer even while knowing this was it. This was all he could give.

His hand began to move in slow, circular strokes across her back. She focused on that, praying the touch would never end. That his touch would dull the pain until eventually, she could breathe again.

CHAPTER 29

*J*ackson squeezed River's hand as he drove them to the gym in her car. "How are you feeling?"

He knew she hadn't slept well last night, and any sleep she *had* gotten was restless. He'd offered for them to stay home today—hell, they'd stay home for as long as she needed if it helped her heal.

River said no. She wanted to be out of the house and focusing on something other than Ryker.

"Still confused."

Jackson frowned. He'd been expecting her to name a million different emotions, but confusion wasn't one of them. "Confused?"

There was a brief pause. "I just…I keep replaying those moments I saw him in my head. In his darkened bedroom the night he…died. Outside the boxing club when that guy attacked me."

Jackson's muscles tensed at the reminder.

She shook her head. "I was just so sure it was him. And even now, I just…I remember those moments, and it's still him, every time."

He swiped her thigh with his thumb. "Sometimes our mind tricks us into seeing what we want to see to protect us from the truth."

They still didn't know for sure who had stopped her attacker outside the gym. But they did know it wasn't Ryker.

Her voice lowered. "Yeah. My mind must be really good at that."

Jackson shot a quick glance toward her then looked back to the road. "On our last mission, after we were attacked and had to find our way back to the US military base, we weren't in good shape. We were all injured and tired. We had no food or water left. The trip was slower than it should have been because we were trying to remain out of sight."

Another swipe of her thigh. "There were moments I thought we wouldn't make it, not while carrying Dec and Cole. My body was screaming at me to stop. Convincing me there was no end in sight. That's when I forced my mind to go black. The mind is powerful, and I knew how easy it would be for my mind to convince me I was done."

Her hand went to the top of his, and she started running a finger along his veins. That simple touch had his skin burning.

"I wish Ryker had spoken to me about that mission."

"Ryker was never a talker when it came to pain. He'd internalize that stuff. Some people get loud when life gets hard. Others turn inward."

She gave a small nod. "You're right. He internalized it until he found the club. Then he used that ring as a way to release it all. The anger. The helplessness. The guilt. Is the ring a release like that for you too?"

"Yes. It's an outlet. A relatively safe place to let everything out. It also allows you to switch off from the outside world." He lifted a shoulder. "The hit of endorphins isn't terrible, either."

She nodded almost absently. Her finger started tracing the

veins up his arm. "I hope the arrests go to plan. I hope they get locked away for the rest of their lives."

He gave her leg another squeeze. "I'm sure they have it covered."

He parked outside the gym, moved around to her side, and held her door open as she got out. Then he took her hand, almost unable not to touch her.

Declan and Cole were already inside the ring. Declan's fist flew at Cole but he dodged it, stepping aside quickly. Cole was more of a defensive fighter, whereas Declan was a dominant aggressor. They were both dangerous. One just as lethal as the other.

The next punch was thrown by Cole. Declan ducked to avoid the hit, then almost immediately grabbed Cole around the middle, sending them both to the floor.

The two big men grappled for a few minutes. It wasn't until Declan jumped to his feet and stepped back that they both stopped.

Cole shook his head, and rose to his feet slowly. "I could have had you."

Declan scoffed. "Sure."

Cole ducked below the rope, grabbed his towel, and glanced at Jackson and River. "Morning, guys."

Jackson dipped his head. "Morning. Been here long?"

Declan scoffed. "Long enough for me to beat his ass more than once."

Cole shook his head. "You wish."

Jackson tugged his shirt over his head, meeting Declan's gaze. "My turn."

At the touch of River's hand on his arm, he turned. "I might pop out and grab some coffees."

"I'll go with you," Cole said, grabbing his shirt and tugging it over his head.

"Double shot for me," Declan called from the ring.

Jackson pressed a kiss to her lips before handing her the keys. "Don't take long."

A small smile touched her lips. It was her first all morning, and it had a bit of the tension in his body releasing.

The second they left, Jackson stepped into the ring. "You need a break?"

Declan raised a brow. "No. You need to warm up?"

"No."

~

"How are you doing?" Cole asked. "And don't give me some bullshit answer about being fine."

River leaned back in her seat as Cole drove to the Penguin Café. "I'm not doing fine. I feel like I need help just breathing right now. When I woke up this morning, all I wanted to do was forget."

He nodded. "I get that. I lost my father when I was a teenager. He was my best friend. It hurt like hell."

River frowned, studying the man. "How did you get through it?"

"I forced the breaths to flow in and out of my chest. I made myself get through each day, one at a time. And eventually, I learned to live with the pain."

"That's what Chele said. That one day I'd learn to live with it."

The problem was, she didn't want to live with the pain. She wanted to flick herself back to a few months ago. To a time when she didn't know the torture of losing her only sibling.

"I'm sorry about your dad," she said quietly.

Cole dipped his head. "Thank you. I was lucky to have had him for sixteen years. Others aren't so lucky."

Others being Jackson. Cole didn't need to say his name for River to hear it.

When the sun glared into her eyes, she pulled the sun visor

down, and immediately her attention went to her reflection in the small mirror.

Yep, just about what I expected you to look like, River. A mess.

She'd barely slept last night, and it was written all over her face. The circles under her eyes were dark. Her skin was pale.

Sick. That's what she looked like.

Sucking in a deep breath, River was just glancing back to the road when she noticed the muscles in Cole's arms flex. His hands tightened around the steering wheel.

"What is it?" she asked.

"That truck a few cars up…" River glanced through the windshield, spotting the truck immediately. "It's the one from Mickey's bar."

River's lips slid open. "Is it supposed to be on the road? I thought the next shipment was Friday?"

"I don't know." He grabbed his phone, pressing a button before putting the call on speaker.

"Agent Widow speaking."

"This is Cole Matthews. I'm driving through Lindeman and I can see the truck Elijah's been using up ahead."

A pause. Then Dwight cursed. "Shit! I need you to follow it in case they're moving early. I'll trace your call and come to you."

The muscles in Cole's arms tightened further, and he shot a quick look at River.

"I'll be okay," she said quietly, knowing she was the one he was worried about.

Cole continued to tail the truck, always remaining at least a car behind. River quickly pulled out her phone and sent a text to Jackson.

River: Cole spotted the truck. Agent Widow asked us to follow.

She waited for Jackson's response. Her phone just started to vibrate with an incoming call when Cole turned a corner.

The truck was right there, stopped in the middle of the road.

Cole slammed his foot on the brake and wrenched the wheel. The tires squealed as the car slid sideways.

Suddenly, the back of the truck opened, and four men jumped out, all armed.

At the sound of guns firing, Cole's hand shot to her head, pushing her down. He cursed loudly. "They're shooting the tires."

He reached beneath the driver's seat, pulling out a gun Jackson must have stored there. "It's not safe in here." He tugged off his seat belt then reached across for hers. "Hide behind the car. Don't move unless I tell you to."

River's mouth opened and closed a couple of times before she forced her voice to work. "Okay."

Cole reached across her body, opening the door, and pushing her out on the side facing away from the shooters. She just about fell on her ass. *Would* have fallen on her ass if Cole hadn't grabbed her.

They both ducked behind the car, and she could hear footsteps.

"That side street to our right," he whispered, gun drawn to his chest. "If I tell you to run, that's where you go."

She didn't have a chance to say a word before Cole rose, pointed his gun, and was shooting. River heard a grunt then the thud of a body hitting the road. Cole ducked again. He waited a few seconds before rising once more, another gunshot fired. Another body down.

"Two to go, but more in the cab of the truck," Cole said as he slid behind the car yet again. "They haven't gotten out yet."

Bullets peppered the metal of her car. She sucked in deep breaths, her fingers shaking.

The next time Cole rose, he swore loudly before lunging and grabbing a guy. Punches flew.

River's mouth opened to scream when she was suddenly grabbed from behind and tugged to her feet, a gun pressed to her head. She tried to fight, but she was pulled backward, her body used as a shield in case Cole decided to shoot. She kicked and punched at the guy behind her, but it did nothing.

When he reached the truck, dragging her up and inside, she fought harder.

What the hell did he plan to do? Use her as a shield before shoving her out when they started driving again? Take her with them? *Kill* her?

The guy was just stepping backward when Cole snapped the neck of the man he was fighting and quickly snatched a gun from the ground.

For a split second, the man behind her trembled, then Cole shot him dead, the bullet narrowly missing River's head.

She took a step forward to jump out of the truck and run back to him when new gunshots sounded from either side of the vehicle.

Oh God. The men in the cab.

Cole ducked behind the car. When footsteps sounded from both sides of the cargo hold, growing closer to the back of the truck, River panicked, knowing they'd shoot if they saw her. She had to hide. The only place to go was behind the kegs.

Sucking in a sharp breath, she quickly moved to the back and crouched behind the tallest kegs. Sweat beaded her forehead. More gunshots fired, and she almost cried out at the possibility that Cole had been shot.

Suddenly, the sound of police sirens grew near.

"Leave him!" someone shouted.

River gasped, ducking lower. She heard two men jump into the back and the door being pulled down. Then the truck was moving.

For a moment, there was only the sound of heavy breathing. Then a man spoke.

"Fuck!"

"No shit."

River tensed. She knew that second voice. It was Jackson's father, Brian.

"The guy killed four of our fucking men! I wanna go back and bury him and that bitch!"

River's eyes shuttered. They didn't know she was here. And it sounded like Cole was alive.

"I think we need to focus on what we're going to say to Elijah," Brian said. "The guy's going to murder us."

CHAPTER 30

*J*ackson caught Declan in the jaw with his fist. The man threw a punch straight back. The hit grazed the side of his head.

They danced around each other, biding their time, each deciding when to strike next, and where.

Declan was just inching closer when Jackson's phone beeped with a message from the desk. Declan stopped, a smile stretching his lips. "Lucky."

Jackson scoffed, slipping below the rope. "Lucky for you. You were seconds from getting your ass handed to you."

Declan laughed. "You keep thinking that."

Jackson lifted his phone and clicked into the message. A chill slithered down his spine.

River: Cole spotted the truck. Agent Widow asked us to follow.

A curse escaped his lips and then Declan was beside him. "What is it?"

"Cole and River spotted Elijah's truck." Jackson lifted his phone to his ear, calling River. When she didn't answer, his fear instantly spiked, and he started moving, grabbing the keys to Declan's rental from on top of the man's bag on the way out.

Declan was right behind him. He tried Cole, but the call did exactly the same thing.

"Shit, neither of them are answering."

He slid behind the wheel, and Declan lowered into the passenger side. Jackson started driving as Declan called the agent. When he didn't answer, he tried Todd. Both men had given them their numbers before leaving last night.

Todd answered on the first ring.

"They're at the end of Raider Street," he said quickly, the sound of a car engine growling in the background. "They'd just turned off Malloy Street when they stopped."

Jackson's heart crashed against his ribs. "Stopped? Why the hell would they stop?"

"I don't know. We haven't arrived yet. Police were called after gunshots were heard."

Todd's words had Jackson's entire world grinding to a stop. He pressed his foot harder on the gas.

Declan pulled guns from their hiding places in the car. He checked that they were fully loaded before handing one to Jackson.

They were almost to Raider Street when the sirens registered. Even that sound had his heart jackhammering into his throat.

The first thing Jackson saw when they turned the corner was River's car. Bullet holes dented every inch of the metal. Every window was shattered.

He'd barely stopped the car before jumping out. The police had also arrived, two of them already beside the car talking to Cole.

Jackson scanned the road, his heart rate tripling. She wasn't there. Had she run somewhere? Was she hiding?

When he looked back at Cole, their gazes clashed—and before any words were spoken, Jackson knew.

"A guy grabbed her and dragged her into the truck," he said, ignoring the police, all his attention on Jackson. "I shot the guy, but people got out of the cab, so she hid behind the kegs."

Jackson shook his head. "*No.*"

"She was boxed in. It was her only choice."

It all stopped. His heart. His breath. His world.

RIVER'S HEART was racing as the truck moved. Her back ached from hunching into a ball behind the kegs. With her head down, she kept her breaths silent.

There was a small light, like one of the guys was using his phone flashlight.

"I can't believe he fucking killed them. All four of them!"

"No shit. I didn't get out because I figured four against one meant the asshole had no chance."

At the sound of a phone ringing, River almost jolted, scared for a moment it was hers. Then she heard Brian speak.

"Fuck. It's Elijah."

The other guy cursed. "He knows."

"How could he?" Brian sucked in a loud breath. "Elijah—"

River heard a loud, angry voice on the phone. It was too muffled and far away to hear exact words, but she heard the fury.

"I know but—"

More words.

When Brian spoke again, his response was clipped, an air of frustration in his voice. "Got it."

A beat of silence passed.

"What did he say?" the second voice asked.

"He knows what happened. We're meeting at the usual spot."

The second guy cursed again. "Would he have preferred we just let the asshole follow us until the cops caught up?"

At the feel of her phone vibrating in her pocket, her heart

catapulted into her throat. The paralyzing fear had almost caused her to forget that she still had her cell at all.

"Did you hear that?" Brian asked.

River bit her bottom lip and scrunched her eyes. Her heart was hammering in her chest as she said a silent prayer that they wouldn't get up and look.

"I didn't hear shit. I'm too busy worrying about Elijah. He's been fucking unstable lately."

The air slowly eased from her chest. Slowly, quietly, she tugged the cell from her pocket, and changed the settings so it wouldn't vibrate again. She also turned the brightness as low as she could.

Brian grumbled. "I know."

As Brian and the other guy continued to talk, River fiddled with her phone, opening her messaging app. The second she saw who it was, tears pressed at her eyes.

Jackson: Where are you? Are you okay?

The small flutter of connection to Jackson, to safety, had her heart contracting in her chest.

With trembling fingers, she quickly typed a response.

River: I'm hiding behind kegs in the truck. They don't know I'm here. Your father's in the back with another guy. We're driving to Elijah.

There was barely a pause before he replied.

Jackson: We're gonna find you. If I call, can you answer and put it on mute? Then we can trace your location. I'll make sure it's silent on my end.

The idea had her stomach cramping. But he was right. It was the best way for him to track her.

River: Okay.

When the call came through, her breath caught, because even though Jackson had said his end would be silent, there was still a paralyzing fear that something would go wrong. That the call would expose her.

Ignoring the pitter-patter of her heart crashing against her ribs, she hit answer, immediately turning the volume off so no sound came through to her, just as extra protection.

Jackson: We're tracking your location now. Hold tight, baby. I love you. And I'm going to come get you.

Some of the anxiety eased in her chest. Jackson knew where she was. If there was anyone in the world she trusted to get her out of this, it was him.

They only drove for another couple minutes before the truck started bouncing. Almost like they were on a dirt road.

When the truck came to a stop, she clenched her fists to ease the trembling. Light filtered into the space as the cargo door opened.

"Elijah isn't here yet," the second guy said.

"Good. Let's do a quick gun check. Make sure they're all here."

The blood drained from River's face—then she heard the men move toward her.

There was no way they'd miss her. The second one of them came over, she'd be spotted.

She slid her phone inside her top, between her bra and chest. She needed it on as long as possible. She needed the connection to Jackson to remain and she needed him to hear whatever came next.

She'd barely lowered her hand again when she saw him. Brian. Standing over her and looking ten times larger than normal.

The second their gazes clashed, his mouth dropped open. For a moment, there was silence. Like the guy didn't know what to do.

Then the second man came up beside him.

"Am I doing this by my fucking se—" He stopped. "What the *fuck?*"

The guy reached down and strong fingers latched into her

hair, tugging her up. River scrambled to get to her feet as pain tore at her scalp. The guy tugged her forward, around the kegs.

"Where the fuck did you come from?" he growled.

When she didn't answer straight away, he yanked her closer. Her eyes watered at the pain.

"I asked you a question, bitch!"

Before she could answer, the sound of a car pulling up had everyone's gazes shooting toward the open back door.

"Goddammit. That's him."

The man tugged her to the edge of the cargo area. She saw the narrowed eyes of a third guy, the one who must have been driving, before she was thrown out of the back. Her knees hit the dirt hard, and pain spiraled up her thighs.

A car was just stopping beside them when she glanced up. Brian hadn't said a word. And if the grit of his teeth said anything, he wasn't happy.

The same guy who'd thrown her jumped down and wrapped his fingers around her upper arm, digging into flesh as he tugged her to her feet.

Three men stepped out of the car. Two of them were well-muscled and tall. The third, the more average-looking man, she assumed was Elijah.

River vaguely remembered them from Mickey's club. The guy she assumed to be Elijah walked toward them slowly. One of his guys followed, while the other headed for the trunk, opening it and tugging someone out.

River's lips separated, a gasp slipping from her throat.

Mickey...

His left eye was swollen shut and the entire left side of his face was bruised and battered. When the guy started to drag him forward, she noticed Mickey could barely hold himself up.

Elijah stopped, his eyes sliding down her body, assessing. River wanted to squirm under the scrutiny, but instead, she straightened, refusing to wither.

When Elijah finally looked to the guy holding her, the air she hadn't realized she'd been holding whooshed from her chest.

"What the fuck happened, and what is she doing here?" he asked.

There was a tense silence. And when she looked at the man beside her, she saw cold, stark fear.

"We noticed a tail. It was one of the Deltas, so we stopped to kill the guy. He got the upper hand, killing four of our men. Before we could finish him, we heard police. So we got out of there."

There was a slight narrowing of Elijah's eyes. When he looked at the truck, unease slithered up her spine.

"And what about *her*?" The guy's words were hard. They made her want to step back, away from the biggest threat here.

It was Brian who spoke this time. "She must have climbed into the truck while we were stopped."

A deadly fury washed over Elijah's face. It had the fine hairs on River's arms standing on end. He tilted his head toward one of his guys.

River's belly cramped, fear fogging her mind as the man approached her. Rough hands skimmed over every inch of her body. When they reached her chest, he dove a hand inside her top, tugging the phone out from where she'd slid it between her bra and chest.

He turned and delivered it to his boss.

If she'd thought the man looked angry before, that was nothing compared to now. He looked ready to kill.

He looked at the phone and pressed the end button before stomping on it.

She glanced to Brian and the other two guys. Their faces were white.

She barely had time to look back at Elijah before the man lifted a gun and shot all three of his thugs between the eyes.

The air cut off in her throat, silencing the scream that tried to escape. Dead. All of them. Including Jackson's father. She glanced down in shock, vaguely noticing the small specks of blood on her arms. Her top.

Elijah turned to his guys. "Move! We need to get as many guns out of the truck as possible and put them in the trunk. They'll be here any fucking second."

The two men got to work, and Elijah turned to Mickey.

"You should've listened when I told you those men weren't welcome in the club." He took a small step forward. "You chose the wrong fucking guy to have a pissing contest with."

The gun rose again, and River quickly shut her eyes before the next bullet was fired.

When she opened them again, Mickey was on the ground, eyes wide and blood pouring from the wound in his head.

She pressed a hand to her mouth as bile crawled up her throat.

When Elijah finally turned toward her, her entire body shook in terror. "Al." One of the men stopped. "Put her in the car. The money we lose on the firearms, we'll make up with her sale."

River lowered her hand slowly, breaths sawing in and out of her chest. "My sale?"

Elijah tucked his gun back into a holster, completely ignoring her.

River couldn't speak again. She could barely breathe. They were going to...what? Drive her over the border to Canada and sell her?

She shot a quick glance the way they'd come.

Nothing. Jackson would be too late.

Out of instinct, she tried to run, the logical part of her brain knowing there was nowhere to go, the terror-filled side needing to try.

Before she could take more than two steps, one of Elijah's guys grabbed her. Then there was a sharp pain to her skull that turned her world black.

CHAPTER 31

"They spotted Elijah's car as it was leaving an old farm."

Jackson sucked in a sharp breath. He'd been sharing River's location with Widow and Todd until the signal from her phone stopped abruptly. "Who's they? And did they stop him? Was River with him?"

Was she alive?

"Two cars with my guys in them," Todd responded quickly. There was the loud sound of an engine over the phone. It rivaled the sound of the car he, Declan, and Cole were in. "One car stopped at the farm, the other continued to tail Elijah. River isn't at the farm."

"Where's the car heading?"

"Toward Easton."

Declan fiddled with the GPS, making sure they were en route toward the town.

"They're driving fast, both of them. We've got local police cutting off all exit points, forcing them to drive through. But we might have trouble once they get to Easton."

"Why? What's in Easton?"

"A fair. People from all over the county are attending. The

good news is, their car will be blocked." Todd paused. "The bad news is, they'll likely run, and they could disappear in the crowd."

Declan pushed the car faster. "We're close."

"I'll keep sending location updates," Todd said.

"She's definitely in that car?" Jackson asked before Todd could hang up.

"She definitely wasn't back with the truck."

Meaning, she had to be with Elijah.

When Jackson hung up, he leaned his head back and closed his eyes. She had to be alive. Jackson couldn't lose her. He just couldn't.

"We'll get her back," Declan said, almost reading his mind.

Cole grabbed his shoulder from behind. "We're not stopping until we find her."

Jackson swallowed, glancing out the window.

When his phone rang next, and an unknown number popped up, he answered straight away. "Who is this?"

"Jackson…"

His entire body froze at the familiar voice. A voice he never thought he'd hear again.

RIVER'S EYES OPENED SLOWLY. Everything was black. For a moment, she thought it had something to do with the pounding in her head. Then she felt the coarse material against her cheeks. There was something over her head, blinding her. A hood maybe. And she was scrunched into a ball with a light vibration beneath her. She was in a car.

"I can't fucking lose him!"

The sound of a man's angry voice had her jolting. And even that small movement made pain shoot through her skull.

She was in the back of the vehicle, but not on the seat. She was on the floor. And even though she couldn't see, she knew the car was moving fast.

The events of the day came back to her in a wave that had her throat closing and nausea yet again sickening her gut at the memory of the men who had been shot dead.

"Shit. There are too many cars up ahead." It was a different voice this time. A voice also coming from the front. "Is this why the exits were closed? Because they knew we wouldn't be able to drive through? What the hell is this?"

Suddenly, the car lurched and her head bounced off something, the middle console maybe, causing her eyes to shutter in pain. She heard the impact of metal on metal, as if a car had hit them.

The men cursed.

"Even if the assholes don't crash us, we're gonna have to stop. There's nowhere to turn off."

The car started to slow. Before she could recover, they were hit again. This time, the men were even louder in their cursing, and she could feel that the driver had lost control. The squeal of the tires grinding against the road was loud, and she scrunched her eyes tight, bracing for impact.

The second the car crashed to a stop, River's head once again bashed against a hard surface. Pain shot through her skull like a hundred tiny daggers.

Suddenly, the bag was tugged from her head. She squinted her eyes, the combination of light and that last hit causing more pain in her head.

Strong fingers wrapped around her upper arm.

"Shoot the assholes," Elijah growled as the creak of a door sounded. "Call me when it's done."

Then she was being dragged from the car. The brightness blinded her, and loud music and voices drilled into her skull. She felt like she was in a daze. She knew she needed to try to stop the man from pulling her, to resist, but was barely able to think, let alone fight.

When the blast of gunshots echoed through the air, it was quickly followed by countless loud screams. The pounding steps of people running.

People ran past her, panicked, looking for shelter. Shoulders bashed into her own.

When the next person ran past, causing her to stumble, she started falling, only to be yanked to her feet again.

Then his voice was in her ear. "You fucking run or I put a bullet in your head. Got it?"

His words were obviously meant to scare her into obedience. They did the opposite. They pierced the fog that clouded her mind, reminding her that she was being pulled away from the crowds. Away from safety.

There were people running everywhere. In a crowd like this, it would be hard for anyone to spot her, but she had to try.

He tugged her forward again, but this time she pulled back, lowering her body for leverage and causing Elijah to stumble. He grunted before firming his grip and pulling her onto a quieter side street. Her body was thrown against a brick wall. Then he was crowding her, his fingers wrapping around her throat, cutting off her air.

"Don't fucking mess with me!" Elijah growled, his head lowering.

When he removed his hand, the air rushed back into her lungs, and her legs tried to cave, but he was already dragging her down the street again.

She sucked in deep, steadying breaths, trying to ward off the dizziness that was hedging her vision. Everything was a blur. Elijah. The path in front of her.

Still, she pressed her heels into the pavement. They both stumbled yet again, but she remained on her feet—just.

The man had barely turned when she raised her leg and kicked him as hard as she could in the knee.

His knee gave instantly, and he shouted in pain, his fingers untangling from her arm as he fell. She ran back the way they came. She got only steps away before a hand tangled in her hair, yanking her back.

More pain splintered through her skull.

Her body was shoved against a wall again, her cheekbone colliding with and scraping against the rough brick surface.

"What did I fucking say?"

She felt the sticky wetness of blood running down the side of her face. The throbbing in her head intensified, hazing her vision further.

When he pulled her back again, she wasn't sure if he was going to throw her against the wall once more or force her down the narrow street.

He did neither. Instead, he gasped sharply—then she was tugged roughly in front of him, the cold muzzle of a gun pressed to her head.

"*You...!*" he whispered.

River's vision was dim. She scrunched her eyes, trying to clear them, but all she could see was a blurry outline.

"How the fuck are you here—and where the fuck are my guys?"

Elijah took several steps back, dragging her with him.

"Your guys are dead."

River's world narrowed to pinpoint accuracy. The pain, the dizziness, it all faded at the sound of his voice.

"And I'm here to make sure you die, too."

Her breaths were coming out in jagged gasps. It couldn't be him—could it? Maybe she'd already passed out. Maybe she was hearing something that wasn't there.

The gun pressed harder to her head. It barely registered. She took two more blinks, and finally, she saw him clearly.

"Ryker…" she whispered.

This time when her vision blurred, it was due to tears. She blinked them away as fast as she could, desperate to keep him in her line of sight.

Ryker's gaze hit hers for a second, his eyes softening just a fraction, before sliding back to Elijah and hardening once again.

Even though she was hurting and tired and probably would have collapsed if she wasn't being held up, for the first time since the agents had left her home, she felt okay. Like her heart had reconnected to her body. Like she was finally whole again.

Ryker had his gun aimed at Elijah, and for every step the man took backward, Ryker took one forward.

"My guy drove you over a bridge! He *killed* you," Elijah growled.

"Only he didn't. I killed *him*. We just made you think I'd died, so you didn't look for me or come after my family."

She could feel the angry, panting breaths coming out of Elijah. "I'm gonna kill you, motherfucker!"

Suddenly, two police officers ran around the corner onto the street. Both looked young. Their guns were drawn, aimed at Elijah, and she could have sworn she saw a tremble in their hands.

She heard the frustrated growl from behind her. Then the gun moved away from her head—and she knew exactly who he was aiming for.

Before he could pull the trigger, River threw an elbow into Elijah's gut. His gun went off. There was the sound of bodies hitting the dirt, men diving to the ground.

Then Ryker was shouting. "Don't shoot!"

But it was too late. Two shots were fired from the direction of the police officers. Elijah roughly shoved her forward and one of those bullets caught her in the ribs.

She crumpled, pain stealing her breath. She was vaguely

aware of additional gunshots from both behind and in front of her, followed by Elijah's loud grunt.

There were footsteps—then she heard a different voice.

"River, talk to me! Rae!"

Jackson. Oh, God. Jackson was here. He'd come from behind them, shooting Elijah, while Ryker had shot him from the front.

Warm hands touched her cheeks. Her arm. There was pressure on her ribs, but the wound was oddly numb.

She closed her eyes, hearing Jackson but too tired to answer. A fuzziness was seeping through her mind.

"River! Don't you dare give up!"

A smile tugged at her lips at her brother's voice.

"I knew you were alive," she mumbled with lips she could barely work.

A breath brushed against her ear. "I am alive. And I need you to stay alive too. Don't give up on me, River."

She tried to nod but it didn't quite work. The fog was winning. And she could only pray that when she woke up, Ryker would still be there.

CHAPTER 32

"*Y*ou ever do that again and I'll kill you myself."

River heard Jackson's voice. It was quiet, like it came to her through a tunnel. She wanted to reach out and touch him. Tug him closer. But exhaustion and a murkiness in her head kept her still.

"I'm sorry." Her heart gave a giant thud at the sound of her brother's voice. "I wanted to reach out, I really did, but Widow and Todd insisted it was safer that no one knew until after the arrests."

Her chest ached. Alive. Ryker was alive. And he was *here*. She needed to wake up. See him with her own eyes.

"Theoretically, it was probably the right call," Jackson said quietly. "But you haven't been here. You didn't see what it did to her when they told her you were dead. She refused to believe it for so long."

There was a moment of silence, and even though her eyes were closed, she could feel its heaviness.

"I hate that," Ryker said softly. "I hate that her, my parents, and you guys all had to attend my funeral. They said it was the only way."

"Tell me about that night," Jackson said.

Again, River tried to open her eyes. She tried to lift her arm. But the exhaustion was insurmountable. In the back of her mind, she knew she was in the hospital. Knew that she must have drugs in her system to help her rest. And those drugs were trying to tug her under again. Trying to pull her away from the voices of the two men she loved most in the world. She hung on to those voices by a tiny thread.

Ryker sighed. "I knew something was wrong the second I stepped inside the club that night. There was this heavy energy. Elijah and his guys kept looking at me, and their stares were... intense. I had a rock in my stomach the entire time."

"They knew," Jackson said.

"It wasn't surprising. I'd gotten too close, and DHS were putting together their sting. I even had the opportunity to see the guns in the kegs and take pictures when no one was watching. Or at least, I thought no one was watching. That's why I went back to my room at River's the night I was declared dead. The phone I'd taken the photos on was in there. I never took it back to the club in case they checked me."

There was a brief pause before Ryker spoke again.

"So, I won my fight, got in my car and left straight away. I'd almost reached the bridge when a guy rose from the back seat. I assume his plan was to hit me over the head and jump out before the car went over the bridge."

"But you saw him..." Jackson said.

"Ducked just before the hit came and grabbed the guy. I barely got out before he went over the bridge in my car. I called Todd. That's when they told me they needed to seize this opportunity, and I needed to be dead. For my safety, and the safety of River and my parents. And so the operation wasn't blown."

The fog started to pull her back under.

No. She tried to stop it but couldn't.

River didn't know how long she slept, but when she started

coming around again, the light behind her lids wasn't quite so bright, and the room was silent.

Slowly, she opened her eyes. And that's when she saw him. The man she'd been told over and over again was dead. The man she'd been told she'd never see again.

Tears flooded her eyes. "Ryker..."

His steely brown eyes shot open, boring into her.

Tears spilled over, tumbling down her cheeks. "Everyone told me you were gone."

Her brother took her hand in his, his face pained, eyes darkening. "I'm sorry. So damn sorry."

"I didn't want to believe it," she said quietly. "And even when those men from Homeland Security came to my house and insisted you were gone, I still struggled to accept it."

His hand tightened around hers. "I wish I could have told you. You have no idea how much."

She swallowed the lump in her throat. "I know. I heard you talking to Jackson while I was barely conscious."

He gave a slow nod, and for a moment, they were both silent. Taking each other in, appreciating that the other person was really there.

"It was you, wasn't it?" she asked quietly. "Outside the gym that day?"

Anger flared in his eyes as he nodded again. "They told me to stay away, but I knew you were looking into things. I needed to make sure you were safe. When I saw that asshole attack you..." His jaw clenched.

"Thank you." She squeezed his hand. "Have you spoken to Mom and Dad?"

Another flash of pain. He nodded. "Yeah. It was...emotional. Even Dad struggled to hold it together. I've been banned from ever working with law enforcement again."

A laugh bubbled to the surface. Laughing with her brother felt good. "I am in full support of that ban."

"They'll be back soon," he said. "I forced them to go home and rest. Seeing you in bed with a bullet wound, and me alive...it was a lot for them."

She swallowed the lump in her throat. "But they know that I'll be okay, and that you're back for good? That everything will be okay now?"

"They know."

"And it will be, won't it? Okay I mean? Because you *are* actually back this time?"

They both knew that even though he'd returned from his final mission physically, he'd never returned in any other way.

Ryker sucked in a sharp breath. "It's over. Mickey's dead and his club will likely shut down. And Elijah and his men are dead."

A small pause.

"And, yeah...I'm back. Jackson mentioned he told you what happened in the Middle East."

River swallowed, giving him a small nod. "I'm sorry you lost people you cared about."

"The pain and guilt will be with me forever. But I need to learn to live with it, to not let the emotions affect me so much."

"I'll be here for you the entire time." He'd know that already, but it was worth saying.

"Thank you." Then he shook his head. "I can't leave you, anyway. You find trouble the second I do."

A small smile stretched her lips. "How else was I going to get you back?"

There was a deep growl from his chest. "You put yourself in danger."

"So did you."

"That's different."

She raised a brow. "Just because I'm not a trained soldier, doesn't mean I'm going to sit by and do nothing when my brother gets himself almost killed."

Another shake of his head. "For every second that Jackson's not there, I will be."

That was the big brother she remembered. "And you don't mind? Me and Jackson?"

A short laugh sounded. "You guys have been a sure thing since we were teenagers. I was just waiting for his stubborn ass to realize."

She smirked. "You and me both."

At the door to the room opening, they both looked up to see the man himself step inside. He held two coffees and was wearing the same clothes as yesterday. Or at least, she assumed it had been yesterday.

Her heart sped up. He looked huge and dangerous, and when his eyes met hers, they were possessive.

Ryker rose from his chair. "I'm gonna go see Cole and Dec for a bit. Erik might have stopped by, too."

Jackson tilted his head toward the hall. "They're in the cafeteria."

"Call if you need anything."

Before he could walk away, she touched his arm. "Don't go far."

"Wouldn't dream of it."

JACKSON TOOK slow steps toward the bed. Her skin wasn't quite so pale, and her breaths were even.

Good. Seeing her shot and unconscious...God, it had torn him in two and almost destroyed him.

He gave Ryker one of the coffees as the man passed. When the door closed, Jackson sat on the edge of the bed, placing the second coffee down and taking her hand.

"How are you feeling?" he asked quietly.

Her warmth seeped into his hand, up his arm, and into his

chest. Jesus, touching her was everything. Seeing her awake, alive... Hell, the only reason he'd left the room to get coffee was because being with her, while she'd been so still, had been killing him. Ryker had noticed, and had kicked his ass out of the room to get them some caffeine and stretch his legs.

"I don't feel any pain," she said quietly. "I think whatever drugs they have me on are strong."

He nodded, words not coming very easily to him right now. Eventually, he sucked in a deep breath. "You scared me." And that was an emotion he wasn't used to. He rarely felt fear. And he'd hated every second of it.

Her eyes softened. "I'm sorry. If I'd jumped out of the truck, I would have gotten caught in the gunfire. I had nowhere to go."

He stroked the back of her hand. "I know."

Her gaze shot to the spot beside her. "Lie with me?"

The woman didn't need to ask him twice. He climbed onto the bed, being careful not to jolt her or touch her injury. His arm went around her, and she nuzzled into him.

This was exactly what he needed after the hellish twenty-four hours they'd had.

"How are you feeling about Ryker?" she asked quietly.

"I can't believe he's alive. Best damn surprise of my life." He glanced down, pushing a lock of hair behind her ear. "You knew all along."

She gave him a small smile. "I'm just stubborn and can't accept that anything isn't exactly as I need it to be."

"You don't give up on the people you love." He pressed a kiss to her temple. "I like that."

"I don't. So if you ever try to disappear like Ryker, I'll hunt your ass down, too."

He chuckled. "I don't doubt it."

She snuggled closer. "So...you still set on staying in Lindeman?"

"Yes." He paused, his thumb stroking a circle around her

shoulder. "In fact, I spoke to Larry's wife. She's getting the papers ready for us to buy her husband's gym, and then we'll reopen."

Her head shot up. "Really?"

"Yeah. Declan, Cole, and now Ryker...they're all keen to do it with me. We're hoping it'll be sort of a refuge for people who need an outlet for their anger. Like Larry gave me. We're going to call the place Mercy Ring."

A slow smile stretched her lips. "After Larry Mercy."

He gave a short nod. "Exactly."

"Does this mean you'll let me go a round with you in the ring?"

He knew she was joking, but he couldn't even crack a smile. "Let's wait for the bullet wound to heal before we talk about you fighting anyone."

Her smile lessened. "I can't believe I was shot."

Jackson's eyes narrowed. The rookie cop who had shot her should have known better than to open fire. It had been Ryker's shot from the front and Jackson's from behind that had been Elijah's kill shots.

She looked up, eyes pained. "I'm sorry about your father."

He gave a short nod. He wasn't happy about his father's death, but he wasn't sad, either. "He made his bed."

She snuggled closer.

"Now that I'm staying though, I'd like you to do something for me."

She looked up. "And what's that?"

"Have another go at making money from taking pictures of the things you love." She frowned as he continued. "I may even have done some research and found the names of some companies and magazines who are accepting nature photography shots right now."

Her eyes softened. "You didn't."

"I did. Give it a go, River. I want you to do what you love."

She sighed. "Okay. I guess I have nothing to lose."

"Absolutely nothing." His hand went to her cheek. "I love you."

"I love you so much that too often I swear I'm going to lose my mind."

He chuckled. "We'll lose our minds together."

Then they were kissing, as if they needed each other more than they needed air. Like any separation at all was too painful to even consider.

CHAPTER 33

"You ever do anything like that again and I'm going to murder you myself," Declan said to Ryker across the table.

He wasn't even joking. He'd hunt the man down and beat his ass.

Ryker dipped his head. "Already heard the exact same from Jackson. If I ever do that again, you have my permission."

Cole shook his head. "We missed you, man."

"I missed you too," Ryker said. "Hell, I missed everyone."

Declan took a sip of his coffee, unable to take his gaze off his friend who sat across the cafeteria table. Ryker didn't want to leave until River did, so this is where they'd all been since the previous afternoon.

"You doing okay?" he asked. "After everything that happened on that last mission?"

Ryker tried to hide the flash of pain, but Declan saw it. "No. But I'm getting there."

He nodded. There wasn't much he could say. What had happened shouldn't have. None of them could bring back the families who'd died. And they didn't have permission to find the guy who'd killed them. That mission was where it ended for them.

Declan tapped his hand on the table before standing. "Right, I need to pop back to the inn for a shower because I stink like hell. Either of you coming?"

They both shook their heads.

Before he could stand, a familiar face stepped into the cafeteria and headed their way.

Declan frowned. "Erik."

He nodded toward them, his gaze pausing on Ryker. "Got a text from Cole saying you were still alive. Thought I'd come down and see for myself. Also check on your sister."

Ryker stood, giving the other man a brief hug. "Good to see you again, Erik. I heard you've spent some time with the team."

He dipped his head. "I did."

Declan stayed for another ten minutes, filling Erik in on everything before he stepped away, moving out of the cafeteria and down the hall.

Ryker was alive. The words didn't feel real in his head. Because the world had told him his friend—his brother—was dead. And he'd believed it. It was only River who had realized the truth.

Now the team was back together. Thank fuck for that, because even one of them being gone hurt like hell. Now that he knew what it felt like to lose a brother, he wasn't willing to leave them. Staying together, staying in Lindeman, felt right.

He tugged his phone from his pocket and checked if there were any messages. His eyes were on the screen when a woman rushed around the corner, crashing right into him. A squeak flew from her mouth and a container almost fell out of her hands.

Declan grabbed the container with one hand and steadied her with the other.

A smile immediately tugged at his lips.

Michele. Her sweet scent of sugar and citrus filled his

personal space. When her gaze finally lifted and met his, her eyes widened. Her mouth opened and closed but no words came out.

Declan's smile widened. So goddamn cute, especially when she got all flustered and quiet. He'd been finding himself thinking about the pretty brunette more and more lately.

She was almost a full head shorter than him, had these cute freckles dusted across her nose and the bluest eyes he'd ever seen.

And her curves...God, they made him want to run his hands all over her.

She was the opposite of every woman he'd ever dated. She didn't fit the MO of loud and extroverted, so his attraction to her caught him by surprise. But he sure as hell wasn't running from it.

"Sorry, darlin'."

Her cheeks reddened and her bottom lip disappeared between her lips. "You don't need to apologize. It was...I mean, I walked into you."

Ran. She *ran* into him. Not that he was complaining.

"Should have gotten my ass out of the way then, shouldn't I?"

A small smile slid across her lips. A smile that had ripples of awareness trickling into his chest.

"You here to see River?"

"Yeah, I, ah...brought food. Hospital food kind of sucks."

Declan laughed. "Kind of? I would describe it as soggy cardboard with a dusting of salt." He nodded his head down the hall. "Come on, I'll walk you."

Her brows rose. "Oh, it's okay. I know where she is."

"I'm sure you do. I want to." His voice deepened, intensity thrumming through his words. He wanted to explore this attraction. See where it took them.

Her throat bobbed, her lips parting. "Um, okay."

He was still holding her container as they walked. His free hand twitched to touch the small of her back. Her elbow. Anything. He clenched his fist to stop himself.

"What did you make?" He inspected the container, needing the distraction.

"Just Moroccan chickpea stew. Nothing fancy."

He laughed, feeling Michele's gaze zip his way. "If the words Moroccan and chickpea are in the same sentence, then it's fancy."

That smile returned to her lips, and he saw the hint of a dimple in her cheek.

"Now tell me how *I* can get some of this," he added.

Her brows rose again. "You want some?"

He wanted more than the stew, but that would have to wait. "I definitely do."

"Pop by the shop anytime you're around."

"You do know we've taken over the boxing gym, don't you? The boxing gym that's right down the road from you. So that could be very often."

She lifted a shoulder. "So come by often, then."

Her quiet words took him off guard. Was the shy woman flirting with him? Parts of his body hardened that had no business doing so in a busy hospital.

As they rounded a corner, Michele's phone dinged—and he could have sworn he saw her shoulders tense. When she pulled it out, the corners of her mouth tilted down, and she quickly clicked her phone off before shoving it back into her pocket.

Unease skirted through his gut. "Everything okay?"

They stopped outside River's room. The door was closed, and Michele turned to face him. Her next smile didn't come close to reaching her eyes. "Of course."

For the first time, he saw little things he hadn't before. Things he'd been too distracted by his attraction to notice. The way her eyes were shadowed and her lips pinched at the corners. The obvious stress. The exhaustion.

He took a small step forward, his voice lowering. "You can tell me if it isn't. You know that, right? I might be able to help."

She swallowed, her gaze flickering between his eyes. "I..." She paused. And for a moment, he thought she might actually tell him something important.

When the silence stretched, his hand reached out, almost as if it had a mind of its own, and cupped her cheek. "I *want* to help."

The electricity that passed through the touch was like a zap of fire. What the hell was it with this woman?

Something akin to need flickered through her eyes. Need to talk to him? Or just need *for* him?

Then she blinked. And when she stepped back, his hand fell. The spell broke. The loss of touch was like a kick in the gut.

"Thank you, Declan." She reached out, taking the container from his hand, her heated skin grazing his, burning him. He was certain she felt it too, because there was the smallest gasp from her before she tugged her hand back and spoke again. "And thank you for walking with me to River's room."

When she disappeared behind the door, Declan continued to stand there for another moment. There was just something about that woman. Something that had him feeling things he'd never felt before. And it wasn't just attraction. It was something that nearly suffocated him with the need to get to know her. Touch her. Protect her.

The last part had him frowning. Did the woman need protecting? His gut told him yes. That there was some sort of danger in her life. He could sense it as well as he could sense anything.

And he was almost certain it had everything to do with her asshole ex.

Order DECLAN today!

ALSO BY NYSSA KATHRYN

JOIN my newsletter and be the first to find out about sales and new releases!

https://www.nyssakathryn.com/vip-newsletter

ABOUT THE AUTHOR

Nyssa Kathryn is a romantic suspense author. She lives in South Australia with her daughter and hubby and takes every chance she can to be plotting and writing. Always an avid reader of romance novels, she considers alpha males and happily-ever-afters to be her jam.

Don't forget to follow Nyssa and never miss another release.

Facebook | Instagram | Amazon | Goodreads

Milton Keynes UK
Ingram Content Group UK Ltd.
UKHW011544050624
443780UK00008B/32